Love and Night

Also by Cornell Woolrich

Novels
Cover Charge (1926); *Children of the Ritz* (1927)
Times Square (1929); *A Young Man's Heart* (1930)
The Time of Her Life (1931); *Manhattan Love Song* (1932)
The Bride Wore Black (1940); *The Black Curtain* (1941)
Black Alibi (1942); *Phantom Lady* (1942)
The Black Angel (1943); *Deadline at Dawn* (1944)
The Black Path of Fear (1944)
Night Has a Thousand Eyes (1945)
Waltz into Darkness (1947); *Rendezvous in Black* (1948)
I Married a Dead Man (1948); *Fright* (1950)
Savage Bride (1950); *Strangler's Serenade* (1951)
Hotel Room (1958); *Death Is My Dancing Partner* (1959)
The Doom Stone (1960)
Into the Night (1987; completed by Lawrence Block)

Story Collections
I Wouldn't Be in Your Shoes (1943)
After-Dinner Story (1944)
If I Should Die Before I Wake (1945)
The Dancing Detective (1946)
Borrowed Crime (1946); *Dead Man Blues* (1947)
The Blue Ribbon (1949); *Somebody on the Phone* (1950)
Six Nights of Mystery (1950); *Eyes That Watch You* (1952)
Bluebeard's Seventh Wife (1952); *Nightmare* (1956)
Violence (1958); *Beyond the Night* (1959)
The Ten Faces of Cornell Woolrich (1965)
The Dark Side of Love (1965); *Nightwebs* (1971)
Angels of Darkness (1978)
The Fantastic Stories of Cornell Woolrich (1981)
Rear Window and Four Short Novels (1984)
Darkness at Dawn (1985); *Vampire's Honeymoon* (1985)
Blind Date with Death (1985); *Night and Fear* (2004)
Tonight, Somewhere in New York (2005)

Love and Night

CORNELL WOOLRICH

⊢⊣ UNKNOWN STORIES ⊢⊣

EDITED BY FRANCIS M. NEVINS

Dennis McMillan Publications 2007

Individual stories in *Love & Night* copyright © 1926,
1928, 1930, 1931, 1934, 1935, 1936, 1937, 1939
by Cornell Woolrich.
Organization, selection, arrangement, introduction, and
other editorial matter copyright © 2007 by
Francis M. Nevins. All rights reserved.

FIRST EDITION
Published December 2007

Dustjacket cover art: "Empire of Light," by Rene
Magritte, copyright © 2007 by C. Herscovici,
Brussels/Artists Rights Society (ARS), New York.

All other artwork in book, and book design by
Michael Kellner.

ISBN 978-0-939767-58-8

Dennis McMillan Publications
4460 N. Hacienda del Sol (Guest House)
Tucson, Arizona 85718
Tel. (520)-529-6636 email: dennismcmillan@aol.com
website: http://www.dennismcmillan.com

Contents

Introduction	i
Dance It Off	1
Mother and Daughter	19
Gay Music	38
Cinderella Magic	56
The Girl in the Moon	70
Between the Acts	83
Clip-Joint	88
No Kick Coming	103
Flower in His Buttonhole	121
Pick Up the Pieces	146
The Clock at the Astor	157
His Nam Was Jack	165
The Girl Next Door	183
I Knew Her When—	201
The Invincible	219

LOVE AND NIGHT: INTRODUCTION

Francis M. Nevins

On September 19, 1968, in a corridor of Manhattan's Sheraton Russell Hotel, a one-legged man in a wheelchair suffered a stroke. He was 64 years old but looked almost ninety. His name was Cornell Woolrich. He was the greatest writer of suspense fiction who ever lived. His two dozen novels and more than two hundred short stories and novelettes had the same wrenching impact, the same resonations of terror and anguish and loneliness and despair, as the darkest films of his cinematic soul-brother Alfred Hitchcock. He had spent most of his adult years living like a recluse with his mother in a New York residential hotel, trapped in a bizarre love-hate relationship with her and in the quicksand of his own homosexual self-contempt. When she died, he cracked, and began his own slow journey to the grave.

Cornell George Hopley-Woolrich was born in New York City on December 4, 1903 to parents whose marriage collapsed in his youth. He spent much of his childhood in Mexico with his father, a civil engineer. When he was eight, his maternal grandfather took him to Mexico City's Palace of Fine Arts to see a traveling French company perform Puccini's *Madama Butterfly*. The experience gave the young Woolrich his first insight into

Introduction

color and drama and his first sense of tragedy. Three years later, on a night when he looked up at the low-hanging stars from the valley of Anahuac, he understood that someday, like Cio-Cio-San, he too would have to die. From that moment on he was haunted by a sense of doom. "I had that trapped feeling," he wrote in his autobiographical manuscript, "like some sort of a poor insect that you've put inside a downturned glass, and it tries to climb up the sides, and it can't, and it can't, and it can't."

During his adolescence he lived with his mother and aunt and maternal grandfather in the grandfather's ornate house on 113th Street, near Morningside Park, a short walk from Columbia University. In 1921 he entered Columbia College as a journalism major, with his father paying the tuition from Mexico City. During a protracted illness in his junior year he began experimenting with writing fiction, scrawling the first draft of a novel in pencil on sheets of loose yellow paper that he scrounged from around the house. From the beginning he was a rapid, white-heat writer. "The stream of words was like an electric arc leaping across the intervening space from pole to opposite pole, from me to paper. . . . It was tiring and it wouldn't let go. . . . You couldn't stop it; it had to stop by itself. Then it fizzled out again at last, as unpredictably as it had begun. It left me feeling spent. . . ."

By the time he was well enough to return to school, he'd become a writing addict. Every evening after supper from nine till midnight, he'd sit in a second-floor room, the door closed, the family out of hearing, a Burmese elephant-head lamp lit on a pedestal in the corner behind him, and scribble furiously. By late spring of 1924 his first draft was done, and he borrowed a friend's typewriter to turn it into readable form. Almost before he knew it, that novel found a publisher, and Woolrich quit Columbia to pursue his dream of bright lights and gay music and a meteoric literary career like that of his and his whole generation's cultural idol, F. Scott Fitzgerald.

Woolrich's early mainstream fiction is saturated with the Fitzgerald influence, especially that first novel, *Cover Charge* (1926), which chronicles the lives and loves of the Jazz Age's gilded youth, the child-people, flitting from thrill to thrill, conversing in a mannered slang which, almost eighty years later, reads like the gibberings of creatures from another galaxy. But if nothing else, the novel is eerily prophetic in the way its protagonist's fate foreshadows its author's. Ballroom dancer Alan Walker winds up alone, in a cheap hotel room, his legs all but useless after a drunken auto smash-up, abandoned by the women he at various times loved, contemplating suicide. "I hate the world," he cries out. "Everything comes into it so clean and goes out so dirty."

This debut novel was followed by *Children of the Ritz* (1927), a frothy concoction about a spoiled heiress's marriage to her chauffeur, which won Woolrich a $10,000 prize and a contract from First National Pictures for the movie rights. He was invited to Hollywood to help with the adaptation and stayed on as a staff writer. Besides his movie chores (for which he never received screen credit) and an occasional story or article for magazines like *College Humor* and *Smart Set*, he completed three more novels during these years. Early in 1931, after a brief, inexplicable, and disastrous marriage to a producer's daughter, Woolrich fled back to Manhattan and his mother. His last mainstream novel, *Manhattan Love Song* (1932), anticipates the motifs of his later fiction with its love-struck young couple cursed by a malignant fate which leaves one dead and the other desolate. But over the next two years he became one more victim of the Depression. He sold next to nothing and was soon deep in debt, reduced to sneaking into movie palaces by the fire doors for his entertainment. What he didn't know was that he was on the brink of a new creative life, that he was about to become the foremost suspense writer of all time.

• • •

It was in 1934 that Woolrich decided to abandon his hopes of

Introduction

mainstream literary prestige and concentrate on the lowly genre of mystery fiction. He sold three stories to pulp magazines that year, ten more in 1935, and was soon an established professional whose name was a fixture on the covers of *Black Mask*, *Detective Fiction Weekly*, *Dime Detective*, and other pulps. The more than 100 stories and novelettes which he sold to the pulps during the Thirties are richly varied in type, including quasi police procedurals, rapid-action whizbangs, and encounters with the occult. But the best and the best known of them are the tales of pure edge-of-the-seat suspense, and even their titles signal their predominant mood of bleakness and despair. "I Wouldn't Be in Your Shoes." "Speak to Me of Death." "All at Once, No Alice." "Dusk to Dawn." "Men Must Die." "If I Should Die Before I Wake." "The Living Lie Down with the Dead." "Charlie Won't Be Home Tonight." "You'll Never See Me Again." These and dozens of other Woolrich suspense stories evoke with fierce power the desperation of those who walk the city's darkened streets and the terror that lurks at noonday in commonplace settings. In his hands even such cliched storylines as the race to save the innocent man from the electric chair and the amnesiac's search for his lost self pulsate with human anguish. Woolrich's world is a feverish place where the prevailing emotions are loneliness and fear and the prevailing action a race against time and death. His most characteristic detective stories end with the discovery that no rational account of events is possible, and his suspense stories tend to close with the terror not dissipated but omnipresent, like God.

The typical Woolrich settings are the seedy hotel, the cheap dance hall, the rundown movie house, and the precinct station backroom. The overwhelming reality in his world, at least during the Thirties, is the Depression, and Woolrich has no peers at putting us inside the skin of a frightened little guy in a tiny apartment with no money, no job, a hungry wife and children, and anxiety eating him like a cancer. If a Woolrich protagonist is in love, the beloved is likely to vanish in such a way that the protagonist not only can't find her but can't convince anyone she ever existed. Or, in another classic Woolrich situation, the protagonist comes to after a blackout—the result of amnesia, drugs, hypnosis, or whatever—and little by little becomes certain that he committed a murder or other crime while out of himself. The police are rarely sympathetic, in fact they are the earthly counterpart of the malignant powers above, and their main function is to torment the helpless. All we can do about this nightmare we live in is to create, if we are very lucky, a few islands of love and trust to sustain us and help us forget. But love dies while the lovers go on living, and Woolrich excels at portraying the corrosion of a once beautiful relationship. Yet he created very few irredeemably evil characters; if one loves or needs love, Woolrich makes us identify with that person, all of his or her dark side notwithstanding.

Purely as technical exercises, many of Woolrich's novels and stories are awful. They don't make the slightest bit of sense. And that's the point: neither does life. Nevertheless some of his tales, usually thanks to outlandish coincidence, manage to end quite happily. But since he never used a series character, the reader can never know in advance whether a particular Woolrich story will be light or dark, will end in triumph or despair—which is one of many reasons why his work is so hauntingly suspenseful.

• • •

In 1940 Woolrich joined the migration of pulp mystery writers from lurid-covered magazines to hardcover books, but his suspense novels carry over the motifs, beliefs, and devices that energized his shorter fiction. The eleven novels he published during the Forties—six under his own name, four as William Irish, and one as George Hopley—are unsurpassable classics in the poetry of terror. *The Bride Wore Black. The Black Curtain. Black*

Introduction

Alibi. Phamtom Lady. The Black Angel. Deadline at Dawn. The Black Path of Fear. Night Has a Thousand Eyes. Waltz into Darkness. Rendezvous in Black. I Married a Dead Man. These titles, all published between 1940 and 1948, make up the finest group of suspense novels ever written.

Those were his peak years, in which he became a wealthy man and a superstar of his genre. Publishers began issuing hardcover and paperback collections of his shorter fiction, which then came to the attention of the story editors of the great dramatic radio series of the Forties, leading to dozens of Woolrich-based dramas on *Suspense* and *Molle Mystery Theatre* and similar programs. Meanwhile Hollywood rediscovered the boy wonder of the Twenties and paid him handsomely for the right to make movies out of large numbers of his novels and stories. These pictures helped shape the uniquely Forties brand of suspense movie known today as *film noir*. But all the money and adulation didn't make Woolrich happy. In a letter of February 2, 1947, to Columbia's poet and professor Mark Van Doren, he seemed to blame his unhappiness on the fact that he was revered only as a mystery writer, not as a literary figure. "I don't like to look back on the Columbia days for that reason; the gap between expectation and accomplishment is too wide." On the other hand, impenetrable as the shield of self-contempt was with which Woolrich had surrounded himself, it's unlikely he would have been any happier if he *had* been acclaimed as another Scott Fitzgerald.

Around the end of the Forties Woolrich's mother became seriously ill, and that combined with his personal problems seemed to paralyze his ability and desire to write. During the Fifties he published very little, but he and his mother continued to live in their comfortable isolation, for his magazine stories proved to be as adaptable to television as they'd been to radio a decade earlier, and almost all the classic TV dramatic series—*Robert Montgomery Presents, Ford Theater, Schlitz Playhouse of Stars,*

Alfred Hitchcock Presents, Climax!, even the prestigious *Playhouse 90*—offered live or filmed versions of his fiction.

The day his mother died, in 1957, was the day he began to die himself, but in his case the process dragged on for more than ten years. Diabetic, alcoholic, wracked by loneliness and self-hate, he dragged out the last years of his life. He continued to write but left unfinished much more than he completed, and the only new work that saw print in the Sixties was a handful of final "tales of love and despair." He developed gangrene in his leg and let it go untended for so long that when he finally sought medical help, the doctor had no choice but to amputate. After the operation he lived for a few months in a wheelchair, unable to learn how to walk on an artificial leg. He had "the stunned aspect of the very old," said science fiction writer Barry N. Malzberg, who was as close to Woolrich at the end as anyone could get. "Where there had been the edges, there was now only the gelatinous material that when probed would not rebound." But his eyes were still "open and moist, curiously childlike and vulnerable."

It ended on September 25, 1968, two and a half months short of his sixty-fifth birthday. Six days after the ambulance took him from the Sheraton Russell corridor to Wickersham Hospital, he was dead. He left no survivors. His funeral was attended by exactly five people.

• • •

Most people who know something about Woolrich tend to think of him exclusively as the man who haunts us with words as Hitchcock haunts us with images on film. The 31 non-criminous tales he wrote during the Jazz Age and the Depression for magazines like *College Humor*, *College Life*, and *Breezy Stories* have long been forgotten even though close to half of them have clear connecting links with his suspense-packed crime fiction. These stories, unavailable for generations, are collected here.

Introduction

Woolrich's career as a short story writer began in 1926, soon after *Cover Charge* was published and while he was still enrolled as an undergrad at Columbia. He described the circumstances in a letter written in 1945:

> I received a telegram...from the editor of *College Humor,* asking for a story. I wrote it at night, knocking off at about 4 A.M., and then went to classes at 9. He sent me a check for $300 for it, so I figured it was worth a few hours of lost sleep. I stopped being so conscientious after that, though, and did the next one in the daytime, on my school time. I made $12,000 in my first full year of writing, but flunked German (I think it was). I never did make up the extra credits I needed for that. It was more fun writing. And a lot more remunerative.

The editor who bought that first short story from him had a different version of their encounter. In the Thirties H.N. Swanson (1899-1991) was to set up shop in Hollywood, where he became the dean of movie agents, representing John O'Hara, Thornton Wilder, John P. Marquand, Raymond Chandler, James M. Cain, F. Scott Fitzgerald, and even on occasion Woolrich himself. In the Twenties Swanson was editing one of the decade's leading magazines of light fiction, *College Humor*. Although based in Chicago, he frequently went to New York to meet and negotiate with writers. Apparently he first met Woolrich early in 1926, when the weather was still chilly. As he remembered the meeting, it was Woolrich who approached him, not vice versa. "One day," he wrote in his autobiography *Touched with Ruby Dust* (1988), "a white-faced, bizarre-looking creature in a black overcoat which reached to his toes came to see me. He said his name was Cornell Woolrich, and stressed the fact that he was a good writer. He pushed a script at me and fled." In a letter to me Swanson described the scene more fully.

> This boy-man looked like he might have stepped out of a Charles Addams drawing. He wore very dark clothes, a long black overcoat that almost hit his shoes, and he had a white face and the appearance of not having enough to eat . . . I think the only money he spent on himself was to sit in some of those gloomy bistros amid the plastic noisy surroundings of a dance joint.

Whoever approached whom, to Swanson belongs the honor of having purchased the first Woolrich short story to see the light of print. Unfortunately "Honey Child" (*College Humor*, September 1926) is just a frothy trifle, more or less in the same vein as the commercial romances that Fitzgerald ground out for the *Saturday Evening Post* and similar magazines of the Twenties to subsidize his novels. The title character is a spoiled New Orleans belle who comes to New York with her black maid for a shopping spree and a round of parties, at one of which a handsome young submarine officer is smitten by her charm. Just before the flirtatious vixen is to catch the train back to Louisiana, she visits the sub, which is moored off Manhattan's 96th Street pier, to say goodbye to her Billy. He however demands that she marry him, and when she refuses, he locks her in his quarters and—at least so it seems—orders the submarine out to sea. This naval maneuver instantly convinces Honey Child that Billy really loves her, and she agrees to become his bride. He then confesses that actually the sub has moved no farther than the 79th Street pier. This kind of story is not included in *Love and Night*.

If *College Humor* was the young Woolrich's best market for short material, his second best was the equally popular and lucrative *McClure's Magazine*. His only other story to be published during the year of his debut as a writer was "Dance It Off!" (*McClure's*, October 1926), a much more mature and meaty tale about the two women in the life of young Wally Walters, a typical 1920s

Introduction

cake-eater and champion dancer of the Charleston. Wally is a man whose spiritual kin pop up constantly in Woolrich's later suspense fiction, a man "always hungering for something out of reach," a man whom no conventional woman will satisfy. In this and several other respects he is a Woolrich self-portrait, and the description of his bleak little apartment, a few pages into the story, brilliantly captures the essence of Woolrichian man. Anyone who doubts that Woolrich and Hitchcock drank from a common spring should note the uncanny similarity between Wally's relationships with exotic and mystery-touched Mimi and nice safe reliable Connie in "Dance It Off" and James Stewart's relationships with Kim Novak and Barbara Bel Geddes in Hitchcock's 1958 masterpiece *Vertigo*. This tale well deserves its place at the head of the present collection.

The next story Swanson bought from Woolrich was "Bread and Orchids" (*College Humor*, January 1927), and later in the year he serialized Woolrich's second novel, *Children of the Ritz*, in four installments running from August through November. Meanwhile two more of the boy wonder's short romances were published in *McClure's*, with "The Gate Crasher" appearing in August and "The Drugstore Cowboy" in October. None of these trifles are revived here, but the opening of "Bread and Orchids" is worth quoting for its superb description of a 1920s hotel lobby.

> Hotels. . . .In the cities of today they rise like magic, thirty, forty, fifty odd stories above the street. All day and all night dozens of lighted elevators rush up and down, like quicksilver in thermometers, carrying people in morning clothes, people in evening clothes, people in sport togs, people in bathing suits. The city could burn down to the ground, and if these hotels were left standing you would still be able to find every phase of life reproduced exactly as it had been on the outside: jewelry shops, haberdashery, fancy diving, bootlegging, florists, marcel waving, millinery, bridge, billiards, and tea for two, or three, or four—but mostly for two (and not always tea either).

In the spring or summer of 1928 Woolrich moved to Hollywood, under contract with First National to work on the silent movie version of *Children of the Ritz*. That year he published no new novels and only a pair of short stories. "Mother and Daughter"(*College Humor*, August 1928), which is included here, resonates with Fitzgerald touches—it's not by accident that the male lead is called Scotty—and with foreshadowings of the *noir* world of loneliness and falling beams from Woolrich's later crime fiction. Our gratitude to H.N. Swanson for publishing it is tempered by amazement that he saw this most downbeat of Woolrich's early tales as fit material for *College Humor*. "The Good Die Young" (*College Life*, October 1928) on the other hand is an absurd concoction which holds no interest today except for the fact that it's the earliest Woolrich story to feature first-person narration by a woman. At least it's more readable than "Bluebeard's Thirteenth Wife" (*College Life*, February 1929), an indescribable hunk of junk which at least two people, Woolrich and the editor who bought it, seem to have thought was funny.

Between the appearance of Woolrich's third novel, *Times Square* (1929), and his fourth, *A Young Man's Heart* (1930), the stock market collapsed and the Depression's choke-hold tightened on the country, but you'd never guess it from his fiction of those years. Nevertheless two of his three short stories published in 1930 are among his best early tales and deserve revival here. In "Gay Music" (*College Humor*, January 1930) we find not one but a pair of glamorous middle-aged women: the protagonist's mother, whose Angel Face nickname will recur again and again in Woolrich's suspense fiction, and a wealthy lady named Zoe, who comes between the protagonist and his young wife. This bizarre story climaxes with a powerful scene evoking the specter of Anahuac that haunted Woolrich all his days and nights. And "Cinderella Magic" (*Illustrated Love*, November 1930) is one of the saddest Woolrich romances, with popular song lyrics like "Here

Introduction

we are, you and I, Let the world hurry by" underscoring the theme that relationships and anguish are inseparable. Between these tales came "Soda-Fountain Saga" (*Liberty*, October 11, 1930), which is interesting enough but not on a par with the other stories Woolrich published that year.

In December of 1930 he married Gloria Blackton, one of the daughters of movie pioneer J. Stuart Blackton, but the marriage quickly proved a disaster (thanks mainly to the groom's homosexuality) and three months later Woolrich was back on the East Coast with his mother. His only fiction to be published during 1931 was his fifth novel, *The Time of Her Life*, and a single short story, "The Girl in the Moon" (*College Humor*, August 1931), the last tale bought from him by H.N. Swanson. The protagonist, Marty, is one more of those Woolrichian men whose woman must satisfy his otherworldly romantic dreams, and the object of his desire happens to have the same name as Scott Fitzgerald's wife.

Woolrich and his mother spent much of 1931 traveling through Europe. When he returned to New York, he found that the worsening Depression had just about wrecked his short story markets. The two tales he managed to sell for 1932 publication— "Orchids and Overalls" (*Illustrated Love*, March 1932) and "Women Are Funny" (*Illustrated Love*, October 1932)—are not worth reviving, but between them came the sixth, last, and by far the most powerful of his early books, *Manhattan Love Song* (1932), in which countless elements from his later fiction of suspense and despair show up for the first time in concentrated form. This all but unknown *noir* classic was reviewed almost nowhere, read by next to no one, and quickly swallowed up in the Sargasso Sea of forgotten literature. In 1933 Woolrich published nothing at all and during the first half of 1934 the only material of his to appear in print was a quartet of very short romances, three of them trivial. The exception, "Between the Acts" (*Serenade*, March

1934), is a neat and cynical gem with which the first half of *Love and Night* comes to an end.

By the time that tale hit the stands, Woolrich was beginning a new life as a writer, a life that superficially seems worlds removed from his earlier Fitzgeraldesque ambitions but that in fact, as these stories show, is more deeply rooted in his previous work than anyone before now has recognized. He spent the rest of the decade writing crime and suspense fiction for the pulps, but in addition he managed during the first six years of his mystery-writing life to whack out fourteen more short romances and a sentimental serial. When I began tracking down these elusive tales, I expected to have to grit my teeth and plow through a pile of Woolrich at his unspeakable worst. Surprise! Although his love stories of the Thirties are not in the same league or even the same world with his *noir* classics, the most interesting of them are intimately connected with his suspense fiction and have a fascination all their own which makes them well worth resurrecting.

• • •

All fourteen of Woolrich's short romances of the period were published in *Breezy Stories*, which had been launched in 1915 by the C.H. Young company as competition for another magazine known as *Snappy Stories*. Both periodicals offered what pulp historian Robert Sampson describes as "mildly risqué fiction about girls who might yield a kiss, or at least think about it . . . and who disregarded moral limits by wearing bathing costumes exposing their ankles." *Breezy* was still a going concern in 1933 when the publisher merged it with the venerable *Young's Magazine*, founded in 1897. During the Depression *Breezy* paid a penny a word for fiction that, according to Sampson, "was rich in compromising situations, casual acceptance of male (if not

Introduction

female) infidelity, and a light-hearted approach to social conduct. Suggestive teasing filled the stories. In spite of all, the heroine remained pure, if barely, and true love resolved all problems, close as the heroine sometimes came to love of the other kind." Most of the fourteen tales Woolrich sold to *Breezy* editor Phil Painter don't fit comfortably within Sampson's description. Some of them are idiotic love stories with sitcom plotlines, but the others, which are included here, have demonstrable links to his past or future suspensers.

Typical of the Woolrich romances from the period which are absent from *Love and Night* is "Don't Fool Me!" (*Breezy Stories*, June 1935). Sophisticated June Bannon takes under her wing a prim gal named Helen Hyde whom she meets at a party. Helen looks like a mouse with spectacles and lacks the simplest social graces but constantly raves about a young man named Marvin Carteret whom no one ever sees but who she claims adores her. Convinced that Helen has made up an imaginary boyfriend to assuage her loneliness, June first invites the prim lass to share her apartment and then sets out to throw Helen into the arms of Tommy Moore, an unattached young man of her acquaintance. Love indeed blooms between Helen and Tommy after what may have been a night of premarital sex—Woolrich's notion of girl talk is so coy that there's no telling for sure—but the punchline comes right after the couple go off to find a justice of the peace. June's doorbell rings and there on her threshold stands "the best-looking thing she had seen since her last Gable picture," asking for Helen and introducing himself as Marvin Carteret. On this note of irresolution the story ends.

In "Clip-Joint" (*Breezy Stories*, August 1935), which is included here, a bit of underworld spice in the boy-meets-girl recipe leads to one of Woolrich's better Thirties romances. The "intimate private club" where patrons are charged $100 per drink and kept locked up till their checks clear prefigures the similar establishment in Woolrich's pulp suspense tale "Crime on St. Catherine

Street" (*Argosy*, January 25, 1936), and the gimmick of the playboy pretending to be a waiter is recycled in Woolrich's powerful 1943 crime novel *The Black Angel*. Though a bit crudely written, this is a neatly cynical story, capped with a surprise ending in the best O. Henry tradition.

"No Kick Coming" (*Breezy Stories*, October 1935) is another romance with crime flavoring, but this one teeters on the brink of *noir* and indeed could almost be described as "Dance It Off!" with the sexes reversed. But even more brim-full of distinctive Woolrich elements is "Flower in His Buttonhole" (*Breezy Stories*, November 1935) with its insult humor and tinny saxophone music and Thirties song lyrics and taxi-dancer protagonist. The opening scene with Faith wearily climbing the stairs to the Broadway dance mill and sparring with the truculent manager on the way in is repeated almost verbatim in Woolrich's suspense classic "Dime a Dance" (*Black Mask*, February 1938), and the climax features a genuine race against the clock as Faith's pal Trixie frantically tries to catch up with her and save her virtue from being sullied. Even without the innumerable ties to Woolrich's crime fiction, this story remains surprisingly readable after 70 years of oblivion.

All three of Woolrich's *Breezy* tales of the following year are connected with his mysteries and all are reprinted here. "Pick Up the Pieces" (*Breezy Stories*, March 1936) deals with the kind of raid on a phony love nest that was common in the days when the only ground for divorce in New York was adultery. More than thirty years later Woolrich recycled the same situation, with murder added, in "Divorce—New York Style" (*Ellery Queen's Mystery Magazine*, June and July 1967). I like the earlier version much better. "The Clock at the Astor" (*Breezy Stories*, April 1936) is one of the most vividly written, cynical, and ironic of all Woolrich's romances, and would be well worth reviving today even if it had no links at all with his classic suspense novels *Deadline at Dawn* (1944) and *Rendezvous in Black* (1948). And several bits and pieces

Introduction

from "His Name Was Jack" (*Breezy Stories*, July 1936) crop up in the unfinished manuscript of *Into the Night*, the novel which, as completed by Lawrence Block, was published almost twenty years after Woolrich's death.

The viewpoint character in "The Girl Next Door" (*Breezy Stories*, July 1937) is a pulp mystery writer living alone in a furnished apartment. Instantly we conjure up memories of the suspenser "Murder Story" (*Detective Fiction Weekly*, 11 September 1937), which Woolrich must have written almost simultaneously with this romance, and also of his bitter retrospective classic "The Penny-a-Worder" (*Ellery Queen's Mystery Magazine*, September 1958). Indeed the lurid tale Ted Cobb is cranking out as "The Girl Next Door" begins is very much like the garbage Dan Moody is working on in "The Penny-a-Worder," and neither is at all like the pulpers Woolrich himself wrote. The title of Cobb's opus is "Murder on a Dark Night," and one fragment of it reads as follows:

> Duke squeezed the trigger and lead whistled at the dick. His own gun talked back in the same bullet-language. Suddenly Dolores was standing there, in the same beautiful evening-gown as when she'd killed Mickey. She had a gun in her hand, too.

Except for the hyphenated compound words that Woolrich instinctively used whenever he wrote, this excerpt could never be mistaken for one of his genuine pulp tales. But the portrait he draws of the hack who's pounding the keyboard perfectly captures the image of Woolrich himself at work: "Cigarette in the far southeast corner of his mouth hanging by a thread, hair a bird's nest, collar open, shoes unlaced, fingers poised predatorily above the keys. . . ." Cobb's furious concentration is broken by noises from the apartment next door, and he starts engaging in a sound-duel with his unseen neighbor, who turns out to be a beautiful professional tap dancer. The upshot of this fascinating little yarn is—well, read it and see.

"I Knew Her When—" (*Breezy Stories,* October 1937) is a strangely moving tale whose first scene may evoke in aficionados of Woolrich's suspense fiction a strong sense of *deja vu.* Jerry Delaney, a young subway guard on the IRT line, gets up early one morning, leaves for work, walks to the station at 125th Street and Broadway, lifts the chain that bars his way, catches a train uptown to the end of the line at 242nd Street, boards the next inbound express, and travels in it down to Fulton Street and Wall Street and under the East River to Brooklyn. This is exactly the way Woolrich had begun his action classic "You Pays Your Nickel" (*Argosy,* August 22, 1936), better known as "Subway." In this version, however, Delaney encounters not a mad gunman but a young woman new to the city. "I was born unknown," Peggy Parker tells him, "but I'm not going to die that way, and that's about all anyone can do for themselves in this life." Delaney of course falls in love with her not in any sexual way but the way a guy might fall in love "with a star over his head in the night sky." In other words, as a Woolrich man loves.

Love and Night ends with "The Invincible" (*Breezy Stories,* January 1939), the last story of its kind Woolrich ever wrote. Sybil Jenkins, ordered by the tyrannical dressmaker she works for to deliver a specially made gown to the penthouse apartment of actress Vivian Lane, finds her in an octagonal mirrored room of precisely the type that, two years later, would dominate Woolrich's *noir* classic published originally as "And So to Death" (*Argosy,* 1 March 1941) but best known as "Nightmare." Vivian offers the princely sum of a hundred dollars if Sybil will impersonate her and go out with a handsome, wealthy, and sexually demanding playboy. What might have been a bitter tale of economic and sexual exploitation ends with a double wedding. Ain't love wonderful?

• • •

Introduction

"I was only trying to cheat death," he wrote in a fragment found among his papers more than thirty years after the last of these tales was published. "I was only trying to surmount for a little while the darkness that all my life I surely knew was going to come rolling in on me some day and obliterate me. I was only trying to stay alive a little brief while longer, after I was already gone." In the end of course he had to die as we all do. But as long as there are readers to be haunted by the fruit of his life, by the way he took his wretched psychological environment and his sense of entrapment and solitude and turned them into poetry of the shadows, the world Woolrich imagined lives.

And so in a sense does he.

Love and Night

This is only the second Woolrich story to be published, but it contains several characteristic Woolrich themes. The obsession with dance, the bleak little apartment, the protagonist whom no conventional woman will satisfy—all will reappear regularly in Woolrich's noir classics of the Thirties and Forties.

DANCE IT OFF!

Wally Walters had been told more than once that he was a cake eater. Now a cake eater is one who having arrived at years of discretion toils not neither does he spin. In other words he lets the bread and butter of life go by him and concentrates on the cake—sugar icing and all. How he gets away with it is nobody's business. But Wally Walters, in particular, wore a three-cornered, low-crowned hat down over his eyes and nose with a little green feather stuck in the band. Being unable to fasten a bow-tie himself, he wore his on a rubber band under the collar of his shirt. It looked just as good anyway. His trousers hung about his legs in folds; they extended to the tips of his shoes, and when he walked he looked elephant-footed. The funniest thing about him, though, was his raincoat. When it rained, and sometimes even when it didn't rain, Wally came out in a soapy looking yellow slicker with a little strap around his throat like a dog-collar. On his back he had a drawing of a bobbed-haired flapper in a pink chemise and black silk stockings, and underneath was the legend "Ain't we got fun" for all the townspeople to marvel at. The blonde cashier at the candy store had done it for him. She had also done some six or eight others. All the boys told her she had a great deal of talent going to waste. She agreed with them.

It is only fair to mention in passing that although Wally Walters was undeniably a cake eater, he never touched cake, or pie either for that matter. He dined in cafeterias whenever he did dine, which wasn't as often as it sounds, and he ate things like ham sandwiches and custards because they cost less and were far more substantial. Several evenings a week he devoted to billiards, but on Saturday nights he was always to be found at the Rainbow, the local dance center, where they took the precaution of searching you for liquor as you went in. Some of the brighter ones got around this by carrying it internally. On Saturday nights Myrtle and Rose and Lily were always to be found there, outdoing one another in the grotesqueries of the Charleston. All that was needed was plenty of room, a pair of strong ankles, and lots of terpsichorean ambition; and these were the very things that Wally Walters seemed to have most of. Consequently he was a howling success and always in demand—as Rose and Myrtle and Lily thought that the cleverest Charleston contortionist was bound to make an ideal husband, in which case they wouldn't have to go out any more but could do their practicing right at home.

But not for Wally. He knew too much about girls. Girls were a necessary evil, nice under Japanese lanterns at twelve o'clock with all their bagatelles and war-paint on, but not so nice at nine the next morning over the cereal and the coffee pot. Wally was an idealist. He had dreams and he hated to see them spoilt. He got a little older and he got a little older and finally he put his trust in one girl and one girl only, a girl in a castle of dreams.

There was Carfare Connie. They called her that because she would ride in anything from a limousine to a mail truck, but she always took along about a dollar and a half for spending money. She called it her emergency fund. She'd had the same dollar and a half for three years now and still her luck kept up. She used to read the motto engraved on the silver half dollar, "In God We Trust," and smile knowingly to herself, and perhaps rub it on her sleeves to brighten it up a bit. Carfare Connie hadn't had any trouble on automobile rides—much—but she believed in being prepared. Every Saturday night she put on a big floppy white picture hat which was nothing but wire and gauze and wended her merry way to the Rainbow, greeting all passers-by en route. She was very fond of Wally Walters. He and she would invent dance steps together.

"Look, cake, how about this one? I thought it up on my way to work this morning."

"Show us it."

"Tum tum, te ta ta," said Carfare Connie with great gusto.

"Yeah," he said, "I see what you're driving at. Only look—tum tum, te ta ta—doesn't that work out better?" Giving his version of it.

"Yeah, you've got it ezactly; that's ezactly what I meant." And a girl has to care a good deal for someone before she'll let him change her pet ideas to suit himself.

Now there were six Lucilles all in a row until one was sent out on the road and there were only five. Lucille was one of those musical comedy heroines who have to wear gingham and tickle dust-mops and scrub floors in the first act, but then in the second act they bob up all covered with sequins and grab the nearest millionaire's son and sing a song all about a platinum lining. And everybody goes home happy.

In this case everyone went home happy except poor Lucille herself. Lucille hated being sent on the road. It put her in bad humor for weeks and weeks at a time. She missed her gorgeous roof bungalow with its mirrored bath, she missed her Hispano-Fiat with its little green baize card table. She missed her borzoi with its concave stomach. Lucille in this instance was Mimi Travers of New York and Philadelphia, but decidedly not of points west. The whole trouble was the producers seemed to think otherwise. All day long on the train she said things about them not meant for little children to hear; and when night came she sat in her dressing-room with shoes scattered all about her and delayed getting dressed for the performance until the curtain of that particular theater was three quarters of an hour late and the stage manager threatened to wire New York. Then she slapped on a make-up helter skelter at the last possible moment and made them omit the "Primrose Path" number from the second act, saying she was fed up on it and didn't give a damn.

And it was this same evening that Wally Walters came north along River Street looking like a million dollars going somewhere to get itself squandered. A brand new electric sign caught his eye and he paused to reflect upon it, giving the dimes, quarters, and halves in his pocket a vigorous shaking up.

LUCILLE
THE HIT OF HITS
ONE SOLID YEAR IN NEW YORK

The lights went on and off, on and off. There was something fascinating in the arrangement of the letters. Lucille, the Hit of Hits. Lucille. What a pretty name. He stood in line to buy a ticket, the six brass buttons on his powder-blue Norfolk gleaming in the light of the lobby—that powder-blue Norfolk that was the pride of his silly, disordered life, that he always wore to the Rainbow on Saturday nights and to the chop suey palaces. And though he wasn't exactly thinking about her just then, there was always this girl in a castle of dreams and bubbles in his heart—which was a good heart as hearts go but all smothered with confetti.

He walked down the aisle to his seat just as the overture was getting under way. A girl in an upper box smiled when she caught sight of him and made some comment to an older woman beside her. He imagined she wanted to flirt with him, so he treated her to one of his studied gazes of approval and smiled wickedly out of the corners of his mouth. For a few seconds she returned his look with impudent disdain; then she and the older woman both laughed in his face. The lights went out like a whip and he sat down, wondering what had been the matter with those two.

The curtain went up on a sea of legs—the musical comedy had begun. Five minutes, ten minutes, twelve minutes passed. It progressed well beyond the first half of the first act with still no sign of Lucille. Who was she anyway, Wally wondered. What was she waiting for, what was it all about?

Up on the stage a garden party was in progress. A bevy of girls with parasols and aigrets and lorgnettes and feather fans made shadows play up and down their legs. They stood in battalions and fluttered their fingers from their feet up over their heads. Then all at once he saw her.

She was in the midst of them. The spotlight picked her out. She was like a guinea-pig among peacocks and flamingoes. Her hair was drawn back into a knot at the top of her head, the way they draw them in the comic strips, and there was a ridiculous little hat perched on top, stabbed with a long pin. Her stockings were red and white wool, striped like sticks of peppermint candy. She had on impossible shoes that buttoned half way up her calves—yellow shoes. She had a little old Irish terrier under her arm; it had been trained to try and get away from her and she had to struggle with it to hold it. The people screamed with laughter. The auditorium fairly rocked with it. It dashed itself against the footlights like spray, wave after wave of it. In the balconies people were standing up to get a better view of her.

But Wally Walters never cracked a smile. He sat there staring out at Lucille's pitiful talcumed face, her clownish face with its blued-in eyes and its blacked lips. The stage beauties circled about her, gorgeous with Titian hair and peach bloom make-up. They studied her through lorgnettes and flicked her with their fans and turned their shoulders on her in contempt. They drew back, leaving her standing alone. Even the little terrier had abandoned her at the first opportunity. There was a hush. A thick shaft of very white light fell on her, powdering her ridiculous padded leg-of-mutton shoulders. She began to sing. She sang about a castle of dreams and how it had come tumbling down. And there was

Love & Night

nothing left, she said, nothing; she spread her hands and let them fall sidewise with a slap and sobbed drily deep down in her throat. Then she went shuffling off in her absurd shoes and striped stockings, and on her way out she pretended to trip over something. That brought the entire house down again.

But Wally couldn't laugh, somehow. He knew how it felt; you bet he knew how it felt. His eyes were stinging him. He pulled his hat from beneath the seat and went trudging up the aisle. People wondered why he was leaving so early. Once he looked back over his shoulder. She hadn't come out again. They were doing a Charleston to the little tune she had sung so wistfully; they were clodhopping among the ruins of her dream castle. It didn't matter to him that she was to come back later with a diadem in her hair and paradise tufts on her shoes. He knew how it was when you felt that way. Who would know better than he, always hungering for something out of reach—and not cake either. He stood out in front of the theater, looking aimlessly up the street without seeing anything. He lit a cigaret and tried to pretend that it was the smoke getting in his throat that made it so dry.

He went home to his room—the "budwa" he called it—and lay on the bed, shoes and all. It was a true image of his life, that small room. Disarranged, meaningless, pitiful, choked with trifles, trying hard to be gay but sad at heart. There was a picture of a motion picture actress, Clara Bow, clipped from a magazine and pasted to the wall. There was a tambourine hanging on a nail and a gilt false-face hanging from its elastic on another. There were girls' telephone numbers scribbled everywhere although the landlady was furious about it. On the dresser there was a ten cent store doll with blue cotton batting for hair; someone had penciled a mustache along its upper lip. There was in addition a nickel-plated pocket flask lying on its side, a feathered bamboo tickler from one of the Chinese restaurants, several menus, a bottle with a little hair grease turned rancid in the bottom of it, and the remains of a package of cigarets. Also a copper ash-tray with chewing gum stuck to it, and one of orange clay with collar buttons and a toothbrush in it.

Somebody was knocking on his door. He bobbed up. "Who is it?" he demanded. He scratched the back of his head.

"You're wanted on the telefoam," cried the lady of the house through the panel. He heard her go away again.

He unlocked the door and went down to the foot of the staircase. The receiver was hanging on its cord, so low that it almost touched the floor. He had to stoop to pick it up.

"Yeah?" he said constrainedly.

"Oh, hello!" said a girl's voice. "This is Connie. Connie speaking."

"I know," he remarked dispiritedly, fishing the while through several pockets in the effort to locate a cigaret. When he had found one he held it between his lips without lighting it—a dry smoke—and it bobbed up and down each time he had anything to say.

"I'm up at the Rainbow," she said. "Why didn't you show up tonight? Anything wrong?"

"Na," he said, closing his eyes for a brief moment. He felt he couldn't stomach Connie this evening, nor any of the others either. The sound of a band, infinitely small and far away and blurred with other noises, came through the receiver.

"Hear that?" said Connie. "Doesn't it make you itchy?"

"Hm?" he said, not caring much.

"I'll keep my eye open for you," she went on. "How long will it take you to get here, cake?"

"I don't know," he said. "I'm not coming. No, not for tonight. I'm all fagged out."

"Why, what's gotten into you all of a sudden?" she demanded in surprise. "Are you trying to kid me? You know yourself you couldn't keep away from here even if you wanted to."

"That's what you say."

He shut his eyes and pressed his forehead against the wall.

Love & Night

"They're going to have a Charleston contest and everything," Connie was saying. "I entered your name for you. You better see that you get here. The leading lady from 'Lucille' is coming up after the show to award the prizes—"

"Hell she is!" he burst out.

"What's the matter," protested Connie angrily, "are you trying to crack my eardrum?"

"Wait for me," he cried. "I'll be over in a jiffy. Meet you in the foyer—" and hung up.

"Men sure are changeable," sighed Carfare Connie, powdering her nose with a puff the size of a postage stamp.

Meanwhile in Wally's room a toilette was in full swing. He crowded his number eight feet into number seven dancing shoes, with spats to cap the climax; he soaked his hair with glycerin—oh, there's no use denying Wally tossed a mean toilette once he got going. And as he went out, carelessly banging the door shut after him, the draft brought the movie star's picture fluttering down from the wall.

There was a taxi standing in front of the Rainbow with its engine going, waiting for someone. It was unusual for a taxi to be here at that hour. Most patrons of the place arrived on foot, or if they rode at all it was in trolley cars and the front seats of moving vans. Wally knew who had hired it without being told. He bought his ticket of admission at the box office and went in. At the inner door he was frisked for possible concealed liquor and brushed by them impatiently. He checked his coat and hat and bought twenty-five cents' worth of blue dance tickets at a nickel a dance. The lights were all swathed in yellow and orange gauze, and from each corner of the gallery a colored lens was directed against the dancers below. Connie was sitting waiting for him at a tiny table which held her elbows, an imitation rhinestone purse, a limeade with two straws, and a zigzag of undetached blue tickets. She waved and he went over to her.

"Hello, cake. How are you, honey?"

"'Lo."

She looked at him happily. "I saved all my tickets until you got here."

"Thanks," he said. "I bought some."

"You didn't need to, honey. That's what I kep' these for."

His glance wandered all around the place. "Did that girl from the show get here yet?" he wanted to know confidentially.

"Yeah," said Connie. "The manager took her over to introduce her to the leader. She's going to award the prizes."

Wally looked down at his feet.

"You'll make it," nodded Connie, reading his thoughts. "You have it cinched."

"What is it, a singles or a doubles?"

"Singles. That's why I stayed out of it. I didn't want to go against you."

He pressed her hand under the table. "Good kid," he said, which was as close as he ever got to tenderness with her.

Connie felt herself tingle with loyalty. She offered him a straw. "Let's finish this drink together," she said.

They bent down over the glass, their faces close together. Connie's eyelids fluttered with the nearness of it but she didn't dare look up. They made a slight gurgling sound. "You take the cherry," said Wally generously.

There was a crash of cymbals from the gallery upstairs. Connie and Wally raised their heads. The orchestra leader was holding a megaphone to his mouth. "Ladies and gentlemen," he boomed, "the Charleston contest will now begin. Entries are by name only. Each contestant will be limited to a five-minute performance. Miss Mimi Travers of the 'Lucille' company has consented to act in the capacity of judge of this contest. The winner will be awarded a silver loving cup, donated through the courtesy of the United Barber Shops' Association." He held the cup up by one handle and a round of applause followed.

"Isn't it beautiful?" beamed Connie, craning her neck. She put

Love & Night

her arm around Wally's shoulder. "It'll be pie for you, honey. They might as well hand it over to you right now."

He smiled—but the smile wasn't meant for her. It was for Mimi, standing beside the orchestra leader. Mimi was beautiful—she was almost too beautiful to live.

"Ladies and gentlemen, Miss Mimi Travers." She and the orchestra leader took a bow apiece. With an almost imperceptible movement Wally freed himself of Connie's encouraging arm. He was clapping his hands vigorously. "Yea, Mimi!" he shouted.

The contest began. Rose and Myrtle and Lily took turns twisting their legs into unbelievable positions while the band played on.

"Faster and funnier," called the onlookers. "Spread yourself. Do that thing!"

Rose and Myrtle and Lily spread themselves. They did that thing. They did a lot of other things with it. They skipped like devils. Mimi Travers had come out on the floor to get a better look at them. She was sitting gazing over the back of a chair with her chin resting on her arms. There was a gold bracelet around one of her ankles. Rose and Myrtle and Lily were through now. They were panting like grasshoppers. Also they were considerably disheveled.

"Mr. Wallace Walters," shouted the orchestra leader. The music began again.

"Oh boy, Wally," Connie was saying excitedly, "go out there and tear that floor to splinters." She gave him a push between the shoulders as he got up.

Wally was out there now and the whole hall was spinning around him like a merry-go-round. He could hear them chanting:

I wonder does my baby do that
Charle-stun! Charle-stun!

Wally saw red. He'd show them whether their baby did that

Charleston! Mimi was beating time with her hands. Clap-clap, clap-clap. "I never saw anyone like him," she turned and said to somebody. "Where did he get that from?"

Wally began to skate as though he were on a pond. A tinkle of small sleigh-bells immediately followed from the musicians.

Connie was almost following him around the floor. "Come on, cake! Eat it up, eat it up!"

"Give him room!" they cried.

"Get that girl out of the way," ordered Mimi imperiously. "What does she think she is, the tail of his shirt?"

Wally was hopping around like some funny little three-legged animal. He went down gradually like a corkscrew going into the neck of a bottle. Then he straightened up and the music stopped sharply.

Connie was waiting right beside him. She threw both her arms around his neck and kissed him.

"Bless your little soul!" she cried ecstatically.

"Bless both my little soles," he panted.

Mimi Travers was talking very animatedly to the orchestra leader. Everyone was watching her curiously. "Hurry up, make up your mind," growled Connie under her breath.

Finally Mimi stood up and took the leader by the arm as though they were going to head a cotillion together. "Miss Travers wishes me to announce," intoned that individual, "that the prize goes to Mr. Wallace Walters as winner of this contest. Will Mr. Walters kindly step this way?"

"Boy, oh bay-bee!" hissed Connie, and she pinched him on the arm. "Do you get that?"

There was an explosion of handclapping. Wally made his way across the floor from group to group, showered with complimentary remarks. Rose and Myrtle and Lily came over to congratulate him—not that they were any the less envious.

"I liked it!" said Rose.

"I loved it!" said Myrtle.

Love & Night

"I adored it!" said Lily.

It was a cake eater's triumph. But Wally, who had had many such moments in the course of his career, was thinking of Mimi and her castle of dreams. They were standing face to face now. He could see a golden flame quivering in the depths of her heliotrope eyes. She handed him the ice-cold silver cup and for a moment their warm fingertips touched over its frosty surface.

"Good luck," she said. "You did beautifully."

"Thank you," he answered. "Glad you liked it." He bowed from the hips.

"Hold it up so everyone can see it," she said, taking in the entire assemblage at a glance.

When it was all over, he found himself seated with Mimi at one of the little tables, somehow. And on the table there was an empty glass with two broken straws in it, and someone's rhinestone purse, and a string of blue tickets. Mimi extracted a perfumed cigaret from a small tortoise-shell case and moistened it with her lips. Now almost anyone at all could have told Mimi that smoking was against the rule, but it so happened that the unpleasant task fell upon Wally.

"I don't think they let you do that here," he mentioned as casually as he was able.

Mimi didn't like being told what not to do. "Let you do what--smoke?" she demanded coldly.

He nodded dolefully and made an unpleasant face.

"Oh, yes they do!" she assured him. "They do me at any rate."

He looked rather doubtful and shrugged his shoulders, having had more than one fair companion separated from her nicotine just when she was beginning to enjoy it. "Well," he said, "if you think so, go ahead—"

"I don't think so. I know so," remarked the fiery Mimi. "I'll tell you what; call the proprietor and we'll see."

He tried to grin his way out of it but this time Mimi was out for blood—that and publicity. "Very well," she said, "then I will!" She stood up and beckoned. "Call Mr. Nathan," she told one of the hostesses.

"Good evening," said Mr. Nathan a moment later. "Anything I can do for you?"

"Yes," said Mimi in a clear voice. "I'd like to smoke this cigaret. Have you a light by any chance?" She stared at him defiantly.

Mr. Nathan saw a neat little sign tacked against a post. It read "Absolutely No Smoking." But "Certainly, certainly," said Mr. Nathan, and dug a little gold lighter out of his pocket. When he tried to light it, though, it shed sparks all over the place.

"Be careful of my dress," cautioned Mimi sharply. Wally, sensing his opportunity, whipped out an everyday case of matches and accomplished the thing in no time at all.

"Thanks," she said, with a sullen look at the proprietor.

"I don't know what's the matter with it," he apologized. "It never stalled like this before."

"No," she agreed cynically, "never."

"Something must be wrong with the tinder," he mumbled to himself as he moved off with his neck bent over it. Wally and Mimi looked at one another and smiled pityingly.

"Isn't he the wet one!" said Wally.

"He's dripping," she agreed.

At this juncture Connie appeared before them with a decided pout on her face.

"I'm ready to go now, cake," she announced, pulling the rhinestone bag from underneath Mimi's nose.

"Well," he said ungraciously, "and what am I supposed to do—break out in a rash?" And Mimi, guessing that the dance tickets were also Connie's property, pushed them angrily off the table with her elbow. They fell to the floor.

"Say, look out what you're doing," snapped Connie, bending over to pick them up.

"I beg your pardon?" said Mimi haughtily.

Love & Night

"You certainly should," Connie told her. She turned to Wally. "Well, make up your mind," she advised him.

"What's all the rush about?" he remarked. "What do you think you are, my time-table? Wise up to yourself."

"All right, cake," she said easily, almost tenderly. "You'll get over it in time."

She turned her back on the two of them. At the door Mimi saw her crumple the tickets in her fist and throw them away from her. But Wally only had eyes for his Mimi. She was the same and yet she was not the same. The clown make-up was gone. She was neat and restful to the eyes. She had lavender silk stockings; she had a gold ring around her ankle; she had a bang slicked down to the bridge of her nose. But he couldn't forget how she had looked with the little terrier clasped in her arms. He couldn't forget that she had stood there on the stage and everyone had laughed at her while her heart was slowly breaking. He kept telling himself that her castle of dreams had come tumbling down just as his had, over and over again. Therefore they were brother and sister under the skin.

"Don't take it so hard," laughed Mimi, thinking he was worried about Connie. "She'll come back; they all do." She stood up, and she was very tall and slim. "Afraid I'll have to go now."

"Can I see you to the door?" he asked.

"Only to the door?" she said, and her eyelashes swept him good-naturedly up and down.

"I meant to your door."

And as they went out, he could hear the band playing softly and sweetly:

*It must be love, it must be love,
That makes me feel this way.*

• • •

The following evening the fun-loving Mimi Travers, of New

York and Philly but still not of points west, was the center of interest of a very lively group of friends who had gathered in her dressing room before the beginning of the show.

"He thinks," she was telling them, "I'm really the way I'm supposed to be when I sing that song. Sort of dumb and weepy, know what I mean?"

"He must be goofy," they chorused. "What a sap. What a bone."

"He is," Mimi assured them. "Probably he likes them that way. So when I found that out, I started right in to emote. Last night when we were coming out of the dance hall a stray cat came along and began rubbing itself against me so I broke down and cried for his benefit—"

Screams of laughter drowned her voice. The idea of Mimi crying about anything seemed to strike them as being extremely funny.

"You should have heard me," she protested. "All I kept repeating was 'What's the use, what's the use, 's a cruel world,' and he dried my eyes and called me his Cinderella. How's that for a riot?"

"Horses!" they gasped hysterically, burying their faces on one another's shoulders. "Oh, you Red Riding Hood! Little Eva!"

There was a warning knock on the door. "Curtain goes up in five more minutes." Mimi quickly wheeled round and began rouging her cheeks with a rabbit's paw. But she was still smiling at the huge joke.

• • •

At the end of the one week stand Wally was walking on air and living up in the clouds. But Mimi was all packed and ready to leave with the rest of the company. He was sitting out front again the night of the farewell performance—he had seen the show every night that week—and as the house lights went on, he edged his way out through a side door and around to the stage

Love & Night

entrance. Backstage everything was in an uproar: sets being taken down and moved about, people getting in each other's way, stagehands in overalls rubbing shoulders with girls in gorgeous evening gowns. He found Mimi's door and knocked.

"Hello?" she called out. "What do you want?"

"It's me, Mimi."

There was a slight hesitation in her voice as she answered. "I'm busy right now. Can you wait?"

He noticed the drop in her voice. He opened the door and went ahead in.

She was in a tailored traveling suit with a red patent leather belt which made her look about fifteen. Her baggage was piled in a heap in the center of the room, and she was sweeping things from the dressing table into the last open suitcase.

"Didn't you hear me tell you I was busy?" she said angrily. "What's the grand idea? What do you take this place for, a corner drug store?"

"I've got to talk to you," he said.

"Haven't got time to talk."

"I thought you were coming up to the Rainbow with me. It's Saturday night."

"I wouldn't care if it was Christmas Eve. I've got to make that train." She saw the look on his face and it softened her for a moment. "What's the matter with you, cakie? You knew this was a one-week stand all along. We're due to open Monday night—"

And now the castle of dreams really came tumbling down, with a terrible crash that no one could hear but himself. He stood there dazed while a couple of stagehands came in and carried her baggage outside for her.

"Get a taxi if you want to take me to the train," she said shortly. Her one moment of sentiment was over and gone.

They got into the taxi and drove to the railroad station. He looked out of one window and she looked out of the other. Neither of them spoke. When she was comfortably installed in the Pullman, she took off her hat and straightened her hair without paying any attention to him.

"Stay over just one more day—" he pleaded.

"My reservation's paid for."

"I haven't told you, but can't you guess why—why I hate to see you go?" he faltered.

"Sure I can guess," she said confidently. "You're keen on me, is that it?"

"That doesn't begin to describe it. All my life I . . . waited . . . wanted . . . dreamed . . . about someone . . . like you are . . . Oh, if you'd only let yourself be the way you seemed to be the first night I saw you!"

"That's sweet and pretty," she told him, "but what good does it do to think about things like that? Castles in the air never did anybody any good—not so you could notice it." She patted his hand. "There goes the whistle, sugar. The best thing for you to do is go back and dance it off."

Outside on the platform the conductor was swinging a green lantern back and forth. "All aboard!" he wailed dolefully. "All aboard!"

"Kiss me good-bye," exclaimed Mimi, "and forget all about me."

Their lips met for the first and last time. The cars started to move. "I'll go with you!" he cried, swept by a wild momentary impulse.

"What? And me lose my job?" answered the prevaricating Mimi. "I should say not. Jump or you'll never make it!"

He ran to the lower end of the car and swung clear of the steps. The sound of his voice came trailing back to her: "'Bye, Mimi." She pressed her face against the window pane, but it was too dark outside to make out anything. She gave a little sigh.

• • •

Love & Night

He picked himself up and watched the red tail-light on the rear car grow smaller and smaller until finally it disappeared altogether. Mimi was gone and he would never see her again. He dusted himself off and went back to his room.

But when he opened the door to the "budwa," he found Connie sitting there reading a magazine.

"How did you get in here?" he asked listlessly.

She looked up. "Did you see your friend off?" she wanted to know innocently.

"Yes," he said, "she's gone away. Let her go."

"I been waiting for you to come back," Connie said. "There's going to be a big masquerade at the Rainbow next Sa'ddy night. They're going to give prizes for the best costume. How about us going?"

He didn't answer. For a long time he stood looking down at her as if there were something about her he'd never realized before.

"Cake," she said, "are you angry at me?"

"No," he said. "Something's just come over me. I didn't see how I was going to stand it . . . I thought it was going to be lonely . . . I thought it would kill me."

"Sure, honey," she said gently. "I know how those things are. I have it myself—"

Suddenly he sank down alongside her and buried his head in her arms. "But it was you all the time, Connie. It was you all the time."

She caressed his hair with the tips of her fingers.

"Cake," she murmured.

"Connie," he said softly. "Dreams do come true . . . sometimes."

[*McClure's*, October 1926]

How this most downbeat of Woolrich's stories got published in a magazine called College Humor *I can't begin to comprehend. But in light of his youthful enthusiasm for the author of* The Great Gatsby, *there's no mystery about why the main male character is named Scotty.*

MOTHER AND DAUGHTER

In the days when the two-step was tottering upon its throne and weird mulatto dances were creeping out of the Brazils to replace it, she and her partner had won fame as ballroom artists. London knew them, and Paris, and the old lobster belt, reaching in those days to Churchill's at Forty-ninth. She was a child of seventeen then, very tall, a little too thin, wore low-heeled shoes and short skirts before their time. He was a man in his middle forties, much divorced, a little made up around the eyes. Together they rose like rockets and went out in mid-air. Paris and London had stopped dancing; they had no time any more.

Georgia, her career cut short, had turned around and married, married well. She had literally made herself a bed of golden dollars and intended to abide by it. The man of her choice was Jordan, who had made a fortune out of peanut brittle simply by removing the shells from the peanuts before they went into the brittle. What he did with the shells after they were removed was never made clear. Georgia used to say he stuffed mattresses with them.

She let her hair grow and amazed the world that had copied her dancing by having a little girl. Going over to add to her collection of chiffon stockings and perfumery, the ship was torpedoed a little after daybreak one morning, and Georgia woke up to find a thin layer of water spread over the carpet of her stateroom. She quickly drew on a *crepe de chine* negligee, then changed it for a

Love & Night

black dinner dress, determined to look her best. The skirt of this was too long, though, and she finally discarded it in favor of an orange tailor-made suit, just the thing for shipwrecks. Then she called the maid, who slept in the next room, and they hobbled out on deck like frightened deer. The moment they were in the open a whole assortment of the ship's officers lifted Georgia bodily in their arms and put her into a lifeboat. The maid was doing her best to climb in after her when Georgia tearfully commanded: "Go back and wake my husband, Marie." Then she added in an undertone, "And for heaven's sake, see if you can't get hold of some face powder for me. It's sinful, with all these people around."

Marie began to weep and said she wasn't going back to be drowned like a rat.

"You're not, eh?" said Georgia, narrowing her eyes. "You're discharged. Get out of this boat."

By three the following afternoon Georgia had found out she was a widow. She took it greatly to heart. "Poor Jordan!" she said. "What will become of the peanut industry now?"

The peanut industry, however, did very nicely. In fact it flourished exceedingly, so that by the time Jicky was ready to come out into the world she needed a rake in each hand to tidy up the dollars that came fluttering down about her like green and yellow leaves.

Jicky was the daughter. Homely mothers frequently have beautiful children, but it also works the other way around. Georgia's mother before her had been undoubtedly attractive, even with all the obstacles of apparel that had to be overcome in her day. But when it came to Jicky, the beauty in the family seemed to have run out. Georgia had eyes that were mixed with star dust. Jicky wore convex lenses in front of hers. Georgia could make her hands talk. Jicky could make hers drop things at critical moments. Georgia could wear a twenty-dollar gown and make it look mysterious. Jicky could wear a two-hundred dollar one and make it look terrible. Georgia could make the traffic part in the middle to let her through, like the Red Sea. Whereas taxi drivers had been known to foist their cabs upon the sidewalk in their efforts to run Jicky down. Georgia walked like a dream, like a lotus borne upon a sacred pool. Jicky walked into things.

Everything Georgia did was done right. If she stroked a dog, the dog stayed stroked for the rest of the day. No one else could do it as gracefully, as full of charming little nuances. If she poured coffee, you asked for a second cup just to see her pour it over again. If she played cards, you forgot your game, so absorbed were you in the delicate shivery way she shuffled.

Jicky? Jicky spilled them all over the floor and dealt them face up. And once, mind you, once, Jicky had been known to trump her partner's ace. She tried to explain later that was all she held in her hand. It was no use though; appearances were against her, and the legend went all over the country club.

Now at about this time there appeared on the scene Scotty Tryon, about twenty-nine or thirty and untroubled as yet by poor digestion or feminine attachment. Jicky met him out at the club one day when a long distance telephone call had broken up a game of doubles. When first seen he was wearing a gray flannel shirt with a package of cigarettes squaring the pocket and a web belt that went up on one side and down on the other. The web belt decided her. A man who didn't worry about the hang of his trousers ought to play a good game. She pressed him into service.

If there was one thing Jicky was good at, it was tennis. I mean, she had nothing to lose by acting in front of the net like a dervish out on a spree. Perspiration or rumpled hair didn't count with her. And when you have nothing to lose, why hold back? She didn't. Consequently, when she smacked the ball, it took your mind off a great many things at once. She looked better in flat shoes than she did on high heels anyway, and the green shade over her eyes did a lot for her face.

Love & Night

Her game took his breath away. Later he asked someone who she was.

"That? Oh, that was Jicky Jordan. Her pillow's stuffed with goldbacks at night. She's supposed to be a man hater. It oughtn't to be hard with a face like hers."

"I wouldn't say things like that if I were you," Scotty remonstrated, creasing his forehead. "Isn't called for, you know." Thinking how she played, for a girl.

They had an appointment to play again the next day, and the next after that, and so on through the weeks. They were really the best foils for each other either one had yet encountered, and in athletics admiration is the closest thing there is to love. Then too, they had begun on a rock-bottom basis. She had never seen him when his shirt wasn't plastered to his back, and he had never seen her when her hair wasn't flying in all directions and her toes curved out. She became vain of her very untidiness, clung to it as a token of her sexlessness. She would run her fingers through her hair and purposely tousle it before coming out of the locker room to meet him in the mornings. She could no more picture him with a collar and tie on than he could imagine her with lipstick and face powder. This was ideal but it couldn't go on forever, naturally.

She had him up to the house one day to show him her collection of rackets, which they handled and discussed avidly over two tall glasses of iced tea out on the veranda.

"Coming out to the club dance tomorrow night?" he asked offhand.

"I believe I'd like to," she said without a moment's hesitation.

He bit his lip and looked off in another direction. "Suppose I call for you at nine," he said, seeing there was no help for it.

"Fine," she answered, and turned around and ran into the house as though she were afraid he'd change his mind if she stayed out there too long with him.

There was a noticeably dejected air about him as he got back into his car and slumped down until his chin met the wheel.

• • •

The girl who is sure of herself is always late. The girl who isn't gets ready too soon. Jicky was ready to go to the dance from eight-thirty on and knew every square inch of the mirror by heart. Six hundred dollars wouldn't have bought the silver slip she had on with a solitary orange poppy over one hip. And she never wore the same dress twice. Her stockings were so spidery you had to look again to be sure she had any on. But she wore her glasses.

When she came downstairs at two minutes past nine without having been called, she found him standing there talking to someone. He had come without a hat apparently, but he had the collar of his coat turned back in the approved manner. She passed him her shawl and he draped it lightly around her.

"Don't catch cold, dear," her aunt said. "Be sure to put your shawl over you if you go outside between times."

Jicky smiled ruefully. A wallflower formerly had been a girl who couldn't get partners to dance with. Nowadays the wallflower was the girl who danced every dance and was never coaxed outside for a while in the moonlight.

The club, seen through the trees, was like a grotto of fireflies, and long rows of cars were drawn up outside. The moon was the color of champagne and from the gauzy clubhouse came music of *Show Boat* and *Good News* like the patter of furtive raindrops on a sheet of tin.

Inside they separated, she to seclude herself in a room already sugary with cologne and sachet odors. Other girls were there, reddening their lips, fumbling with the hems of their skirts. When they saw the silver lace on Jicky, they sighed enviously and gave one another looks. She took her glasses off and wrapped them in

Love & Night

her shawl although everything looked blurred to her. She knew she was taking a chance. She might go up to the wrong starched shirt outside the door. That was what reading hundreds of books in sunlight and firelight and lamplight when you were twelve and thirteen did for you. As she stepped outside into the glare and excitement, she had a feeling she was dowdy, even though she knew her dress to be an original and her heels were as tall as an infanta's. Some girls could take a piano cover and a rhinestone shoe buckle and get better results.

Not knowing her and not knowing the club, one might have mistaken Jicky for someone immensely popular, the way the young men gathered around her. True, she knew everyone. But it was only a synthetic popularity as far as Jicky was concerned, and no one realized it better than she herself. They knew they would have to dance with her sooner or later in the course of the evening, and the trick lay in getting it over with as soon as possible. Afterwards, when the center of gravity shifted to the cars outside, she would be left high and dry on the dance floor. She could distinctly recall having been left behind in places where the only other living beings were the musicians and possibly the caterers.

"Let's go outside," Scotty suggested at eleven-thirty.

Nights of unforgivable neglect had taught Jicky nothing, however.

"I don't think I should," she said coyly.

He took her at her word.

There was a telegram waiting for her when she got back. She crossed the corridor with it and knocked on the door. "Aunt Pauline," she said, "are you up yet? We'd better pack. We're to go back to New York in the morning. Mother's coming in Wednesday on the Aquitania."

• • •

They had been back about six weeks when the telephone interrupted their breakfast one morning. Georgia, who had an extension beside her bed, immediately got on. A moment later she called Jicky into the room. There was a note of surprise in her voice. "Oh, I'm sorry. It was meant for you, dear." This was something new to her.

Jicky arranged herself on a chaise longue, giving a very inept imitation of the way Georgia did it so often herself.

"Ye-es?" Her voice rose, musically tremulous. She tried to prop a cushion over her shoulder and the receiver fell into her lap.

Georgia bit her lip to cover a smile. "Relax, dear, relax," she suggested.

"Been meaning to call you," Scotty was saying in Jicky's tingling ear.

"Oh, dear, how nice," she said inanely.

Georgia curtained herself behind a sheer of cigarette smoke, doing her conscientious best not to be present. She felt too deliciously lazy to get up, and there was a cup of coffee-and-chocolate on her knee to be considered.

Jicky hung up and kept the telephone in her lap as though she couldn't bear to part with it.

"It was Scotty," she said. "The one I told you about. Wait. I think I have his picture inside."

"Oh, is that the kind he is?" remarked Georgia facetiously.

"No, no," Jicky hastened to assure her. "I cut it out of a sporting magazine. He does a lot of tennis. And what do you suppose he does with the cups?" Her eyes grew enormous. "He uses them to put his old razor blades in."

"How extraordinary of him," breathed the satirical Georgia.

"He's coming up Friday to dinner. I want you to meet him," Jicky exclaimed vibrantly. "Oh, he's simply dandy."

• • •

Love & Night

Friday at half past eight she made her entrance by stumbling over and lifting the edge of the jade-blue rug. "Mother, this is Mr. Tryon," she heard herself saying a trifle nervously.

Georgia, in the decorous instep skirts of the second empire, was trying her best to be motherly, was ready to forego all restful crossing of the knees that evening for Jicky's sake. She held herself demurely in the background, doing things with a little jet fan she had brought out with her and eyeing the cigarette dish longingly from time to time.

Jicky was frozen with shyness and shrilly voluble by turns. No one had ever had an effect like this on her before. During dinner she upset her wineglass and the stem snapped. She sighed gloomily. Georgia and Scotty were too deeply engrossed by this time to have noticed anything. Every other word of his was addressed to Georgia and every other word of Georgia's was directed toward Jicky in what began to look like a desperate attempt at keeping the balance of conversation even.

Georgia excused herself at ten, and a half hour later Jicky found her in her room nestling in chiffon and devouring cigarettes.

"Why didn't you come back? I'm sure he thought it was strange. He asked what had become of you once or twice."

"Wouldn't have intruded for anything," murmured Georgia, going ahead with the book she was reading.

"Now I've told you you weren't; why do you keep saying that?" said Jicky. "How did he strike you?"

Georgia, feeling that some comment was expected of her, did her conscientious best. "Oh, rather nice." She had a vacant air about her, as though she were not paying strict attention to what she was saying.

Jicky gazed upward through her glasses in rapture. "I think so too," she remarked. "I think he's just dandy."

• • •

He asked them to the theater shortly after, binding Georgia's attendance by the announcement that it was to be a party of four. The friend, Russell Bain, was so patently cut out for Jicky by years if not by inclination that it seemed only natural for Georgia and Scotty to gravitate toward each other. Afterwards, at the supper club, Scotty danced the first number with Jicky, during which she got spells of rigidity and it became next to impossible to budge her, and all the rest with Georgia, who tried to minimize her performance by saying something to the effect that she had once had to earn a living at it.

It was with quivering eyelashes that Jicky that same night said the orchestra had been simply awful and she would have preferred remaining at home.

"So would I," agreed Georgia with the sigh of a martyr.

• • •

The Bain boy, pursuing Jicky with phone calls and engagements in the weeks that followed, managed to get himself a little mistrusted by her. A suspicion came over her at times that perhaps he had been coached beforehand in the part he was to play, as far as tying her hands most effectually was concerned. Here was admiration and she didn't want it; here was tenderness and it bored her. She was seeing very little of Scotty these days, and yet he was continually stopping in for a cocktail. It was all very puzzling, and then after a while it was not nearly so puzzling any more. She began to see things in their proper light.

"What do you think of Mother?" she asked him once.

"Remarkable looking, isn't she?"

"Isn't she, though! Everyone has always thought so—" All at once she stopped, as though someone had bored a little hole in her and let all her enthusiasm out. They never discussed Georgia between them after that.

And then one afternoon she wandered into the topaz-lighted

Love & Night

room at the Madrid, and there was Georgia sitting over on the other side next to the wall. Jicky started across toward her, and just as she got about halfway, the waiter who had been arranging the tea things at Georgia's table stepped to one side and revealed Scotty, all smiles as he leaned forward to say something more or less pleasant. Jicky stood still for a frozen half moment; then she turned around to walk out as though she had forgotten something. Georgia looked up just at the wrong moment. She came hurrying after her and stopped her just over the threshold.

"Jicky! Didn't you see me sitting there?"

"Of course I did," said Jicky, "but I thought—"

"What silly notions you get," Georgia exclaimed. "Don't make a scene like this. We've ordered another pot of tea for you."

Scotty half rose and bowed her into her seat.

"Marvelous to run into you like this."

"Isn't it, though," she replied uncordially.

"We called up to have you join us but you had gone out," Georgia said.

"No doubt," answered Jicky with cryptic intent.

Georgia, seizing her opportunity, gathered up her purse and gloves. "Mind if I run along now? Some things I must do."

Jicky, her teacup still filled, was held trapped. She stared resentfully as she saw Georgia go out the door.

"We happened into each other quite accidentally," Scotty related, "so I suggested coming here."

"Rather nice to meet you both." This latter word sticking its head up like a thorn. She said very little else during the course of the next ten minutes. Her napkin reappeared above the table. "I'll say goodbye. I have a headache."

"If you must go," he said.

She did a lot of thinking when she got back that afternoon. It is safe to assume she had never concentrated quite so wholeheartedly and painfully on any one thing in her entire life before. When Scotty called that evening, Georgia was not in.

Neither was Jicky, sitting alone in the living room swinging her foot and humming in a carefully guarded voice. The sequence in which he had asked for them had nothing to do with it, she assured herself.

They sat facing each other at luncheon a day or two later, and Georgia unaccountably dropped her hand to her lap. Not quickly enough, however. "A new ring, isn't it?" Jicky observed. She extended her hand and Georgia, disengaging hers, reluctantly submitted the tips of her fingers for examination.

"Isn't it darling," said Jicky in a hoarse voice.

Georgia laughed embarrassedly. "I hardly know what to say," she admitted. "In fact I—I'm not free to say anything just now."

In her own room a few moments later, Jicky took her glasses off for the last time. As a matter of fact, she threw them on the floor and dug her heel through them. She had a hairdresser and his assistants up and spent her afternoon undergoing elaborate rites of beautification that left her looking at least ten years older. Then when Russell Bain called up, she accepted the inevitable with what amounted to stoic philosophy.

As she crossed the foyer on her way out, she came face to face with Scotty, handing his hat to the maid. He took in the mandarin coat and rhinestone vanity case at a glance.

"Good evening," she said briefly. "And by the way, allow me to congratulate you."

He stared at her blankly. "What for?"

"Announce the gentleman to my mother, Leila," she said, and closed the door on him. She went down in the elevator with the feeling that somehow her evening was definitely spoiled even before it had got under way. She caught the gleam of something liquid on her lashes in the beveled mirror facing her.

"Where to?" asked Russell, sitting waiting for her in the car with his stick between his legs.

"Don't give me a minute's time to think tonight," she warned him, "or I'll fold up on you and die."

Love & Night

• • •

Two days later the count appeared. Georgia's room meanwhile had become a bower of flowers overnight. "Count Riano," she explained, weaving a pattern in the air with her atomizer. "A dear friend of mine from Paris. Won't you come out and say how do?"

Jicky groped to straighten her glasses. Then she remembered that they were gone.

He was sitting in the half light of several lamps, slowly turning the leaves of a book without attempting to look at it. He laid the book aside and stood up, his shoulders orange in the evening light.

"My daughter, Jocelyn," said Georgia.

"But how charming," said the count.

• • •

When Georgia came in that night, there was a droop to her; she was crestfallen as Jicky had never seen her crestfallen before.

Jicky patted her on the shoulder.

"Did he dance terribly, shake like a leaf and all that? Did he spill things when he ate? Something went wrong, I can feel it. Won't you tell me, dearest?"

"Oh, no," Georgia answered simply. "He carries himself like a twenty-year-old with the antics left out. It's myself. I never realized it until tonight. It's—it's over eight months since we've seen each other, you know."

"You mean he found a change in you?"

"'How fresh and youthful all your American women are,' he said, and then he looked at me. 'My dear,' he said, 'I don't believe New York agrees with you. You were not so pale last year in Paris. You have a harried look—"

"Oh, well," said Jicky bitterly, "if he insists on throwing a roomful of debutantes in your teeth, let it go at that. I think the average person seeing you out together would take him to be your father."

"No," said Georgia pensively, "you're very good to me, but something's got to be done. It's for my own satisfaction, you understand. There is this new treatment everyone is beginning to talk about," she said. "I wonder—Sondra Clark was telling me about it only yesterday. Some kind of heliotrope rays—I don't know what they're called—that vitalize the muscles of the face. It's really an electric bath."

"Things like that can be dangerous," said Jicky. "Please don't."

"How absurd," said Georgia. "This is 1928. Things are perfected beyond the point where any risk enters into them. Didn't that dancer do it when she wanted to acquire a tropical sunburn?"

• • •

A week later she was beginning the experiment. Brimful of enthusiasm, she could talk of nothing else. "But I do look better, don't I?" she would ask Jicky half a dozen times in the course of a day. Jicky was undecided whether it was the process itself or her enormous faith in it that gave her an undeniably quickened reaction these days. The treatments were rather early. As a rule Georgia was gone before anyone was up.

One morning the count put in an appearance just as Jicky had finished breakfast. She recoiled in synthetic modesty, but he seemed not to see her. Obviously pale and shaken, he went directly to the wall cabinet and poured himself a small glass of cordial with a wrist that trembled so exaggeratedly it almost suggested a stage effect.

"*Vite.* Get yourself dressed," he said hoarsely.

Love & Night

"What's happened?" she said. "Where's Mother?"

"I beg of you get yourself dressed," he said. "The vibrator have been accident."

She had no sooner left the room than she was back with a coat thrown over her, tears beginning to form in her eyes. They hurried out together, leaving the door open behind them.

Georgia was already under ether in one of the emergency wards. She lay coifed in gauze like a nun. The count led Jicky from the room after a while, and all afternoon long she paced back and forth in the little waiting room outside. Toward four o'clock they held a consultation over her and announced there was no immediate danger. Skin grafting would be undertaken, they gave Jicky to understand.

"There will be marks, unavoidably, but we will do everything in our power."

The count shook his head morosely as they seated themselves in the car and started back.

"The marriage will have to be postpone."

"Marriage?" echoed Jicky.

"She no have told you of our engagement, then? *Mon dieu*, since last year in Paris already."

"I've seen the ring, I think," said Jicky.

"Ah, yes, the ring," he agreed indifferently.

At her door he handed her out of the car with elaborate politeness. Something told Jicky, as she watched him resume his seat and carefully button one chamois glove, that that was the last they would see of him.

• • •

Six weeks later, in her own home, the shades drawn and the light carefully tempered, the bandages were finally removed from Georgia's face and throat. Jicky had taken refuge in the hallway outside that significantly closed door, her chilled wrists in Scotty's keeping. There was an air of fatality about the apartment. A sickening stillness that gave pause to some ominous thing about to happen. In the other room the light footstep of a nurse was heard, the doctor's voice in a guarded murmur, and then a silence, utter and obliterating, that lasted hours, it seemed.

A scream, short and swift as a knife thrust, rang out behind Georgia's door. It held an element of surprise, of a sharp indignity thrust upon one. It could have been the death cry of a woman's vanity.

Jicky was in Scotty's arms now, trembling, her face buried on his shoulder.

"My dear, my dear," she choked, "I can't bear the thought of it."

"Go in to her," he urged. "You'll have to, you know. You've got to see her through it."

She left him and went toward the door, conscious of a bitter resentment against herself. "You won't have to be envious of her now, you rotter."

There was a slight tinge of drugs in the air and the nurse stood unobtrusively over in a corner. There was no one else in the room but Georgia, a pathetic Georgia, her hands lying limply beside her on the covers, palms up.

"Mother!" said Jicky.

"Is it true, Jicky?" she said. "Is it true—I have to be this way from now on?"

"Mother, Scotty's here with me. You want to see him, don't you?"

"How can I? Oh, no, how can I?"

"Dearest, Scotty's your friend—"

This was the test, to try not to gloat when Scotty saw what had happened to Georgia's looks, to try to feel sorry for him and sorry for her, sorry that the thing he had valued above everything else was gone, sorry that the thing she had been was blighted.

The door opened and he came in.

Love & Night

He gave one swift look as though the bottom had dropped out of something, and Jicky's heart died within her. He must have cared then, to look that way about it.

Georgia's voice from the bed, trying to be gay, pleading desperately, then all at once breaking off.

"Is—is anything noticeable? They told me it was the shadow in the glass. Oh, Scotty, I'm so afraid—"

He was standing beside her looking down at her.

"You know better than that," he said softly. He reached over and put one finger to her brow as if in whimsical camaraderie.

"You're—you're marvelous. What did you expect? How could you be otherwise? You think just a little gauze and cotton is going to change you?"

He turned to look at Jicky and there was some kind of detached wistfulness in his eyes she could not fathom. And as they stole out of the room together, Georgia turned her face on the pillow trustfully up to the nurse. "He would tell me, wouldn't he?" she murmured.

Jicky stood with her back to the closed door. "You're a brick," she faltered gratefully. "Poor Mother."

"A woman will believe what she wants to believe," he answered.

• • •

In the weeks that followed and the months they totaled, he never ceased importuning her to go out with him and she hardly ever went. There was always the shadow of this thing between them. The count had gone back to France, alleging pressing business matters, and was one man very different from another when it came to things like these, Jicky asked herself? Scotty might besiege her with telephone calls and drop in at every turn, but would he have turned to her if what had happened hadn't—

come between? She crushed the thought to her like ground glass and bled herself sick over it.

It was only the two of them now. The dreaded confirmation of her worst fears to be met with in keen strange feminine eyes would still be spared Georgia for a while. Her pleading had to be met too as well as Scotty's on these occasions.

"Please, dear. Won't you go with him for my sake, just this once?"

"But there's nothing I'm fit to be seen in."

"Wear one of mine then."

"Oh, what's the difference? I'll look like a pig anyway."

And then Jicky, unhappy to the core, going in to vent her dissatisfaction on him with the particularly ungracious comment: "Mother wants me to, so I'll go with you."

• • •

At the Lido one night in an atmosphere of cigarettes, aigrettes, and Lehar waltzes, he told her how much he cared for her and she began to cry, blindly furious at herself, without letting him see it, somehow. She would have killed him if he had noticed it. Her chin almost touching her chest, she studied the finely spun web of brilliants that constituted the upper part of her dress, a surface that at close range dislocated the rays of vision and went slightly out of focus, coruscating like some dazzling boiling substance.

This crowd of pretty things around him, such pretty things they were, and he could sit there looking at her guiltily sparkling lashes and talk this way to her? Every jeweled heel that touched the floor spurted its ice-like reflection downward into the heart of the glassy paneling. And women over their partners' shoulders breathed not air but blue notes that stung their nostrils to a rhythmic frenzy. It was such a good looking crowd, such a good looking crowd. A bandeau of rhinestones and aquamarines

Love & Night

fronted Jicky's brow and behind it a strange swift prayer began to surge.

"Oh, God, make me beautiful in his eyes. Beautiful. In his eyes. In his alone." And the ultimate admission, wrenched from her with a suffocating sense of humiliation. "Make him love me as I love him." After which there was nothing more to be prayed for.

"I want you to say that you'll marry me," he said. "A man wants all the beauty he can get into his life and so—I want you."

So he wanted beauty too. But he was not like her, not selfish; he wanted it from outside of himself. The thought of those long-forgotten mornings on the tennis courts came back to her, with her hair wind-blown and just a woolly white sweater on her. So he really found her beautiful after all. In that case, why, she must be, in some hidden way overlooked by everyone else until now. Perhaps in that tennis court sort of way, and without all these brilliants and this paint. It was up to her then. She would have to forget about being beautiful and just be beautiful. For beauty, she had heard, was in the eye of the beholder.

Jicky raised her head and looked at him and at everyone else as though she saw them for the first time. She forgave him everything she had ever done—her doubts and her jealousy and her humiliations. She could have forgiven him anything, for they were both alike in this: they were both beauty-mad.

• • •

Georgia was sitting up, the exquisite light from a cluster of electric grapes at the head of the bed tinseling her shoulders, when Jicky stopped in the doorway. This was a new Jicky. She held her head high; she was vibrant with courage and a new sort of vindication that still left her puzzled but was more welcome than she could ever know. The bandeau sparkled but under it you noticed the more lasting sparkle of her eyes. The fringe at her shawl dropped to the floor about her in a sort of gentle silver rain. She stepped into the room, carrying her youth like a chip on the shoulder. She took an amber-backed object from the table and put it in the drawer and shut it from sight.

"For us there'll be no more mirrors. Mirrors lie."

"Mirrors lie," agreed Georgia. "They've lied to me all my life."

Jicky turned around to look at her and the shawl dropped to her feet in a foamy pool.

"Mother, I'm beautiful, and I'm going to marry Scotty. Beautiful—"

She stood gloriously erect for a moment, then crumpled over across Georgia's knees. Suddenly she burst out crying.

"He thinks I am, so I am. Oh, Mother, help me believe it; help me believe it! There's beauty in me now, real beauty, where there was only wretchedness."

They lay with their arms around each other, their cheeks pressed together like two children, staring over at a far corner of the room as though they could see themselves there as they believed themselves to be.

"I don't blame him. Who could help loving you? Oh, if you could only see yourself as I see you."

"And you, my dearest, you," purred Jicky, "you're beautiful. The most beautiful mother in the world."

Said Scotty, a woman will believe what she wants to believe.

[*College Humor,* August 1928]

The mother of this tale's protagonist is called Angel Face, a name that Woolrich later used in several noir classics, including The Black Angel *(1943). If nothing else, the evocation of the specter of Anahuac that had haunted Woolrich since adolescence would seem to have disqualified the story for a magazine with* Humor *in its title. The miracle is that it didn't.*

GAY MUSIC

When he was eighteen, Gerald Jones found out things about himself. A gypsy woman told him, a gypsy woman with gold coins in her ears and cigarette-stained teeth and a cerise petticoat and an apple-green scarf about her head. He came across two of them trudging along by the roadside one day, and had pocket money with him, and noticed that they were noticing him.

"You a very good looking boy," one of them remarked.

"Oh, sure," he scoffed, but it didn't make him angry nevertheless.

The one that had spoken to him squatted down until she was no higher than his knee. Her gaudy petticoat settled itself around her in a splashy circle like red ink soaking through the macadamized road. She produced a pack of cards and began to tell them out before her on the ground in a double row.

She said: "I read your fute."

"Read my foot?" he asked in astonishment. These foreigners could get so embarrassing.

"Fooch," she said.

"Oh, future, you mean."

She squinted up at him. "You got money?" she wanted to know.

He became cautious at once. "Uh-huh."

She had all the cards face downward on the ground and began to turn them over here and there as though at random. A number of twos and threes made their appearance.

"You gonna not be very rich," she said.

"Aw," he sighed, "and I wanted a yacht with a little brass gun on the deck of it."

Two queens came up, one of hearts and one of diamonds.

"Two lady," said the gypsy woman, "gonna loave you."

"Both at one time?" he gasped. "What'll I do?"

She shrugged her shoulders and laughed.

• • •

In college he was called Jonesy. Everybody knew Jonesy. One of those sporty snap brim hats always pushed back on his head, always going somewhere, always just back from somewhere else, always a wee wisp of something on the breath, always chewing cloves. Everybody liked Jonesy. The night of the prom a girl named Jemima Marsh, Jimmie for short, was his room guest. They had danced themselves almost to death. Toward three in the morning they went down to the gymnasium for a breathless leave-taking. It was pitch dark, and not exactly deserted either. They found a bench with the aid of a match.

"Jonesy," said Jemima with a mouth full of kisses, "I think you're awfully mean."

"Wuff, wuff," said Jonesy.

"Only don't muss my hair," said Jemima. "It took me all afternoon to get it brilliantined."

"Oh, if that's the way you feel about it—" Jonesy turned his back to her and stuck his hands in his pockets and sulked exquisitely. "Conceited," he remarked over his shoulder.

"Thanks!" said Jemima angrily.

There was quite a silence between them. Jonesy tapped his

Love & Night

foot and Jemima tapped hers and they both sighed and they both went ahead tapping and they were both very angry at each other.

All at once Jonesy felt a smooth fairylike little hand, smelling of dew and rosewater, travel down one side of his face and up the other in a scary, tentative sort of way. It was her way of telling him she was sorry. He pulled her down to him and kissed her with great enthusiasm and very little technique. Somehow she seemed a little different from what she had been before. It seemed she had lost weight, and he couldn't quite recall the perfume she had on. There was a different aura about her. The kissing went on just the same, however. He heard someone say "Ooh, the nerve of you!" right close beside her ear, and then he got a terrible slap over one eye.

Suddenly Jemima's voice rang out. "Wha'd she do, slap you? Here, don't you slap him—he's with me."

"Then he shouldn't grab hold of me like that," said the other one.

"Well, go 'way from us," answered Jemima.

There was a sudden loud splash directly in front of them, so that they were both bedewed.

"Oh, Lord, she's in the pool!" cried Jonesy excitedly.

"I know," answered Jemima calmly. "I pushed her. What she really needs is to cool off a little."

He started throwing off his coat and the sleeves got caught.

"Take it easy," advised Jemima. "She probably can swim a lot better than you can."

"Just the same," said a muffled voice from below, "I didn't come down here to swim. You'll pay for my dress."

"See my lawyers," said Jemima disdainfully.

The girl in the pool began to cry and the low ceiling for the place made it echo and reecho so that she really managed to make some noise what with splashing around and sobbing out loud and saying things to them. Jonesy got down on his hands and knees and reached out for her.

"No," she said. "You'll say you saved me and you didn't even jump in after me."

"What are you doing out there?"

"I'm treading water."

"Well, why don't you come on in?"

"Well, where are the lights?" she wanted to know.

"They were disconnected on purpose at the beginning of the evening," he admitted.

He caught her by the wrists and drew her slowly out like a captured mermaid. She was slim and supple. She kneeled on the edge of the pool and wrung out her dress behind her; then she got to her feet.

"Very fine thing you just did," she remarked in the general direction of the red dot made by Jemima's cigarette. "What do you think you are—a traffic cop?"

"You're all wet, lovey," was the only answer Jemima deigned to give.

"Better take my coat," offered Jonesy.

She did take it but not the way he wanted her to. She took it and flung it into the water, where it did a Sir Walter Raleigh.

"There!" she said. "Now I feel better."

"But I didn't do anything to you," he pleaded.

"I don't care," she said. "You didn't jump in after me, did you? You're a total loss."

"You're nothing to rave about yourself," observed Jemima.

"Who was with you?" Jonesy asked.

"Nobody was with me. I was trying to get away from somebody. That's how I came in here."

Someone lit a cigarette lighter. Then a moment later the lights went on all over the place. The gymnasium was full of people, of the indoor sport variety. A young couple standing under a dry shower fixture jumped guiltily. In the center of everything the water, cause of all the disturbance, was heaving rebelliously under a surface unbroken as oil. It was acid green, and deep down in it swam the quicksilver reflection of the arc lights overhead. The coat had gone to the bottom but a white carnation had disengaged itself and remained afloat like a lotus on the infinite placidity of some Nirvana.

They saw each other for the first time. Beads of water clung to her lashes and her dress was like a huge cabbage. Her short hair was down over her eyes in a jet black bang that gave the look of a Japanese billiken. The pink on her cheeks had run a little bit. In fact her whole make-up had slid down toward her throat; it was lengthened out of all proportion. She looked funny. She looked cute. She looked adorable. She seemed to be about seventeen, but in all probability she was twenty. Her name was Sharlee. "Sharlee," someone said, "what happened to you!" That's how he knew her name was Sharlee. It was honey to the palate to say that name.

Sharlee sighed. "Keep away from me, McLaughlin, for the rest of the evening. My nerves are all woozy." She shrugged her wet shoulders in horror and antipathy that seemed exaggerated, but most likely she was sincere.

Gossip was leaping up on all sides like wildfire. She wouldn't have done it if she hadn't been tight in the first place. My dear, certainly she had been tight, what then? She had said this and she had said that earlier in the evening. Dearie, she only did it because she thought her form showed up better under a wet frock. Kitty, kitty, nice kitty.

At length Sharlee covered her ears with her hands, walked backward and forward a couple of times, and cried out: "I'll jump in it a second time if you don't all clear out of here."

The music started in to play again upstairs. They slowly faced around, two or three at a time, and turned toward the door. Their pocket flasks and Yale haircuts, their arched backs and panniers and flounces, their calves and jeweled heels, their perfumes and their whisperings, went up the stairs that youths in bathrobes and in running trunks were accustomed to use.

"I'm Gerald Jones."

"Go away."

"I'm Gerald Jones."

"Go on away, I tell you."

"But you'll catch cold."

Jemima came back. Jemima felt sorry. "I got this shawl for her," she said. "I don't know whose it is, but I got it anyway."

Jonesy took it and put it around the unresistant and slightly shivering form that stood looking down into the depths of the water, brooding over the carnation that was slowly disintegrating petal by petal.

"Thanks, Jimmie, old top," he said.

"You better give her some of our private stuff," said Jemima. "I'm going back up and dance. See you later."

Nothing was said for several moments.

"It isn't bad," Sharlee remarked, handing him back the flask. She went out on the diving board and sat down, swinging her feet above the water. "Gerald Jones, I like you. You're a nice person."

He crept out beside her. "Where're you from?" he said.

"New York."

"That's funny. I'm from New York too."

Sharlee didn't say anything. She looked down into the water, and her eyes swam with the reflection of it.

"I'm s'posed to go back there too," he added ruefully.

"I hate it here. I wish I hadn't come," said Sharlee. Her lip doubled over into an ugly pout.

"I'll take you back with me."

When he said that, she turned around and looked at him. A swarm of honeybees winged their way from her eyes and hovered about his head. He almost fell into the water.

Love & Night

"But I can't walk a step," said Sharlee. "I lost one of my slippers in the pool."

"I'll carry you to the train," said he.

Upstairs there was no one on the floor any more. They were out in the moonlight doing a snake dance, hands on shoulders. Their legs rose and fell like pistons; they resembled figures from an Egyptian bas-relief. Jonesy with sleepy Sharlee in his arms tried to break through. Sharlee began half to laugh, half to whimper. They held their heads close together while jeering faces went around and around them in maddening succession.

"Nice Gerald Jones," said Sharlee dreamily.

• • •

In New York Gerry went to see Angel Face, his mother. She lived in an apartment house that contained forty-two dogs and three monkeys but would not admit children under fifteen years of age.

"I'm Gerald Jones," he told the maid at the door.

"Step in a minute," said the maid. "She usually doesn't see people at this hour of the day."

"But I've come all the way from upstate."

The maid came back and said: "She's getting up," and she gave him a look as of one who had seen a miracle performed. "It'll take her a little while. She said for you to amuse yourself until she's ready. You can turn on the radio or do anything you please."

Gerry didn't need the radio; there was music enough in his veins. He jumped onto a big divan with both knees and buried his face in the cushions. Through all the doors and all the windows Sharlee came in until the room was full of her and his heart was full of her too.

Then he saw that Angel Face was standing there looking at him curiously, with a blue and silver cap on her head and ribbons under her chin. "I've been standing here at least ten full minutes watching you," she said. "And you never even saw me. It's discouraging to think one is that thin."

"Dearest!"

"Ger-ruld." She deepened her voice purposely. Eyes blue as the skies of Paestum at high noon, blue as the fabled moon that is said to come once in a while.

"Sit down on my knee?" he wanted to know.

"I should say not."

"Cigarette?"

"Never before noon."

"Want me to go 'way again?"

"You can stay until half past ten," she said. "A car is coming to call for me at eleven. You can stay all day for that matter," she added, "only there won't be a soul here." She sat down to breakfast and immediately pushed her orange aside. "How was the prom?" she wanted to know. "Soaking wet, I suppose."

"I have some news for you. I got married last night. Or rather early this morning."

"What for?"

He looked at her for a long time, a long, long time, to gauge precisely what she had in mind. Then he said: "What does anyone marry for?"

"We won't discuss that now. Who is she?"

"Sharlee."

"Sharlee." She seemed to be tasting it on the tip of her tongue. "Do I know her?"

"No."

"When did you meet her?"

"Last night."

"And when did you marry her?"

"Last night."

She stood up and went to the window. "What are you anyway," she said, "one of these minute men?" She walked back to the

Love & Night

table and rested her hands upon it, leaning forward. "Where have you left her?"

"At the Plaza."

"On what?" Her voice rose incredulously.

The crisis. "That," he said, "is what I've come to talk to you about."

She smiled. "I'm sorry," she said, "I'm not in a position to—" She held her peach-colored nails close to her face and studied them. "You see, you never came to me for advice."

"Oh, I understand," he said politely.

"Won't you have more breakfast?" she urged. "I love to watch young men eat; they do it with such native enjoyment."

"Thank you, no," he admitted. "You've taken my appetite away."

"Naturally you won't go back to college?"

"Hardly, under the circumstances."

"Well, is there anything you can do? Anything you think you can do?"

"Last summer I organized a jazz band among some of the fellows and we got a season's engagement at an amusement park. We made out very nicely—"

"Would you be willing to go ahead with that sort of thing?"

"Why not?"

"I may be able to help you," she said. "I had a letter from a friend of mine in Florida—"

• • •

Each afternoon at cocktail time Mrs. Harry Werner sighed a sigh, batted an eye at the gaslight-blue Florida seas, and got up from her beach chair.

"Time to get dressed," said Mrs. Harry Werner, emptying her cheeks of smoke.

A colored man, whose people had been in the country two

hundred odd years before Mrs. Werner's, folded her peppermint-striped umbrella for her and picked up the book she had recklessly thrown away.

"Never mind," said Mrs. Werner. "It has no pictures."

"Yes'm," said the colored man, showing his teeth delightedly. Most of them were porcelain but some were gold. All were horrible.

Mrs. Harry Werner moved toward her hotel with great deliberation, sowing seeds of envy as she progressed. Her Lido pajamas fluttered about her like tattered rags, which was precisely what they were meant to do. As she walked along with the colored man at her heels, the Albuquerque Playa loomed in sight like a cliff of sandstone. It had six hundred and twenty-five windows overlooking the sea and a fountain with goldfish in the patio. Mrs. Harry Werner was not interested in goldfish, though. Neither was she interested in the sea. The sea was no affair of hers, she felt. It could take care of itself as far as she was concerned. Indeed there was only one thing that mattered very greatly to Mrs. H.W. and that was herself.

As the tea hour lengthened to a close, she made her appearance in the pavilion, escorted by two chevaliers of the five to seven. She, as the wife of a very wealthy man, felt herself to be above suspicion. Consequently she courted it at almost every turn. Playing with fire was one of her chief characteristics, and Phoenix-like she rose from the ashes of each disappointment with renewed confidence in her own loyalty. Mrs. Harry Werner, choosing a table close beside the dancing space, put out the coral taffeta light and said "Bitters." By way of afterthought she added "Orange bitters." She put a finger to the end of each eye. "I am so tired," she said. Then she said: "I wonder what makes me so tired." She waited a little while and observed, "Oh, it's you, you people make me tired!", at which they both laughed engagingly like sleek tomcats with collars around their necks.

The sea was deserted. From blue it had become green and

Love & Night

from green grayish-yellow. In a short while it would turn purple and then black. But no one was at all interested. They were not down here to study nature. Instead they were studying Mrs. Harry Werner a considerable part of the time.

Mrs. Werner got up to dance with one of her friends.

"I see they have a new orchestra down here this year."

"They've been here ever since the holidays," he informed her. "I don't think much of their playing, do you?"

Now anyone who knew anything at all about Mrs. Harry Werner would have known that to run anything down in an effort to distract her attention was the most fatal thing imaginable. Mrs. Harry Werner was stubborn and used to having her own way too much for that sort of thing to be at all successful.

"Why, I don't see how you can say such a thing!" she exclaimed at once. "I like their playing very well."

"Everyone's taste is different," murmured her partner.

"In that case you have a great deal to account for," said she.

When they sat down, she looked out at the obscured sea for a long while and her well-etched brown eyes seemed a thousand miles off. Then all at once she came to life again, borrowed a pencil from the waiter, and wrote a few words on the back of a card. This she wrapped in something crisp and yellow below the level of the table and passed it to the waiter, folding her small hand over his.

"A new leader," she murmured into her cigarette. "How challenging!"

Presently she got up to dance once more with her friend. A tender sobbing filtered through her consciousness.

"Do you recognize that?" she said. "It's the Meditation from *Thaïs.*" And she added with a touch of bravado: "They're playing it for me."

"What a heavy title," observed her partner. "You'd think they'd call it the Deep Thinkin' Blues or something like that."

As they passed Jones, baton in hand, he caught their eyes.

48

"Thanks," smiled Mrs. Harry Werner cordially.
"Thank you," he answered with a slight bow.

• • •

Every afternoon Zoe Werner stopped for luncheon at the Casa Madrid. The sands of the Albuquerque Playa knew her no more. Each day she drove nine miles to and fro for the cold asparagus tips and convent-like gloom of the Madrid. Is it reasonable to suppose she knew her own mind? Leaving her car, she entered and looked about her, accustoming her eyes to the cool shadowiness that pervaded the place. The floor was of pinkish sandstone and the patio partly open to the sky. There were plants and vines and Moorish water jars. Zoe Werner sat down at a nearby table at which Jones had been seated for some time past. They shook hands above the sapphire glassware.

"Wasn't the water chilly this morning?" she remarked casually. "Have you had your dip yet?"

"She comes here every day at this time," a Dillingham chorus girl confided to her chum. "He's the orchestra leader at the Albuquerque Playa."

"The butcher, the baker, the candlestick maker," observed the chum philosophically.

"I wish you wouldn't insist on this place," Jones was saying. "It's frightfully expensive."

"Don't let that trouble your little heart."

His eyes followed a mountain of cotton batting drifting painlessly over the sky in the direction of the West Indies. She had a flair for romance. She went over his face inch by inch like a surveyor.

After a while they renewed a discussion that had been going on between them for several days in succession.

"Then you want me to believe you are married?" she smiled.

"What makes you think I'm not?"

Love & Night

"Oh, it wouldn't be right somehow," she cried impatiently.

"Haven't I a right to be married as well as the next fellow?" he said dryly.

She smiled into the corrugated blue glass. "You can't convince me."

"I can't, eh?"

They laughed foolishly into each other's faces.

"Not even if I were to tell you my wife's right down here with me?"

Zoe Werner choked with mirth. "Absurd!" she cried. In the emotional intensity of the effort to convince her, he took one of her hands. Neither of them appeared to notice.

"She has charge of the perfumery counter at the Albuquerque."

Her fire-red lips were ever so slightly ajar. She seemed puzzled. She drew her hand away. "I think I know who you mean. That baby-faced thing with the boy haircut."

"She wears a ring around her throat, an alabaster ring I gave her."

Zoe Werner made a little fist. "I'm going to ask her," she cried rapturously.

He meanwhile was fumbling with the inside pocket of his coat and growing red in the face. She watched him with an expression that seemed to say "Yes, I know."

"Try one of the side pockets," she suggested, looking down shyly.

He put his hand in and felt a small envelope that had been left open.

• • •

Mrs. Harry Werner had sent down to say that she wanted to make a selection of toiletries. Sharlee was shown into her suite at ten the next day, carrying a tray loaded with flasks and vials strapped over her shoulders.

"Send her in here to me," directed Mrs. Werner from an inner room. She was on the bed but not in it, her ankles crossed on the coverlet. She wore her hair in a Grecian knot at the back of her neck.

She looked Sharlee over. "What have you got there?" she asked indifferently.

"Coty, Caron, Bourjois—"

"I, ah, was speaking to your husband yesterday evening," proceeded Mrs. Werner without stopping to listen.

Sharlee nodded obediently. "He leads the orchestra."

"You both of you seem so well bred," observed Mrs. Werner. "I can't quite grasp the situation."

"I came down here to be near him. Everyone has to make a living, you know."

"Yes, we lunch together quite often," mused Mrs. Werner dreamily.

"I know," said Sharlee spiritedly. "Mr. Jones tells me everything."

Mrs. Werner treated her to an indulgent smile. "Not quite everything, my dear."

Sharlee looked at her as though a rattlesnake had just bitten her. She could hardly wait until she got away.

"Will that be all?"

"Yes, that will be all."

• • •

That evening Gerry stood with his back to the dance floor, shaking spasmodically first one leg then the other, resting the baton against his waistcoat, leading his saxophones like whimpering panthers. And all about him danced Zoe Werner, a thing possessed, devils in her eyes, a bacchante brave with silver

Love & Night

and with jet. They played *Poor little rich girl, Poor little rich girl, Better take care.* Diluted breezes came in under the scalloped awnings. This pitiful music drowned out the sound of the sea for a little while only, but the sound of the sea would last forever.

"Look, Gerry, how's this for real dancing?" Her hair began uncoiling and then all at once tumbled headlong down her back. She gave a hilarious scream of dismay and ran out of the room.

A little while after that there was an intermission, and Sharlee met Gerry on his way out through the lobby for a breath of air.

"Gerry, I haven't seen you all day."

He murmured something about being called back.

"There's loads of time," she said. "You won't have to play again for another half hour."

He lit a cigarette with a trembling hand, but she could see that he wasn't even thinking of her; he was all keyed up to the intrigue set for him, looking over her shoulder toward the elevators all the time.

"What?" he said absently.

"Gerry Jones," she lamented in a peculiar sing-song, "you're the talk of the season, you two. I've stood all I can. You're the laughing-stock of this place—"

"What are you doing—trying to start a scene with me here?" he demanded angrily. "You couldn't pick a better spot, could you?"

"I'm not trying to start any scene," she repeated in a trance-like calm. "I've got my ticket to go back to New York."

He woke up to what she was saying then.

"That night we met," she went on very earnestly, "must have been a mistake. I've thought it over." And going over to the perfume case she switched off all the lights.

At this point Mrs. Werner, her hair freshly done up, stepped out of one of the elevators, a black velvet cape gathered jealously about her. Her eyes were particularly Venetian this evening.

Poor Gerry Jones, trying to unravel his destiny in a few broken whispers. "You make me feel like two cents, sweetheart—"

"Say it with your music," said Sharlee. "You're so weak you're not worth saving." And she walked off.

Zoe Werner's candle-like fingers closed on Gerry's arm. "What's all the shooting for?"

"Sharlee just told me she's going back to New York."

"Oh, you silly children. You sil-lee, sil-lee children."

"Dear lady," he told her, "we are children. Why did you ever meddle with us?"

She regarded him gloomily. "The good die young," she said with a touch of sarcasm.

Gerry went back to his music. People wanted to dance; they wanted gay music to shut out the sound the sea was making. Gerry stood up in his place and trembled spasmodically, shifting his weight first to one leg then to the other, and swung the baton dreamily before his chest. Before him swam the image of a beautiful woman in beautiful clothes. A vain selfish woman, the sort of woman Zoe Werner was.

And at first he thought she was more beautiful than an artery of mauve lightning in an angry sky. Every day for days and days of her life she had rubbed creams of almond blossom and of orange blossom, essences of honey and heliotrope dew gently, ever so gently, into her skin. Every day for days and days of her life she had bathed her shoulders in steam and jasmine, pressed a sponge choked with ice cold water to her heart, touched a glass rod with a drop of liquid violets and French chemistry to her lashes and the lobes of her ears. She had protected herself against drafts with spun silk and with lace of Ireland and of Flanders. She had protected herself against cold with the skins of leopards and of seals, with shawls of Persia and Seville. She had protected herself from darkness with electricity in rose and pearl and amber globes, and when the globes burst, it was seen that there was no light to be had from them at all, only an illusion.

Love & Night

And all at once he looked closer and saw that there was no face there at all, only grinning decaying teeth and eyeless sockets and the worm-eaten bridge of a nose. It was a death's head. The mouth was painted and the cheeks, and the ears were colored shell pink. She even had a gardenia in her hair. And with it all she was a ghastly looking thing. The gay music wavered, then broke, and the bottom fell out of it. The dancing outlasted it only a matter of a second or two. People came to a halt and looked at one another uncertainly, not knowing what to make of it.

"Water!" said a voice at the far end of the room. "He's fainted. Take him outside."

• • •

Sharlee was upstairs, getting ready to go away. She took time off from her packing to bury her head in the pillows and sob. Then there were voices outside and someone knocked on the door.

"Yes?" said Sharlee, jumping up and dabbing at her eyes.

The door opened without waiting for her, and she saw a corridor full of people, all staring at her. They brought Gerry in, very pale, with his eyes closed, and put him down on the bed.

"My honeyboy!" Sharlee gave an agonized little whimper, and all thought of New York vanished completely as she bent over him and kissed him. She got everyone out of the room and closed the door on them, but her back was no sooner turned than the door opened again and a voice said: "Mayn't I help? I've brought my spirits of ammonia in case—"

The Venetian-eyed Zoe Werner had insinuated herself into the room.

"If I thought I could trust you to take the right care of him," said Sharlee bitterly, "I wouldn't spend another night in this hotel."

"He's overworked," Zoe murmured, not noticing. "The hours here are too long."

Sharlee snatched up her valise and took long hysterical strides to the door. "Stay here if you want," she said, half strangled with sobs. "I'm going to New York."

"You needn't go," said Zoe gently. "I'm leaving in the early morning for Jacksonville." She passed her, and on the way out said softly, "Tell him goodbye for me."

• • •

The sea was blue as only the Florida seas can be: acetylene blue. It reminded Gerry of the eyes of Angel Face, his mother. A dripping mermaid came splashing out of the surf to greet him.

"I saw you leave the hotel," said Sharlee, "and I was afraid you might want to try the water. I don't think it would be good for you just yet."

They sat down on a little hillock of sand, and their arms went around each other.

"We will go away from Florida," said Gerry.

"We can't," said Sharlee, grinning up at the sky. "I wired Angel Face and she's on the way down. She says she wants to dance to your music. Go in and dress, and I'll sit out here listening, and when you play, I'll know it's all for me."

[*College Humor,* January 1930]

> *This downbeat tale of love between a "shanty Irish" young woman and a wealthy young man echoes Woolrich's sad relationship with the woman whom in his autobiographical* Blues of a Lifetime *he called Vera Gaffney. As so often in his noir novels and stories, popular song lyrics underscore the anguish.*

CINDERELLA MAGIC

Sometimes it all seemed like a dream, one of those things that happens in books and talking pictures, but not to her, Patty Moran, of Sixty-Eighth Street and Ninth Avenue. Ninth Avenue, where the "El" trains rumbled by in front of the parlor and people ate corned beef and cabbage and had worries. Maybe it happened because she was eighteen. When you're eighteen, dreams have a way of coming true.

First there were just the two of them, Laurence and Patty. No one ever knew where he ever got that name. Spelt with a U in the middle, too. He hated it. If you wanted to be his friend, you had to call him Larry, if you knew him well enough like Patty did. Or else just plain Mr. Cogan.

Patty was the one who could call him Laurence (with a U in the middle) and not risk getting a punch in the nose. Sometimes she did it when she wanted to tease him. He'd look at her and smile. After a while she found out he liked it. He'd call her up on the telephone and say, "This is Laurence with a U in the middle." They'd been going together steadily for quite some time, nearly a year. And they knew they'd have to keep on going for another year, or maybe two, before there would be enough money to—if you know what I mean. But they didn't mind that.

For all they knew, they were the only two in the whole wide

world. Of course there were mothers and sisters and brothers and people like that—but they didn't make Pat's heart beat any quicker, the way it was doing right then, for instance, at the telephone.

"And what's on your mind, Laurence with a U in the middle?" Pat said, pretending to be very matter-of-fact. "Admitting that you have one."

"It's about that dance, sweet Patty Moran," he said. "They couldn't get Killarney Hall for tonight, so they're giving it downtown instead, at an armory on Park Avenue. I'll wait for you at the door. Are you ready to leave soon?"

"No," she said. "I'll have to change my dress first. I forgot I was seeing you tonight."

"Shame on you!" her mother laughed. "Standing there in your silver shoes and all, telling him that." And she tried to take the phone away from Pat and say, "Don't believe a word of it, Larry!"

Pat climbed up on a chair, phone and all, and winked at her. "How will I know this armory?" she said to Larry.

"It's as big as a castle," he said, "with a great wide awning over the door. Will you remember the number?" And he gave it to her. Pat called it out so her mother could write it down on a piece of paper for her. "I'll be seeing you then," she said, and ran inside just to take one more look at herself in the glass. But when she asked her mother for the number, Pat found she hadn't written it down at all.

"I didn't have any pencil," her mother said, "but I kept it in my head for you. It's 240."

"I think he said 420."

"If it isn't one, it's the other," her mother said. "That's easy enough."

"Sure it is," Pat said sarcastically. Her mother didn't know very much about taxi fares. And Pat was going to take one because this was one night she was dressed the way she would have liked to go looking all through life, even if the total outlay was only about $18.50. She borrowed half a dollar from her mother and a dollar and a half from her big brother (who told her not to buy a Packard with it), bringing the total expense up to $20.

"Stop at 420 if it has an awning over it," Pat told the driver. "If it hasn't, go right on to 240."

He looked at her to see if she really meant it, but she said, "You may proceed!" in her haughtiest manner, which took him so much by surprise, coming from anyone at 68th Street and Ninth Avenue, that he didn't dare say another word.

When they got to 420, it had an awning over it, sure enough, and there were people going in dressed in furs and velvet.

"How do those girls do that on twenty a week?" Pat wondered. "Well, some of them may be making twenty-five; that explains it all. Stop here; this is the place," she said to the driver, and saw by the meter that her money wouldn't have lasted until the next address anyhow. And when an individual with gold buttons and braid all over him held the door open for her, she knew it was the armory, because she remembered that armories have something to do with men in uniform.

She didn't see Larry standing anywhere so she went on in to look for him. And first there was a big glass spinning-door, with someone to turn it for you, and then there was a flight of marble steps to be climbed, and after that came miles of velvet carpet with palms growing along the side. But no Larry anywhere. Pat was afraid she couldn't find her way back to the street by now anyway so she just kept on walking. Until a velvet rope stopped her. And still no sign of Larry.

Then a young man wearing a flower in his buttonhole stepped up to her and said, "Your invitation, please?"

Pat didn't at all like his speaking to her without a proper introduction, so she decided to become very haughty once more. "My invitation was by wire," she said. "Laurence asked me down." Before she had time to give him Larry's last name, he had let down the rope and passed her on to a lady wearing black beads and eyeglasses.

"A friend of Laurence's," the young man said. "Invitation by telegram."

Pat hadn't meant telegram at all, she had meant telephone, but the lady said, "Oh, of course. Come with me, my dear. I'll show you where Laurence is," and took her to a room full of mirrors and girls powdering their noses. Pat looked at each one in turn, but their gold and silver and crystal dresses didn't seem to matter so much after all because none of them were eighteen any more and the only way to look eighteen is to be it. So Pat decided all she must do was not to stand too near a very bright light in her organdy dress.

When she had left her wrap behind, the lady with the eyeglasses said: "Now I will bring you over to Laurence, and then I must hurry back on the receiving line. There he is, over there."

Pat didn't see him, but she followed her across a room nearly as big as the Roxy where dancing was going on, and suddenly she was standing in front of someone Pat had never seen before in her life and saying: "This is a good friend of yours, Laurence. See that she has a good time." And without even waiting to be introduced, the lady walked off and left them. And the band played "Here we are, you and I, Let the world hurry by."

For a minute he was as surprised as she was. "It isn't Florence, is it?" he said. "No, she was blonde. It can't be Bernice—she was shorter than you are. Or are you the girl I taught to dive at Miami last winter?" He was young and nice, but his eyes were a little sad as if he always expected to be disappointed and always got what he expected.

Pat stamped her foot decisively. "It's me, that's who!" she told him. "And where's Larry?"

"I'm Larry."

"You are not! Don't try to fib!" she cried.

"Yes I am," he said. "Laurence Pierce."

Love & Night

Pat nearly fainted. "Why, I must be in the wrong place," she said. "Isn't this an armory?"

He seemed to think that was very funny. He could hardly stop laughing. "I must tell that to mother," he said. "It ought to hold her for a while."

"Do you mean to say you live here?" Pat gasped.

"Yes," he said apologetically. "Just forty rooms but it's home." And he seemed kind of unhappy about it.

"I didn't know," Pat said. "Excuse me! I wouldn't have walked in here like this for the world." And she turned around to go, but he followed her and took her by the arm.

"Can't we pretend just for a little while that this really is the place you were going to—and I really did invite you?"

"No," said Pat firmly.

And she walked away a few steps farther, and again he came after her.

"Won't you stay if I invite you here and now? I'm afraid I've been rude to you. Won't you stay and let me make up for it?"

"Oh, I couldn't—" Pat started to say. But she was already standing still and not moving any nearer the door.

"There's something so real about you. Most of these girls here are just like dolls." He looked down at the floor and said in a low voice: "No one that was real ever came near me before. And then you walked in the door."

"The wrong door!" she said.

She should have gone while she still wanted to. But she didn't want to very much any more. She thought of Larry Cogan waiting for her at the armory. But he could wait a little longer. His eyes had never looked as sad as this, so he could wait just a little longer for her tonight. He'd see her every other night in the year.

"Please stay," he said. And he looked at her and she knew she would.

He called the orchestra leader over to them and he said: "Lower the lights and let's have a waltz." Then he looked at Pat's dress that wasn't gold or silver or crystal at all and added: "Play Alice Blue Gown."

And then they were dancing and it all seemed a dream.

At eleven he said: "You haven't told me who you are yet."

Pat said: "I'm Patty Moran of 68th Street and Ninth Avenue."

"I'm going to like 68th Street and Ninth Avenue," was all he said to that.

At twelve she said: "I'll have to go now."

At one she was still saying she'd have to go.

Finally at two she went.

He went with her as far as the spinning glass door, and she saw a big car waiting outside.

"I can't go with you," he said, "because it's my sister Agatha's coming-out party and she'll scratch and bite. But Bob will see that you get home safe."

"Goodnight, Law."

"Goodnight, Pat."

That was all they said. They didn't have to say much. Pat lifted up the speaking tube and said, "Sixty-eighth Street and Ninth Avenue," and she took a rosebud from the crystal holder and held it in her fingers and looked at it for a long time. "Little flower," she said finally, "what am I going to do about this?" But the flower didn't answer.

Her mother was sitting by the open window fanning herself with her apron when Pat got in.

"Look at me!" she groaned. "You see me in the condition I'm in, all weak and warped, from answering that blessed telephone the livelong night. If Larry Cogan's suicide is announced in the papers tomorrow morning, you'll have yourself to thank for it. Your brother Tom counted the calls and he says there were twenty-eight of them. Myself, I think there were one hundred and twenty-eight."

Love & Night

Pat threw her arms around her and hugged her. "Bless you for getting that address wrong."

"I'm not asking you what happened," her mother said, pretending to be very much offended, "because Mrs. Moran's daughter is above rayproach, but I am asking you, daughter or no daughter, the next time you decide to break an appointment, see that your poor old mother doesn't have to make all the excuses for you."

"Mother," Pat asked her, sitting on her lap, "can a girl love two people at the same time, both in a different way?"

"If she does," her mother answered, "one of them gets left in the end."

Pat thought a good deal about that before she went to sleep.

• • •

The next day two things happened. The first was Larry's (her Larry's) phone call before she was even awake.

"What did you do that to me for last night?" he demanded.

This went on for quite some time. Pat's mother even brought the coffee out to the telephone so she could drink it while they were arguing and not lose any time.

"You must have money to burn," Pat said among other things, "throwing nickels away like you did, just to keep my mother awake half the night."

He went on and on. "You ought to know by now without being told," Pat said. "Well, if I have to say it, all right then—I love you. And don't think for a minute that means you can boss me as much as you please."

"For the like of those three words," he said, "I'd gladly live the night over again, worried and jealous and all, glad of the chance."

"Well," said Pat, "no one's asking you to."

• • •

And that night at supper-time the doorbell rang. Tom went to answer it, and when he came back to the table, he said to Pat: "There's a chauffeur out in the hall with a message for you." She jumped up and when she got there found Laurence's chauffeur standing in the door.

"Mr. Pierce sent some flowers over with his regards," he said, touching his cap. "Can I have them brought up?" And without waiting for her answer, he went out to the head of the stairs and called down: "All right."

On second thought Pat wasn't at all sure she liked the idea. Presents the first thing when they had only met the night before for the first time. If he had been poor, it wouldn't have mattered, but he was rich and it didn't look right. She knew her mother wouldn't say anything, but she didn't want to give the neighbors a chance to talk. In fact she was just about to ask him not to bring them upstairs when in they came, a whole heap of them, and behind them Laurence himself, looking pleased and just a little embarrassed as though he didn't know whether she'd be glad to see him or not.

"I had to," he remarked, throwing the flowers in a corner without even giving them to her. "Been thinking about you the live-long day, ever since I first woke up."

So had Pat but she didn't say so.

"Are you angry because I came here without being asked?"

"I did the same thing at your house last night," Pat laughed. "But you didn't have to bring a whole florist shop with you just to come and see me."

He was still out of breath from coming up those stairs of hers, and he was just like a little boy with his eyes so eager and all. "I'd like awfully to have you ask me to dinner," he said.

And they walked in together and Pat said, "Mother, I have

Love & Night

company for you. This is Laurence Pierce of 420 Park Avenue, and he's staying to supper."

And Laurence sat right down in the first empty chair and tucked a napkin in his collar the way Tom had his.

Pat's mother fussed with her hair and looked nerved for a minute, but Laurence said, "My, that stew smells good," and she looked pleased and proud and helped him to some of it.

Then afterwards, while they were all sitting in the front room and Tom was pumping a music-roll through the pianola, in walked Larry Cogan.

"I dropped in to take you to a movie," he said to Pat matter-of-factly.

"I can't tonight, Larry," she said. "We have company. This is Mr. Pierce—Mr. Cogan."

Larry hardly shook hands with him at all. He had understood even quicker than Pat thought he would. She could tell he didn't want to stay, but he was awkward and didn't know how to get out of the room now that he was in it. So he sat around and tried to ignore Laurence.

Pat's mother asked her to come out in the kitchen and help her serve some cakes and homemade wine. Pat didn't think it would be a very good idea to leave the two of them alone like that. "If they fight in my sittin' room, I'll throw them both out with my own hands," her mother observed.

But when Pat hurried back to them, she found them standing around the pianola singing, or at least trying to, while Tom pedaled. That showed her what kind of a person Laurence was, that when he wanted to make people like him, they liked him in spite of themselves.

Larry left soon after and she went out into the hall with him. "Do you like Laurence a little better now that you know him?" she asked anxiously.

"I'd like him a whole lot better than that even," he admitted, "if it wasn't for his coming between you and me."

"Don't say that, Larry," Pat begged. "He hasn't."

"Maybe you don't know it yet," he said, "but he has. Anyway, think it over good and carefully first."

"Larry—!" she called after him, but he had already gone down the stairs.

• • •

Pat had known Laurence about a week when he started to bring up the subject of marriage. Their marriage. Pat laughed it off mostly, with her heart doing all sorts of queer tricks inside her. One time she simply remarked, "Don't let's build castles in the air."

He had lots of answers to make to that, oh lots of them. He made them, all right. Pat saw that it was up to her to bring him back to earth again.

"Did you ever stop to think what your family might have to say?" she suggested.

"It doesn't matter what they say."

"It matters a great deal to me," she told him.

"Why should it?" he asked curiously. "You don't even know them."

"But don't you know what they'd say—what everybody would say—if you married me?"

"That I was the luckiest boy alive, if they knew you as I do."

Pat turned her head away. "No. They'd say I married you for—for your money. Oh, I wouldn't blame them," she said quickly. "I'd think that too if I heard it about some other girl."

"Maybe it would be true about some other girl," he answered, "but it isn't true about you."

"When Ninth Avenue marries Park Avenue," she said, "no good comes of it."

"We'll see about that!" he said determinedly. "We'll show them they're wrong for once."

Love & Night

The very next day he said to her over the phone, "Don't make any engagements for Thursday night. You're having dinner at my home— I want you to meet my family."

As she hung up, Pat said to herself, "Here is where I lose him."

And she couldn't tell if she was sorry or if she was glad. Dreams shouldn't come true; you lose them that way.

• • •

Thursday morning a box came. When she opened it, there was a dress inside, of apricot velvet with a silver orchid on one shoulder. And a card—"Miss Agatha Pierce." Pat knew that he had sent it and used his sister's card so she wouldn't feel hurt. She sent it back. "I'm going to be fair to myself and fair to him," she told her mother. "His family will see me as I am, in my little blue dress from Lerner's. The rest is up to them."

And that's the way she went there, in an outfit costing $18.50. He sent the car for her, of course. Pat met his mother and his sister and her fiancé. There were just the five of them. And they were going to be very nice to her, Pat could tell. They were going to be very nice to her and show Laurence how unsuitable she was for him. So she played up to them and helped them along, and she even said and did things that she knew were wrong. She said hello to the butler, and she pushed her spoon toward her instead of away from her when they served the soup. But they didn't seem to notice anything, and after a while she forgot to pretend any more and just became her natural self. And before she knew it, dinner was over and she was alone with Laurence's mother and sister. His mother put her arm around Pat and said, "You're a lovable child. What I like about you is that you're so natural. I can understand how Laurence feels."

And his sister said, "You were right not to wear that gaudy

dress he sent you. You don't need it. You look too sweet this way."

"All we want is to see Laurence happy," his mother said. "And if you really care for him—"

Pat knew what she was going to say. She had seen it in the pictures a great many times before. It was always: "You will give him up if you really love him."

But his mother went on: "When I was your age, I was selling flowers in a restaurant. I don't see what right anyone has to stand in your way if you love each other."

Pat didn't wait to hear any more. She began to cry.

"Oh, I can't pretend any more!" she sobbed. "I don't need to tell you how much I love him. But what am I going to do? You know what people will say."

"About his money?" Mrs. Pierce said. "Well, let them! You're one girl in a thousand and Laurence believes in you. Isn't that enough?" And she gave her a little kiss. "I'll see you and Laurence through this," she said.

And the next day there was a diamond on Pat's finger that hadn't been there before, and Pat kept looking intently at it.

All it seemed to do was bring the tears to her eyes. "My darling Larry!" she said to her mother. "How can I give him up? Oh, it's tough sometimes to be a girl."

"Well, it's either one or the other of them," her mother said, "or else it's bigamy."

And Larry himself wouldn't listen to anything Pat tried to say. "Did you think I'd stand in your way?" And when he smiled at her that way, she could almost hear her own heart breaking inside her piece by piece. "Wouldn't I be the man to do that! He's got a combination hard to beat—love and money. Don't throw yourself away on Mrs. Cogan's little boy."

And he took her in his arms and kissed her, the first time he'd ever done that in all the time they'd known each other. Greetings and farewell!

Love & Night

"Say the word," Pat sobbed, "and nothing matters but you."

"Good-bye's the word," he murmured.

• • •

Sometimes a little thing makes up your mind for you. Molly Reardon, who lived on the floor below, walked in one night about two weeks before the wedding. Pat had never liked her much anyway.

"What's all this going on around here?" she said to Pat's mother. "A snappy car parked in front of the flat every night and reporters snooping around trying to find out who the lucky girl is. I hear Pat has caught a swell. Pretty soft for her. How'd she do it?"

Pat was in the other room drying the supper dishes when she heard her say that. She dried her hands and went in to them then. And a minute later Pat's mother had to call out at the top of her voice, "Tom! Tom! Come in here quick before that sister of yours breaks all my best plates!"

Molly Reardon ducked once to the right and once to the left, and then she managed to escape into the hall in a big hurry, followed by a salad-bowl.

"Didn't I tell you?" Pat sobbed when they had calmed her down. "That's what they'll all be thinking. Caught a swell, have I? Just because he's rich and I'm poor. And maybe some day he'll begin to think so too. That's what I'm afraid of. Some day he'll forget and think it was the money."

"Not if he loves you he won't," her mother assured her.

"I want to keep this dream," Pat told her. "It may be the only one I'll ever have. I want to keep him forever, just like he was this one month I've known him."

And she called up Laurence's house, but she asked for his mother, not him.

"You said you used to work for your living when you were my age," she said, "so you ought to understand. Make him understand too."

And when she was all through, Mrs. Pierce just said, "Poor Laurence" and hung up.

Then Pat rang a certain other number. Corned beef and cabbage for the rest of her life.

"Larry," she said, "I'm to be married, and I want you there."

"You know I'd do anything for you," he said, "even this. Where is it, 420 Park Avenue?"

"No," Pat said, "68th Street and Ninth Avenue. And don't keep me waiting because you're to be the groom."

[*Illustrated Love,* November 1930]

In this story we meet yet another Woolrich man whose woman must satisfy his otherworldly romantic dreams. It's not by chance that the woman in the tale has the same name as F. Scott Fitzgerald's wife.

THE GIRL IN THE MOON

A big round moon leaped up, quivered a little, and then steadied itself, half of it bent flat on the boards, the other half upright against the backdrop. It glowed rose, tinted with yellow, perfect as a hot-house peach but more ideally round than any peach could ever have been. A girl came through the curtain.

It is impossible to characterize Zelda. To everyone in turn she represented something different. To that comfortable woman with the pearls in her ears sitting in the second row on the aisle, she was one of the lucky ones who weighed one hundred pounds and could climb stairs without seeing black spots in front of her eyes. To the woman's husband she brought to mind that summer of 1923 when his wife had been away in Maine. He would have liked to meet her. He would also have liked to have his hair back and be President of the United States. To the wise gum-chewers up on the shelf, she was simply a good act, nothing more. To which their flour-faced friends retorted, not without acidity, that they had seen better. To the orchestra leader, she was someone who flew into rages at Monday morning rehearsals and who darted deadly looks at him under her long lashes if he began vamping an encore when she wasn't in the mood for one. To the man in the wings, she symbolized drudgery, painting itself in bright colors and fooling the world for fifteen minutes each night but not fooling him.

Her method was not subtle. She had to score and score quickly, and she knew it. She began to sing something popular. She had all the mannerisms that went with it. Palms out in the direction of the audience as though pushing it away from her. She gave a sly little turn of the wrist, pointing with one finger, and the moon that had been following her about like a big cartwheel rolled glibly off the stage and perched obediently on one of the upper boxes.

There was only one person in the box. She had chosen it so there would be no division of interest on the part of the audience. He seemed turned to stone. In all that glare he never batted an eyelash. After a moment he let his chin sink forward until his jaw rested more comfortably on the back of his arm. He gave the absurd impression of taking the whole proceeding seriously. The audience by now was convinced he had been planted there for her act. They expected witty repartee, and when it failed to come, they could not understand why it was being withheld.

To cap the climax, when she remarked in a wheedling voice, "Darling, you do love me, don't you?" (as part of the patter chorus) he nodded his head affirmatively, and the girl on the stage, more disconcerted than anyone guessed, almost forgot to gesture for a moment. She had expected almost anything but not this. Instead of wriggling adolescents stumbling over each other in a mad rush to get out of the light, or some jeering salesman sitting through it with an air of assumed bravado, she had unearthed an enigma.

She could efface him swiftly and at once. Lift her little finger and the moon would come floating back to her. But she didn't. It wasn't businesslike of her in the least. She knew that. She needed all the moon she could get in the short time she was out front, and yet she let it stay up there on him. Her nerves were crying for a well rounded performance, and she couldn't get it. As intended comic relief he was no help at all, had simply ruined the number. A professional plant at least would have had a line of back talk ready to throw at her.

Love & Night

She began to work harder than ever, angrily determined. "Look at his eyes, folks. Aren't they beautiful? Do you blame me, girls?"

She had to give in at last. With a limp gesture of farewell she finally called the moon off him and took her bows. It had gone over immensely if the smacking was any criterion, but she had that empty, that "all gone" feeling she had known she was going to get. She glared daggers at the leader and frightened him out of an encore. As it was, she had to feed them something about her gratitude.

She brushed by Jack in the wings on the way to the dressing-room. "Some fool up in one of the cages rattled me."

"Maybe you'd like a screen around you," he suggested uncharitably.

• • •

The next show she received a note in her dressing-room. This was no novelty, certainly. She put down the grease stick to look at it. Miss Zelda Grayson, care of Bandbox Theater. She opened it with a pair of manicure scissors.

"Sweet peas," said Jack, sticking his head in at the door. "Going to open an undertaking parlor with them?"

"Yes," she said crushingly. "Send your head around some time for embalming."

After the show she thought it out. She would be very hard-boiled about this. That was the thing to do. And though she hated to admit it, she knew she wasn't at all hard-boiled underneath and never would be. But she had acquired the manner to perfection and that helped some. She knew all the mean little stencils that could take the warmth and kindness out of things instantly like the cut of a whip.

She was smiling rather venomously as she bound a towel about her hair and put on a street make-up. Tamper with her act, would he? She'd see about that. Not that there had been anything disrespectful in the note or the gift of flowers (sweet peas, she admitted to herself, were not expensive enough to be very insinuating); it was simply that she intended to repay him in kind. Especially since he laid himself open this way. It was too good to miss.

Dressed and ready to leave, she selected two or three of the flowers and pinned them to her coat. She emerged into the obscurity of the alley backstage, with its single light in a wire basket throwing a pool of light downward over the cement, and reached the street at the end of it without meeting a soul. It was a little too early yet for them to be coming out.

There were not more than four people waiting in the lobby when she got around to the front of the house. Two of them were women and one was a colored man with a mop and pail, which made the task of identifying him much simpler. He was, if anyone, the individual peering through the oval panes at the end-numbers of the show. He turned around just then and she lowered her head to smell the flowers on her coat. He caught the signal they had agreed upon and came over to her at once. They studied each other for a split-second like a pair of prizefighters measuring distances at the stroke of the bell.

"Good evening," he said.

"What makes you think you have the right to speak to me?" she asked, detachedly curious.

"I haven't the right, only the wish."

"Well, your wish has been granted." She pretended to move away. "Good night," she said. That, she knew, would bring him after her. It did.

"Wait!" he said. "You're not going so soon?"

"Why not?" she answered. "Do you think I came out front here on purpose to meet you?"

"Yes," he said gravely. "You're wearing the flowers to identify yourself."

Love & Night

She unpinned them and threw them away. He picked them up and put them in his wallet.

"I suppose now you'll carry them around with you for the rest of your life," she said mockingly. "Until you fall for somebody else."

"I'm not that kind," he said.

"What do you do?" she asked.

"When your partner goes in to buy a shirt," he said, "why, I wait on him."

"No, you don't," she corrected. "He's only got one and the last time he changed it was when the boys came back from overseas. The other night the collar-band dropped off and started to walk away of its own accord—he just stepped on it in the nick of time."

He laughed appreciatively.

She was finding it harder to dislike him as the minutes wore on. He made a good listener at any rate. The show was out now and the lobby was filling with people.

"It's warm," she said. "I'd like a Coca-Cola."

They went to get one.

"Listen," she said, "why did you crab my act last night? Don't you know that wasn't regular? You should have played up to me."

"I wasn't thinking of the act, I was thinking of you."

"Now really," she said, "isn't that going a little too fast?"

"The first night I came, I bought one of your records in the lobby to take home with me. And when I put it on, it wasn't you at all; it was someone else singing it."

"Were you disappointed?"

"I never got to the end. I broke it right then and there."

Who wouldn't have been very gentle with him after hearing a thing like that? And she was not so hard-boiled inside herself after all. She knew that now. Through barely parted lips he heard her murmur, "Almost thou persuadest me." As they walked out of the drugstore together, she was certain of only one thing—she would not do what she had planned to do to him. She stopped him at the door with a little gesture.

"You stay here, and don't look which way I go. Tomorrow night if I am thirsty, I may drop by here for another Coca-Cola."

• • •

Tomorrow night she was thirsty.

She did not have to pin flowers to her coat now, or identify him by eliminating everyone else nearby. In the taxi driving to the theater she had said to herself, "What is the matter with me?" and could find no explanation. She made one last feeble attempt to fight off this thing that she had sung about so often from the boards and was now meeting for the first time. "If you're a dreamer," she said, "you'd better get someone else for your dreams. I can't see you any more."

The next night she found that she needed a new lipstick and she stepped in to buy it. All he said was, "How lucky for me you needed that lipstick." She refused to admit even to herself that she had just thrown a brand new one away in the alley in back of the theater. They were Marty and Zelda to each other now. And Coca-Cola no longer seemed a very commonplace drink.

At times she still stopped a moment and tried to understand what it was that had happened to her. "It seems that this is love," she said. She wasn't laughing at this the way she would have a little while ago.

• • •

A week from the night they had first met, they were married. They had their whole future planned in the fifteen minutes it took to drive to the theater, holding hands in a black-and-white cab.

Love & Night

"But you want me to, don't you?"

The old story: "I want you all to myself. But are you sure you won't regret it later?"

"I'm never sorry for what I've done," she said. "I'm a good sport."

She gave the stage manager notice. And then she had to tell Jack. She stopped him in the wings. Distant hand-clapping filled the air like hundreds of little firecrackers all going off at the same time.

"Listen!" he said. "Is that for you?"

"I suppose so," she answered absent-mindedly.

"You've got them eating out of your hand!" he cried joyously. "Go on out there!"

"No," she said. "This is my last show. I was married this afternoon."

In the dim light his face was a cipher to her. "Now? You're going to quit now? After all I've done for you? I didn't think it was in you to act like this!"

She kissed him lightly on the cheek. "It's love, Jack, love! Do you want to know why I went over so immense just now? He was out front. I wasn't acting, I was living my number."

"I give you a year of that," he called after her. "They all come back."

"Good night, Miss Grayson," the doorman said.

She smiled and opened her purse. "It's Mrs. Martin now, Dave, and it's good-by."

He watched her step out into the alley under the dim light and walk away on her husband's arm.

• • •

The flat (Brooklyn because "Where else could you get it for fifty-five?") had a shining white refrigerator that purred like a kitten and made little frozen dice in a pan. It had a radio that hissed and spit if anyone crossed the floor in front of it but at other times poured forth the sweetest music mortal ears had ever heard. Furthermore, it had a dumbwaiter that miraculously disgorged itself of cans of peaches and cartons of cigarettes while a voice hidden somewhere in the bowels of the earth called up "Four seventy-five, please!" Zelda, used to hotel rooms all her life, brought no caustic comment to bear on ten cent cups and saucers and a sofa secured by a five dollar deposit; found in them the essence of the ideal, and crowed delightedly at the implication of personal ownership in all this. The lily needed no gilding, but for ornament there were her own striking wrappers and the Chinese lanterns she conscientiously fastened to all the lights.

The first weeks went by in a flurry of excitement. There were things to be bought. There were things to be done, things to be learned. How to make coffee, for instance. The only way she had known was to pick up a telephone and say "Room service." And over and above all this there was love, breathless and absorbing. Until weeks grew into months and the excitement was less. Love did not grow less, but the excitement did.

Hers was to be no busman's holiday. She stayed away from the places she had known. No more midnight lunches in restaurants filled with shop-talk. No more of friends who called her "honey" but would have cut her throat professionally. Once her costumer called her. "It's all of silver fish-scales and just the thing for you. Lily de Vrie is wild about it, but I thought I'd give you first chance at it."

"Let her have it," Zelda said. "Haven't you heard that I've quit?"

She didn't want gold or silver or anything shining any more. Her eyes were a little tired of glitter. Diversion was to sit in a room, her very own room, with him there, with a lamp and a book and a cigarette there, and not have to sing for people, not have to smile. And if one stocking slowly dropped below her

Love & Night

knee, it was luxury; it was better than a diamond-studded garter. She took pride in demonstrating her newest accomplishment now, made a cup of coffee as a special treat just before they retired, while the announcer's voice was signing off to soft faraway music. If they had drained the pitcher of cream between them, she would scrawl a little note, "Borden: Leave us a bottle of cream tomorrow," and curl it up in the neck of a bottle outside the door.

A few of Marty's friends came out from time to time. She wanted to like them, tried to make them feel at home, but they invariably asked her to sing, entertain them in some way.

"I have a headache," she would say. "Not just tonight, some other time." They seemed to feel they had been snubbed.

"Don't let's have them any more," she pleaded. "They're always asking me to perform."

"I'm afraid you don't like my friends," he said.

"They keep an imaginary spotlight on me all the time. If I walk into the room to say hello to them, they make an 'entrance' out of it somehow. They stop being just callers and turn into an audience right away. They want a show."

"But I thought you liked the stage—"

"The stage is just a habit, and now I've broken the habit. Think what it means, to stay in one place all the time, to forget there are things like trunks and trains and eight o'clock shows." She raised her chin as though it hurt. "See these little lines here? I had them when I was seventeen. I'm not old, but I'm so tired—"

She was a little different now from what she had been when he first saw her. And soon she was a whole lot different. He couldn't understand what had happened. Every evening, rushing home under the East River in a crowded train, he thought of her as she had been, in the heart of that electric moon, a two-dimensional being, a product of lights and music, a stage effect, but bringing beauty into his life and his heart, a warmth that would linger there for the rest of his days. And every evening, when he got there and opened the door, he saw her as she was. It was a little hard to fit the two together. He thought: "Did I marry this girl? What is this girl doing here?" He couldn't think of her in a kimono, loose ends of hair straggling about her head, sitting, drinking coffee from a thick cup. Couldn't think of her that way at all. And one Sunday morning, as though seeing her for the first time, he said: "Why, you're no different from anyone else this way."

She sighed and said: "Do I have to be different? Can't you take me as I am?"

And at another, later time she said: "I know. You wouldn't have married me if you had known I would turn into a washout like this."

"It isn't that—" he said. "It isn't that—" She had no right to read his thoughts that way.

But it was that. He knew it and she knew it too.

She had a little plan then. She would look as he wanted her to. He would come home and find the glamorous thing he had married waiting for him. She spent the afternoon getting ready. Had a wave put in her hair. A little perfume but heavy enough to cut with a knife. New eyes, new lips, new lashes, out of little boxes. A baby chandelier dangling from each ear. She saw herself in the glass. "How cheap I look," she said. Men were funny. Maybe she would have to do this once or twice a week. But after she had taken it all off again, there would always be the radio and coffee, each time.

She slipped her hand through one more sparkling paste bracelet for luck. Then the telephone rang. He wasn't coming. They were taking an inventory of stock, get away as soon as he could. She sat down abruptly on a chair and laughed for a very long time. She sat there holding a hand to her head and laughing. They really did those things, then, in everyday life. Rang up home and said they were detained by business when they wanted to take someone else out to dinner. She hadn't believed it until now, thought it just a married-life "gag." One of those funny-paper

Love & Night

jokes. Now it seemed it wasn't. She understood, of course. She knew by his very voice. Probably one of the salesgirls. She shook her head tenderly, was not at all hard-boiled. "Poor Marty. Poor boy. Got to have someone to dream about."

And what about all this she had on? Simply because she felt unequal to the bother of taking it all off again so soon, she got up after a while and languidly called her old theater.

"How's the new show going these days, Jack? I have a hunch I'll drop around tonight. Leave a pass for me in the box-office." Then she boiled herself a cup of coffee and sighed lugubriously. Anyone that would want to leave a cozy flat like this even for an hour must be a fool.

"Dressed up, looking like a Christmas tree," she added aloud. She turned out the lights lingeringly, almost caressingly, and left. The last thing she heard through the door was the purr of the mechanical ice-box. "The darling!" she crooned, as though it were a child.

She got there late. The show had started. And when the house lights went up between the acts, there was Marty sitting precisely one row in front of her, with a friend. Not a woman, though. But even so, he had lied to her.

She left her seat hurriedly, furtively, trailing her wrap across people's knees after her. She wouldn't go back to it again when the audience settled itself for the second half. She was afraid he might turn around and see her. She felt guilty herself somehow—she couldn't quite understand why. Probably because she had caught him unaware. She had once said to him, "I'm a good sport."

Instead of going home at once, she went backstage to talk to Jack. "I don't think my husband cares about me any more," she said, half laughing, half in earnest. "I saw him in the audience just now."

And when she left, Jack was saying, "That'll give you two weeks to rehearse. And the de Vrie woman leaves in ten days. They can put in an understudy till you're set. Now don't forget, tomorrow at eleven!"

"I'll be seeing you," she said wearily.

Marty of course was home before her and pretended to be absorbed in his newspaper. Finally though, because she was his wife and it was the least he could do in all decency, he put it down and looked at her. The way she was dressed and all. His expression never changed.

"What're you all dressed up about?" he asked indifferently.

"I'm going back in the show business," she said quietly. And wanted him to storm and forbid and shout "What, my wife? Never! You'll do nothing of the sort! Your place is home!"

"S'funny, I've been thinking about it too, lately," he drawled, "and wondering if you ever would or not."

Well, she had done all she could.

• • •

A big round moon flamed up against the curtain, wavered a bit, and then steadied itself. It glowed radiantly, too perfect to be anything but a stage moon out of an electrician's box of tricks. Whoever came under its rays bathed in the fountain of youth. The curtain lifted and a girl came through.

To everyone in turn she represented something different. To the man watching her from the wings, she symbolized drudgery, painting itself in bright colors but not fooling him and not fooling herself. To one alone in that entire house, she brought a gift of beauty and glamor.

She gave a little turn of the wrist, and again the moon flashed blindingly on one of the boxes. Marty was sitting in it. In all that glare he never once took his eyes off her. He gave the absurd impression of taking the whole proceeding seriously. "Sweetheart," she sang, "do you love me? Do you want me? Am I in all your dreams?" as part of the patter chorus. And he

Love & Night

nodded his head and sat there mutely adoring. The audience by now was convinced—well, you know the rest.

And every night after the show he was waiting for her to take her home, and there was an air about him of one who sees his dream come alive and walk about before his very eyes.

[*College Humor*, August 1931]

The only Woolrich material published in the first half of 1934 was a quartet of very short romantic tales, of which three are unrevivably trivial, but the fourth (actually the first to appear in print) is a gem. See if you don't agree.

BETWEEN THE ACTS

Russell Barker stood waiting in the crowded lobby of the theater. Half-past eight sharp Stella promised to be there, but she was almost always late. He'd been going out with her for nearly a year now, and she had never yet been on time for an appointment with him. Even though she knew darned well how little he could afford the price of theater tickets these days. Twenty to nine. He put his watch away and started to walk back and forth, looking at the framed photographs of well-known players that decorated the walls.

Stella was a puzzle to him. Did she really care for him or didn't she? Sometimes he wondered if she wasn't just using him as a space-filler until someone more worthwhile—financially, of course—came along. And for that matter did he really care about her either? He couldn't tell. He wasn't as sure as he had once been about—Oh, well, why bring that up now? It was over and done with long ago.

Outside on the wet, gleaming sidewalk in front of the theater, the uniformed doorman was being kept busy as car after car drew up at the entrance to disgorge its smartly-gowned women and stiff-shirted men and then rolled smoothly away to give place to the next. Russell watched them as they sauntered in, these well-to-do occupants of boxes and of first-row orchestra seats, laughing and chattering gaily. They seemed not to have a care in the world. Stella should have been here in time for all this, he realized; she would have enjoyed looking at the women's clothes. She loved clothes so, sables and evening gowns and things like that; she was always talking about them, wishing she owned them. He looked at his watch once more. Quarter to nine. If she didn't hurry, they were going to miss part of the show. Most of the people in the lobby were beginning to filter inside now, and snatches of the overture could be plainly heard each time the inner doors were opened.

Then Stella appeared at last, hurrying toward him, and just as she came in, the biggest limousine of all drew up outside at the curb. Two people got out of it.

Stella greeted Russell in her usual peevish way. "What a night to ask me to come out! If I had known it was going to be like this—!" She cut her complaint short to turn and take in the beauty of an ermine wrap that had just come sailing in, muffling its wearer to the ears. Just behind her came a rather paunchy gentleman.

The wearer of the wrap suddenly stopped short, turned aside ,and came over to the wall as though the pictures on it interested her. She stopped just a foot away from Russell. He saw her face and his own paled a little. But Stella only had eyes for the wrap, envious, longing eyes. "Louise!" the paunchy gentleman remonstrated impatiently. "Come on, we'll miss the show."

"Just a minute," she answered indifferently. "I want to see whose picture this is they have up here." And she raised her finger to her lips as though she were studying the picture critically—but it might have meant simply: "Keep still; don't speak to me—now." And did Russell imagine it, or had a whisper floated toward his ear? "Meet me here between the acts." Suddenly she was gone, had gone in with the paunchy gentleman. Had he really seen her, he wondered, or was it just a ghost—a ghost from out of the past?

Stella brought him to. "Well, come on!" she remarked sulkily. "What are we standing here for?"

As they climbed the two long flights of stairs to the second balcony, she had further fault to find. "I'd like to go to a show just once in my life with you," she said, "and not have to sit way up on the roof!"

Russell didn't answer.

Just before the first act was over, Stella prodded him with her elbow and pointed. "There's that ermine down there, in a box. It's the best-looking thing I've ever seen."

But he had seen it long ago, from the moment he first sat down. The curtain came down for the end of the act. The girl in the box stood up and went outside; the ermine wrap remained behind upon the chair. Stella kept eyeing it hungrily. "That man with her," she commented, "has fallen asleep." Then she added: "I bet he bought it for her. Some women have all the luck!"

"I'm going downstairs and smoke a cigarette," Russell said, standing up. "Wait here, will you?"

• • •

He came out into the lobby a minute later, and they stood face to face, the two of them, the girl who had worn the ermine wrap and he.

"Well, Russell," she said, "let's shake hands anyway. It's been a long time now—"

Their hands met. "Over two years, Louise," he nodded, and asked: "Who's that with you?"

"Oh, someone," she sighed, and explained. "He wants me to marry him—when I get my final decree." Then she smiled and asked, "And who's that with you, Russell?"

"Oh, another someone," he said. "I've thought at times I'd ask her to marry me—when you do get your decree." Abruptly he said: "He's too old for you, Louise."

85

Love & Night

"She'll nag you to death, Russell," she answered. "I could tell that by one look at her face."

They seemed to find it difficult to continue the conversation for a moment. "You came out without your wrap," Russell observed lamely.

"I hate the thing," she said, and added in a low voice: "Like everything else I once thought I wanted so badly!"

Inside, the overture for the beginning of the second act started up with a crash. They grew strangely silent while the lobby around them slowly emptied of people.

"It's funny," Russell mused. "I can remember every little thing we ever said or did—except what caused the final break. What was it? Can you tell me, Louise?"

They both laughed a little and then grew sober. They kept staring into one another's faces as though longing to say something and yet afraid to.

"You used to make such vile coffee—" Russell blurted out longingly.

"You were always such a poor wage-earner—" she sighed wistfully.

"How happy we were!" they both said together.

He felt for her hand and gripped it convulsively without saying anything. She seemed to understand what it meant. "Oh, Russell!" she sobbed all at once, raising her head and looking at him pitifully.

"Louise!" he cried.

• • •

All through the second act a chair in the lower right-hand box where a gentleman dozed and a seat in the second balcony beside which a cross-looking young woman sat frowning remained unoccupied. And when the stage had finally darkened and the house emptied, these two still lingered on in the lobby, he with an ermine wrap slung uselessly over his arm and she with a man's fedora held uselessly in her hand. "And are you positive," said the paunchy gentleman, peering into the box-office for the ninth or tenth time, "that no message was left here for me? Goyter is my name."

"Or for me?" asked the young woman. "Haggerty is mine."

For answer the shutter was slammed down in their faces.

They turned and looked at each other. She glanced thoughtfully from the ermine wrap to the limousine standing waiting outside the door.

"Pardon me—er—may I drop you anywhere?" the paunchy gentleman volunteered.

"That's very sweet of you," she smiled.

"It's a pleasure," he replied, holding the wrap open and folding it gallantly, consolingly about her shoulders.

[*Serenade,* March 1934]

This is the third Woolrich romance which post-dates his debut in the detective pulps and, with its underworld flavor and O. Henry-twist ending, one of his neatest. He recycled the "intimate private club" setting in "Crime on St. Catherine Street" (1936) and the playboy-posing-as-waiter ploy in The Black Angel *(1943).*

CLIP-JOINT

The taxi-driver slowed down invitingly, reached behind him, and threw the door accommodatingly open almost before the man's arm had gone up to hail him. He said, "Yessir! Good evening!"—a courtesy he wasn't in the habit of addressing to every customer. Skip Rogers ducked his head and got in. He took a tuck in each trouser just below the knee, leaned back against the upholstery, and sighed expansively. The uncommonly polite driver reached around a second time and closed the door for him. You wouldn't have thought it was New York at all but for the serial number on the cab's license plates.

He was well-dressed, Skip was; maybe that had something to do with it. The taxi-driver had already had his eye on him from as far away as the corner. He had noted him as a possibility. A man as well-dressed as that wouldn't be very likely to walk when he wanted to go some place—and this man seemed to want to go some place, to want to go some place badly, without knowing just where. Which was just the way the driver liked them to be. In Skip's case it was more than a mere matter of clothes. He had an air about him; he knew how to carry them. On someone else the dark blue chesterfield, the white piqué scarf, the slanted derby would have been just so many articles of wearing apparel; on him they were badges of distinction, insignia of swank. That clothes make the man has been said often enough, but that the man sometimes makes his clothes seem what they are is equally true. It was in Skip's case. The driver considered himself a good judge of character. Here was someone for whom the best was none too good; here was someone who wanted a party, money no object, but didn't quite know how to connect with one. In other words, here was someone who was just what the driver was looking for, made to order.

The taxi-driver turned around in his seat, willingness to oblige written all over his weasel-like face, and said: "Yessir, boss! Where to?" Skip hadn't given him any address yet. If he had, of course, it would have been a different story.

Skip wrinkled his brow in perplexity.

"Suppose you help me out?" he said. "I used to know someone who lived in that house you saw me standing in front of, but—no soap. Guess Annie doesn't live there any more. Now I'm all dressed up and no place to go. Eleven o'clock's too early to go home. Maybe you know of some place where I can get a drink—in the right company?" Then he added quickly: "Now don't get me wrong. I don't mean what you think. I mean just what I say: a couple of drinks, a lot of laughs, and somebody not too hard on the eyes sitting across the table from me. Oh, I know there's plenty of places like that in town, but just when you want to remember the addresses, you can't."

The driver had a hard time keeping a straight face. Was this a pushover? Asking for it, mind you! Coming right out and asking for it! Didn't even have to waste time building it up to him. Who said there wasn't a Santa Claus? However, he decided it wouldn't pay to seem too eager, liable to frighten a good thing off that way and spoil everything. He would go about this carefully.

For a minute he pretended to be at a loss himself. He scratched the back of his head in cleverly simulated cogitation as if he were racking his brains. Then finally he drawled, as his machine moved slowly along and his meter moved quickly upwards, "Let's see, I ought to know of a place like that—" He was, he told himself meanwhile, getting real good at this sort of thing; maybe he should have been an actor. Still, he didn't want to overdo it; keep the guy waiting too long, the sucker might cool off, change his mind. So he took one hand from the wheel and snapped his fingers triumphantly as if it had just then occurred to him. "I got it now!" he said. "I know a real nice place up on Seventy-second. Come to think of it, I took a fellow there only last night."

"What's it like?" the man in back of him wanted to know.

"It's sort of private, know what I mean? But that's all right; I can take you up and introduce you. It's not a loose joint or anything like that—it's just a sort of little club. They don't like too many people to go there at one time because there ain't room enough for them, but outside of that everything's on the up and up. If you don't like to sit by yourself, why they'll introduce you to one of their little hostesses—everything perfectly proper and the way it should be." He paused. Then, just to show how immaterial the whole thing was to him one way or the other, he added: "At least so they tell me. I'm a working man myself, don't get much time to relax." With a superb negligence he questioned: "What d'ye say? Want to go up there?"

"Sure, why not?" his passenger acquiesced. But there was a happy ring to his voice that showed how eager he had become to visit this paradise the driver had described to him.

"I've sold him," thought the man at the wheel. "Sold him out!"

When they had arrived, by means of a roundabout route that gave the meter a thorough work-out, the driver hopped out and held the door open just as if he were a private chauffeur.

"Sorry I took you out of your way like that," he apologized insincerely, "but I wasn't sure of the number myself until we got here just now." Skip however paid him without demur and even threw in a tip for good measure. He was, the driver told himself, getting to be a good picker, a very good picker. "It's on the second floor," he said. "I'll go up with you. I'll tell 'em you're a friend of mine."

It was a rather run-down looking apartment house they had stopped in front of, of pre-war vintage. It boasted an elevator, however, and orange electric lights in the lobby. It had undoubtedly seen better days. The driver ushered Skip in, and the latter missed seeing the knowing look that was exchanged between his guide and the sleepy colored youth who ran the elevator. It was a look that plainly said, "You know and I know but he doesn't know."

They got off at the second floor and went toward the back along a cheap musty corridor paved with white mosaics, most of which had become loosened and rattled as one stepped on them. The taxi-driver stopped in front of a door numbered 2– and rang the bell. He gave two short rings and one long one, then whistled a little.

A chain rattled on the other side of the door, a bolt was thrown back, and the door was opened just an inch, no more. "It's Marty," said the taxi-driver in a low voice, whereupon the door opened the rest of the way and revealed a pasty-faced individual in what is known to hoi polloi as a tuxedo. He had a look that would have turned milk sour, but the minute he saw that Marty was not alone, he put on a great show of cordiality and good-fellowship and aplomb.

"Hello, Marty, old boy," he said, "glad to see you! Where y'been keeping yourself? Come on in and have a drink!" But his eyes were on Skip Rogers the whole time he spoke.

"No thanks," said Marty. "I gotta get back to my cab and earn an honest living. But this is a friend of mine, I want you to treat him right. See that he has a good time."

The orang-outang in the dinner jacket beamed. "Any friend of Marty's is a friend of mine," he proclaimed. "Step right in," and motioned Skip in with a sweep of his arm. Then he attempted to

Love & Night

close the door after him, but the taxi-driver's foot had somehow become wedged in front of it and held it open.

"Not so fast," the latter snarled under his breath. "How about my commission? What do you think I'm doing this for—my health?" And he held out his paw palm upward. A five-dollar bill came out of the trouser pocket of the tuxedo and found its way to the outstretched hand. The foot, however, stayed where it was. "What're y'trying to do, hold out on me?" Marty wanted to know. "This is a real live one I brought you this time." A murderous look passed between them, but two single dollars joined the five. After which Marty removed his foot, the door closed, and the chain and bolt went back in place with a venomous clash.

He stood still for a moment, folding and refolding his ill-gotten gains until the seven dollars had become a wedge not much bigger than a postage-stamp. He then held it to his lips for a second in what looked suspiciously like a kiss and carefully tucked it away in his clothing. "And now back to the warpath!" he grinned cheerfully, and turned away from the ominous-looking door.

When the taxi-driver got to the end of the hall, the elevator was still up, waiting for him the way it always did at times like these. The operator looked as sleepy as before, only now he was holding out a beige palm as if feeling for rain. The steerer tried to ignore it, but it followed him into the cage, and the car wouldn't go down.

"Does I git ma usual rake-off or does I start tawking nex' time you brings one in?" drawled the drowsy African.

"All right, all right!" snarled the steerer and unwillingly fished a fifty-cent piece out of his pocket, holding back the rest of its contents with one hand. The car went down in blissful silence after that.

By this time the companionship-seeking young man who was the innocent cause of all this high finance was already at one of the little tables for two up in 2–, and the gorgeous redhead sitting across from him in the fluffy green dress was looking trustfully up at the waiter and cooing: "—and a very weak one for me, Frank." A wink went with the words. Then she smiled sweetly at her new acquaintance. "Just for sociability's sake, you know. I hardly ever drink, you understand. But you go right ahead; don't let me stop you."

She took time off to glance appraisingly at the cut of his suit and the careless ease with which he wore it, as one to the manner born. He looked better-groomed than ever now that he held a square of green pasteboard instead of his coat, hat, and scarf. Just how expensive that bit of pasteboard was he didn't know yet. A cute little brunette in a doll-apron, who could have pulled your teeth and made you like it, had given it to him on his way in just now and then gone off somewhere with his things. He could just as well have said good-by to them. They were already on their way out to a "fence." The man who had opened the door had tactfully disappeared too after introducing him to "Miss Gordon." Everything was peaches and cream; it was what you might call the lull before the storm.

He and the redhead were alone in the room except for one other couple, a blonde and her table-companion. The latter had already reached the stage of squashing his esses and dropping his t's, as well as part of every drink he tried to pick up. The room had originally been intended for the living-room of the apartment, back when it was meant to be lived in and not used for assault, battery, and highway robbery. Some cheaply flamboyant drapes hid the exact location of the windows if there were any. A midget space had been left clear for dancing. The radio droned lullingly on, a mere blur of sound in the background, "—hands across the table, when the lights are lo-ow." The whole set-up was an aphrodisiac, meant to awaken passion which these vultures fed on. The loose joints that Skip Rogers had so carefully stayed away from tonight were honest and upright compared to this place.

The waiter would come to the door and look in whenever the

Love & Night

re-orders of drinks began to slow up; he seemed to give them about five minutes apiece. He didn't have to do that very often though; the two "hostesses" were there to see to that. He was a six footer like the man who ran the place, and husky as an ape. He brought Skip and "Miss Gordon" their two drinks, the strong one and the weak one, and went away again. The redhead simpered cherubically. Rogers seemed to meet with her approval.

"Here's looking at you!" she said gayly and picked up her glass. If he had looked closely, he would have seen that the amount that passed her lips was scarcely enough to moisten the rouge that lay on them. His tasted like benzine, only not so smooth.

"Where you from, Miss Gordon?" he asked her suddenly.

"Just call me Rose," she begged him and moved her chair over a little closer. Before she could commence her life story, however, something going on at the other table had caught Skip's eye and sent a chill through him. From that point on, although he seemed absorbed in what she was telling him, he actually heard not a single word she was saying. For the rather plastered middle-aged gentleman who was sitting with the blonde seemed to have gotten into difficulties of some kind. The waiter was bending over him. The individual in the tuxedo had also come in from somewhere and was standing menacingly on the other side of him. The stew kept pushing away a small slip of paper, and they kept shoving it back at him. The blonde got up and made the radio a little louder to drown out the angry voices. Rose plucked Rogers by the coat sleeve and dragged his straying attention back to herself.

"Don't notice what's going on over there," she suggested tactfully. "Some people can't hold their liquor, that's all." And she began to talk sweet but fast.

The next time Rogers found time to look over in that direction, there was no longer any middle-aged gentleman in the room at all, and the waiter was softly closing the door he had just passed through. It wasn't the door by which you came in, either. From somewhere further back in the flat came the crash of a chair being overturned and a muffled cry that sounded something like "Let me out of here!" But Rose kept chattering away for all she was worth so it was hard for Skip to tell.

His face took on a stony, set look as if he was using it for a mask behind which he was doing a lot of quick thinking. The fact she wasn't getting across penetrated to Rose presently, and she stopped her chatter.

"What's the matter, honey?" she said caressingly, reaching for one of his hands. "Am I boring you?"

He seemed to make up his mind to something all at once. He leaned toward her across the table.

"I should say not," he protested. "You've got me spellbound." With one hand he raised her fingers lingeringly to his lips. With the other, hidden by the caress, he switched the two new drinks the waiter had brought in a minute ago. "I could go for a girl like you!" he vowed, star-gazing into her mascaraed eyes. They sipped. But now it was he who was talking fast and sweet and low. "I walked in here tonight never dreaming there'd be a number like you off the hook." She didn't have time to notice the shellac she was imbibing and she was only human anyway; they didn't often come as young and good looking as this—not in her racket. She could feel Mickey Mouses running up and down her spine. "All my life I've wanted to meet somebody as lovely as you are—" And the radio: *"Speak to me of love, Tell me the things that I'm longing to hear—"*

"Oh, go wan," she protested, but a dreamy look had come into her eyes just the same. Not for nothing was she red-headed; her own blood was double-crossing her. They sipped again. All he was getting was rancid ginger ale; she was getting the works.

"Always had more money than I knew what to do with, always had everything I wanted, but somehow I never met the right girl—until tonight!" he was going on.

She pricked up her ears at that. Money? Everything he wanted?

"On the level, who are you?" A hiccough marred the intensity of her new-found interest in him, but it was there just the same.

"You've heard of Robbins & Rogers, haven't you?"

She nodded owlishly. "Sure, thass those restaurants where you put in a nickel and—plop! Out comes a sandwich."

"Well, there you are." He spread his hands.

She pointed an awe-stricken finger and covered her mouth with her other hand. "Then you—you must be the old guy's son or something! Rogers' son!"

He dropped his eyes modestly. "Why go into that? All that matters is I'm completely sold on you; nothing would be too good for you, if you'd only let me—"

He leaned entreatingly forward again and began exploring her fingertips with his lips. They tasted of nail-polish, but it was an improvement over the liquor.

She was doing a lot of quick thinking now on her own account. A millionaire's son had fallen for her! It was the chance of a lifetime, might never happen again. If she let anything happen to him here tonight, where would she be? He'd be through with her, never look at her again. All she'd get out of it would be a lousy ten per cent commission. On the other hand, if she got him out of this jam, saved him for herself, who could tell what it might lead to? She'd be a fool not to think of herself first, and the hell with her employers!

"Wait a minute—wait a minute. I gotta think!" she said to him, and held his head in her hands.

He smiled a little out of the corner of his mouth, but she didn't see that. He went right ahead singing his love-song close to her ear: "—diamonds and orchids and a mink coat and a penthouse way up in the air to which nobody but me would have the key. There'd be nothing too good for my baby! And at night—you'd have love!"

She rumpled her blazing hair and smote herself distractedly on the forehead.

"I gotta get you outta here! I gotta think of number one. Sh-h—not so loud, don't let 'em hear you or we're sunk!"

"Spoken like a lady," he agreed humorously. "You're—you're just an angel in an evening gown."

She had sobered up all at once. She glanced furtively around over her shoulder.

"Nurse your drink; make it last," she said out of the corner of her mouth. "You're in the red enough as it is. I've got to think of an out for you—for both of us. You shouldn'ta come here. Do you know what this place is?"

"I knew the minute I came in," he said calmly, "but it was too late to do anything about it by that time. What could I do?"

"Here's the set-up," she hissed, her shoulder touching his. "They're going to clip you a century apiece for every drink the two of us have had. You say no to them and you get the beating of your life. They hold you in the back of the flat until your check has a chance to go through at the bank in the morning. Then they give you knock-out drops and you come to riding around in a taxi somewhere. It's no use trying to catch up with them after you've come out of the repair shop; we change addresses about once a week." She clenched her fist and brought it down on the table-top. "They're not going to make a dent in my baby's bankroll, not when I've got all those fancy trimmings coming to me! Once they find out who you really are, they'll clip you twice as much. They won't leave you anything but your shorts—"

"You've been peeking," he observed dryly. He almost seemed to be enjoying himself, but she failed to see any humor in it.

"Tear up any cards or means of identification you've got on you, quick! If worse comes to worst, we can say you're just a poor hash-slinger at one of your father's restaurants, out on a spree; you haven't a dime; you borrowed the clothes from a friend. But I can think of a better way still, a way that we won't have to do any explaining." She rose from the table. "I'm going inside and get my—my powder-puff." She gave him a wink. "You sit tight here, keep everything under control until I get back. Don't get into any argument because you're no match for them. They carry blackjacks and brass knuckles." He saluted her with two fingers, and she disappeared out the back way. Skip sat there grinning at his own thoughts, which seemed to afford him considerable amusement. "The old oil," he remarked to himself. "The same old oil gets all of them."

The waiter stuck his head in and glanced meaningfully at the two half-empty glasses. Skip gave him no encouragement. He sauntered over and leaned both hands heavily on the table. Skip stared up at him coldly. He may have been amused by the antics of Rose Gordon, but he didn't seem to find this funny.

"Who sent for you?" he demanded brittlely.

"You drinkin' any more?" rumbled the waiter.

"Who wants to know?" countered Skip, starting to breathe faster.

"Then suppose you pay off. We're closing up—"

"Fair enough," said Skip, dangerously calm. "How much do I owe you?"

The Caliban of a waiter didn't bother jotting anything down. "Three hundred and fifty dollars," he announced matter-of-factly, his pig-eyes boring into Skip's.

Skip Rogers drew out a crumpled five-dollar bill. "Bring me four dollars change," he ordered contemptuously, "and consider yourself damn lucky!"

The waiter didn't waste any more time. He simply turned his head and whistled warningly over his shoulder. Instantly the man in the tuxedo appeared in the doorway. He was coatless now and rolling up his shirt-sleeves preparatory to going to work. Behind him was another gorilla, appearing on the scene now for the first time. They both made for the table, nice and slow, nice and easy, as though there was no hurry about this at all. Skip's chair went over backwards with a bang and he was on his feet, facing the three of them. The waiter swung at him, a blow that would have felled an ox. Skip ducked it nimbly and came back like a flash with a less powerful but better aimed jab that landed on the Frankenstein's nose. Blood spurted and he gave an animal roar of fury.

"Here I go!" thought Skip philosophically as the other two spread out fan-shape on either side of him.

Suddenly Rose Gordon's voice rang out sharply from the doorway, harsh and strident maybe but sweeter than the song of Lorelei at such a time.

"Turn around! Get away from him, all of you! This is one guy you don't touch! Hand over the key to the front door, Shorty, and hurry up about it!" She had her hat and coat on and she was holding a small revolver in her hand, waving it at the three of them. Her eyes were menacing slits. No one looking at her could have doubted that she would have used it without hesitation. The three of them slowly backed away from Skip Rogers, hands at shoulder-level. The one called Shorty drew out a door-key and tossed it down on the floor. "Grab that," she ordered Skip. "I'll hold 'em until you get the door open!"

"Ladies first," he countered. "I'll do the holding. You unlock and wait for me down on the street."

She passed the gun to him and slipped out, the key in her hand. "We'll get you, baby! You'll be sorry for this!" the erstwhile manager breathed virulently after her as she went. The sound of a most undignified but effective "raspberry" or Bronx cheer came drifting back from the hallway.

When Skip joined her on the sidewalk in front of the house five minutes later, he had somebody else with him, the unfortunate middle-aged gentleman who had been sitting with the blonde earlier in the evening. His collar was torn, he had a black eye, and he was almost dazed by his sudden release. Skip shoved him into a taxicab, then hailed another for his rescuer and himself.

Love & Night

"I'm going home with you tonight," he told her matter-of-factly. "They may try to come after you and—well, I owe you that much anyway."

If his words were strangely un-loverlike, she didn't seem to notice. She snuggled down contentedly against his shoulder and sighed. She was visioning herself in a bathtubful of eau de Cologne in a penthouse twenty stories above the street, with him pacing impatiently back and forth outside her boudoir.

When she woke up in the morning, he was gone and it seemed hard to believe that he had ever been in the dingy furnished room with her. She looked around it, and she knew she was getting out right then. Not only because there were better things in store for her but also because it was dangerous to stay there alone; her former employers were liable to look her up at any moment. She packed the few things she had and told her landlady with an air of noblesse oblige that she could keep the balance of the week's rent.

"I'm moving to Park Avenue," she said. "I don't know the exact location yet, but it'll be somewhere along there, don't worry!" Skip hadn't left any note for her but that didn't matter; she knew where to find him. It didn't even occur to her that there was anything strange about it. He'd gone home to change his clothes, that was all; you couldn't expect a rich man's son like him to stay in the same rumpled clothes after being out all night.

She reached the main Robbins & Rogers restaurant, a few blocks from where she had formerly lived, just a little after the breakfast-rush was over. She marched in, suitcase in hand. She was being very tactful about this; it wouldn't have been ladylike to march right up to where he lived—at least not that early in the morning. Besides, for all she knew he mightn't be exactly anxious to have his people know anything about her; she'd been around enough to know how those things worked. Also she wanted to give him time enough to make the arrangements for the penthouse; he would have to sign the lease for it and so forth. The rest of the shopping—for the car, mink coat, furniture, et cetera—they could do together later on. So she had lots of time. Meanwhile she would tie on the feed-bag at his old man's expense, here in this place. He didn't know it yet, but she was practically his daughter-in-law already.

She set her suitcase down beside an empty table in spite of the sign that warned Not Responsible for Personal Property. Then she stalked, swaggered you might say, over to the steam counter and ran a contemplative eye along its display of dishes as though she already owned it. "Fry two, sunny side up," she commanded across the counter. "Two, bottoms up," echoed the counterman to the short-order cook. "You can bring them to me," she added haughtily, "over to that table, there." If she was going to have a penthouse and a dinge to manicure her dogs, she might as well get used to being waited on right now. Huh! The owner's son's sweetie should carry her own food to the table? Not by a long sight!

"Sorry, lady, gotta pick 'em up yourself, this is self-service—" the counterman started to remonstrate. She didn't stand there arguing about it. He didn't know who she was, that was all.

"See that you don't keep me waiting!" was all she said, and she turned, went back to her table, sat down, and began to fan herself indolently with a paper napkin.

"These yours?" At the sound of his voice she whirled around on her chair as though she had been bitten.

"Skip!" she started to exclaim joyously, and then stopped short. Her mouth dropped open and stayed that way. She just sat and stared up at him. He was holding her platter of eggs all right, and he was wearing a soiled, crummy white jacket—the same service-jacket all the helpers and bus-boys wore in the Robbins & Rogers restaurants.

"I saw you come in," he said. "I'm not supposed to do this. If they catch me at it, they'll fire me, but you wanted table-service and it's table-service you're getting."

Love & Night

"Wha—what're you doing—dressed up like a hash-slinger?" she gulped. She just slumped down in her chair and stared up at him like a fish gasping for air.

"Funny," he observed, "but that was what you wanted me to tell them last night, wasn't it? Well, it so happens that I am. They wouldn't have believed you, but it would have been the truth. I was dressed up in somebody else's clothes and was shooting a whole month's wages on a one-night spree. Is it my fault I look like a million bucks every time I put on a clean shirt?"

Her voice rose hysterically. "But you told me—" she shrieked furiously. "You made me believe—you promised me—!"

He looked at her sorrowfully but with an undertone of humor. "Is that all you cared about—what I promised you, what you thought you could get out of me? Or was it me, myself, you liked? Because I haven't changed. I'm the same guy who whispered in your ear last night. But I'm glad I found out if that's the kind you are."

She was nearly choking on her rage. "Why, you small-time, petty-larceny, no-account—Do you think I'd waste five minutes of my time—"

He sighed, but whether with regret or relief is problematical. "Well," he assured her, "I can't treat you to a mink coat or a penthouse on my wages but I can do this much for you—have these on me; it's my treat!" He put down the platter of eggs at an angle and the yolks splashed out in all directions.

"Show this lady out," he remarked to the other employees who came running up, "and don't spare the shoving."

When she had gone, howling imprecations, and her suitcase had been sent flying after her, Skip Rogers started to unbutton his white service-jacket. He turned to the manager, standing beside him wringing his hands, and said:

"Here you are; give this back to whoever I borrowed it from. And whatever you do, don't mention this little masquerade to Dad. He might think I really want to go to work here!"

[*Breezy Stories*, August 1935]

Published in Breezy Stories *just two months after "Clip-Joint," this is the most overtly crime-linked of all the Woolrich romances and indeed teeters on the brink of noir. Wouldn't the young Cagney have been just right for the part of Eddinger?*

NO KICK COMING

They were walking home in silence together. He takes all the kick out of everything, she thought, by the way he does things. If he would only give more snap, more suddenness, to what he does!

She knew, almost word for word, step by step, and move by move, what the wind-up of their evening was going to be like. At the last corner before her house he would say, "Did you have a good time?" Then when they were at the door, he would say: "Well, here we are. See you night after tomorrow." Always that unnecessary "Here we are!" As though they could be any place else but where they were!

As though he had ever failed to call for her every other night in the week!

Then for a dramatic climax, he would follow her just inside the doorway, strike a match so that she could fit her key in without any trouble, and after the door was open and the match blown out ask: "May I kiss you?" Once, to her intense surprise, he had varied this by saying "Mind if I kiss you?" But two nights later he had gone back to his original wording again and never changed it after that. Why, oh why, did he have to ask like that each time and rob the kiss of all its kick? She shook her head as she walked along beside him. It wasn't, no, it wasn't very thrilling, that was all.

Love & Night

They arrived at the last street corner. Here it came now, always at this same spot, right where the electric lamp-post was standing. "Did you have a good time?"

"Very," she answered patiently.

They stopped at the door. Say it! she thought irritably. Say it and get it over with!

He didn't fail to. "Well, here we are," he said. And then, "See you night after tomorrow." She just smiled drearily at him and turned to go in. He came after her and struck a match and held it while she put her key in the door. Then "May I kiss you?" he murmured. It made the whole thing as tame as a handshake. She held up her face, coolly, briefly, and then slipped in and shut the door after her.

Inside the flat she flung her purse down with a violent, explosive gesture. Immediately the light flashed on and her roommate sat up in bed suddenly.

"Hello, Ivy," she said. "You woke me up. What time is it?"

"It's the usual time," said Ivy sullenly. "Not a minute later, not a minute sooner. Everything's run according to a schedule with him, you see."

"Have a good time with Walter?" her roommate yawned.

"Oh, gorgeous!" snapped Ivy.

"You don't sound like it. What happened? Did you have a quarrel?"

"A quarrel would be something at least," Ivy exclaimed, running a comb repeatedly through her hair in what looked like a vicious attempt at scalping herself. "He hasn't even got spirit enough to quarrel with me." This was said complainingly rather than admiringly.

"Why, Ivy!" the roommate admonished, sinking back on the pillow and ruffling her hair in time with Ivy's frantic combing. "He loves you. What more do you want? A steady, reliable fellow who's devoted to you and intends settling down with you. You have no kick coming!"

"That's just it," agreed Ivy dismally. "I certainly have no kick coming!" She abruptly snapped the light out.

• • •

The next day, in a starched muslin frock and a peaked white cap to go with the surroundings, she waited on tables. The final touch of old Holland, the wooden shoes, had fortunately been omitted as conflicting with the necessary rapidity of movement. In this atmosphere, redolent of such native Dutch dishes as griddle-cakes and shredded wheat, the long hours slipped past her. The evening of the second day was one of Walter's Saturdays. A picture show on Tuesdays and Thursdays, dancing on Saturdays. That was as immutable as the laws of the Medes and Persians. That they should go to a picture on Saturday, for instance, and dance together on one of the other two nights, why there was much more likelihood of the sun shining at midnight or snow falling in August than of that ever happening! Instead of feeling the way girls do a month or so before they get married, she thought rebelliously, I feel the way they do years afterward— all disinterested and blah! She was meanwhile preparing herself in a listless way to be ready at half-past eight, the hour when he would call for her, with no excitement and no anticipation.

All the faces would be the same, the tunes would be the same, for he always took her to the same place. And at the very same spot on the floor, where that thick post was set, he would go out of step again trying to get past it. It was difficult to recall, it seemed so long ago now, that she had once laughed about this, saying: "We'll have to have that removed!" And that a week later, when the same thing happened, she said: "Here's our old friend Mr. Post." Now she no longer said a word. It was—well, just a part of Walter; it had to be taken for granted along with everything else that he stood for: good-hearted, reliable, devoted to her; altogether a calendar of virtues. But a calendar without

Love & Night

a red-letter day for her. Her friend came in at eight, home from toil.

"You certainly are," she remarked with a glance at the familiar pale-blue Saturday night dress, "getting your money's worth out of that thing. Aren't you afraid Walter will get tired of seeing you in it so much?"

"It's just the other way round," Ivy corrected her. "I wear it each time as a special favor to him; he's asked me to time and again, doesn't like me in new things. That night I wore the other one for a change, his face dropped and he said something about having to get used to me all over again."

"Well," observed her friend enviously, "he's just about ideal. You don't have to worry about what to wear to go out with him. Are you lucky!"

"So I've been told," Ivy agreed desperately.

Eight-thirty came, then went again. Thirty seconds past, then a whole minute, then two—and for the first time in months the doorbell didn't give its familiar ring. He had never been as unpunctual as this before.

"I honestly believe," Ivy said hopefully, as though discovering a new trait to be admired in him, "he's going to be all of five or ten minutes late. And yet it can't be possible; it must be our clock that's fast."

"I'm not put out," she was saying a quarter of an hour later. "At least for once he's done something to break the awful monotony. It's a habit should be encouraged."

The telephone rang. It was Walter. He had been unavoidably detained. He was apologetic, almost abjectly so in fact. He was on his way now.

"Instead of your coming all the way up here," she suggested, "I'll wait for you at the place instead. That'll save time."

When she came back to the room, she remarked, "I'm going to do something I've wanted to do for months."

"What?" asked her friend, slightly alarmed.

"I'm going down there alone to that place, ahead of him, and find out what it feels like to dance with somebody else for a change."

"Ivy," her roommate remonstrated, "you're just doing this because you're peeved at him. You don't really want to go down there without an escort—"

"Don't I!" said Ivy. "Don't I? If you only knew! Listen," she said intensely. "I have an enemy down there, and tonight is my chance to get even. Don't get frightened," she added as her friend's eyes widened. "It's only a post, but tonight for once in my life I'm going to get past that post without having a hitch thrown into my dancing!" Then she flung the door open and departed, leaving her roommate to close it after her with a puzzled look on her face.

• • •

Ivy bought her own way into the dance hall and seated herself in the first vacant armchair she came to. "No," she said almost at once, over her shoulder, and then "No" again, and still a third time "No" with an added "Thank you" by way of afterthought. She hadn't come there to indulge in flirtation; those who had noticed her on former occasions in the company of Walter and now approached with a doubtful, furtive air about them wouldn't do at all.

"He's got to come up and stand right before me, whoever he is," she told herself, "not sneak up sideways hoping no one will notice."

Her glance wandered across the sleek floor to the opposite side of the room. There's someone, she thought, who would do nicely. Almost as though he had heard her, he started over, then and there, neither hurriedly nor yet slowly, cutting directly across the vacant floor with an air of assurance that was all to his credit. I shouldn't have looked over at him, Ivy thought remorsefully, now that it was too late. She turned her face away. Even when she knew that he was standing there, she pretended not to see him.

"The next?" he said in a resonant voice.

"What would you have done if I had refused?" she asked curiously once they were out on the floor.

"Just what I'm doing now," he said. "Dance with you anyway."

"With somebody else, you mean?"

"With you, I said," he corrected. "When I want to dance with someone bad enough to ask them, I dance with them!"

"Well!" she said, a bit rashly. "This is something, anyway! I have no kick coming so far."

The famous post bore down on them. Instinctively she bunched herself together, waiting for the misstep that was to come. There was no misstep. Expertly he detoured in a half circle, and it receded harmlessly in back of them. There, she thought triumphantly. I've accomplished what I set out to do tonight—now I'll leave him as soon as the music stops and wait for Walter.

She did leave him as soon as the music stopped, and the next time it stopped, and the time after that too. In fact, each and every time it stopped, she left him to wait for Walter, and each time it began, no matter how inconspicuous and out-of-the-way a refuge she had chosen for herself, he found her and dragged her out into the open again. She said "No" and "No more tonight, thanks," and found herself dancing with him anyway.

"You've been saying for nearly an hour now," he objected, "that you expect your friend any minute. Well, he isn't here yet." He came to an abrupt decision. "Come on, let's go," he ordered. "I didn't dance with you all evening to turn you over to someone else! I'm taking you home myself."

"Leave here with you?" she gasped. "Why, I should say—"

"Come on, no use arguing about it," he repeated impatiently, and taking her by the elbow lifted her to her feet.

After all, she decided, it was no more than Walter deserved for being so late. He'd kept her waiting here for him for nearly an hour. "You'd make a good kidnaper," she told him tartly. But at the same time she inconsistently let him lead her toward the entrance and out of the place. It was rather nice for a change to have your mind made up for you. It put the blame for whatever you did on the other person and not on yourself. It made you feel carefree and irresponsible.

"Well," she said ungraciously as they reached the street, "now that you've had your way, what next?" And shot him a look that was meant to be cold and disapproving.

"We'll go and get something to eat," he said.

"No we won't," she said immediately. "I'm not hungry."

"I am," he told her, "so we'll get something to eat."

"Didn't I just tell you—?" she began. By the time she was through telling him, they were already seated at a table somewhere.

"And a chicken sandwich for the lady," he informed the waiter.

"Nothing of the kind!" Ivy corrected bitingly. "I'm not having a thing."

"And like I just told you, a chicken sandwich for the lady."

The man nodded and went to get the order; he seemed to have no doubt as to which voice of the two was the deciding one.

"He can bring it," said the irate Ivy, "but that doesn't mean I'm going to eat it!"

Somewhat later, after she had replaced her fork on the empty plate, they stood up to go. "He thinks he's good," she told herself knowingly. "I simply changed my mind, that was all."

On the way to her house they passed a jewelry store, the same one Walter always stopped to look at whenever he brought her by there.

"Wait a minute. Let's see what they've got here," he said. But he didn't have as much trouble as Walter did making up his mind, he did not bother calculating how long it would take at the rate of five dollars down and five a week or anything like that. All he did was point to the very biggest diamond ring on the tray and say: "There's a beaut. Want me to get you that?"

"Are you crazy or something?" she gasped. "We've only seen each other tonight for the first time!"

He looked at her in surprise. "What's wrong about that?" he wanted to know. "Isn't that the way to do things, right on the dot? I happen to like you!"

That was the way she had always felt about it herself—make life a breathless, thrilling thing. But this was going too far.

"Not so fast, slow down," she said coldly.

"Why, we're just cut out for each other." But she had turned resolutely away from the window and wasn't listening any more. "I'm going to get that for you," he said briskly, coming after her, "that one I just showed you."

"Better forget it," she smiled. "It's priced too high."

"When I want something," he said stubbornly, "I go ahead and get it!"

They passed the lamp-post on the corner.

"I enjoyed myself tonight," she said suddenly, without being asked.

All he said was "What'd you expect?" as though that was to be taken for granted; it was needless to mention a thing like that.

"But, Ivy," her friend asked when she let her in a few minutes later, "what on earth possessed you to pound on the door the way you just did? Didn't you have your key with you?"

"Yes," gasped Ivy, "but I didn't have time to use it. It's a good thing you came to the door when you did!"

"That's not like you at all," her friend persisted. "And poor Walter has been ringing up constantly all evening long saying he couldn't locate you—"

"Walter?" said Ivy with an effort. "Oh, yes—I forgot."

∙ ∙ ∙

She had a mid-afternoon station at the Old Dutch Corner the next day. As she was walking along leisurely toward the restaurant in the two o'clock sunshine, something made her stop and stare in surprise. There was the familiar jewelry shop, but quite a change had come over it. Two boards, crossed to form an X, protected the place where the glass showcase had been until now. And where the glass showcase had been, there were just splinters and jagged ends sticking out of the frame, with the sidewalk below it well iced with innumerable fragments of broken glass. A policeman on guard before the doorway kept advising loiterers to move on and not stand there.

Which advice Ivy took herself only when she found herself being addressed in person. Held up! she thought, continuing reluctantly on her way. I wonder what Walter will say when he hears about it? Then suddenly a horrible intuition that had nothing whatever to do with Walter flashed through her mind and was quickly dismissed. "I'm imagining things," she told herself. "He wouldn't dare."

She entered the Old Dutch Corner, made her way to the back, and descended the narrow stairs that led down to the waitresses' locker-room. When she came up again, she was in the muslin frock and peaked cap. "The six tables along the wall in back," the manager directed her. "And fill the sugar bowls. People have been putting wet spoons in them all morning." Into the fray she plunged for the next five or six hours. Endless hours of serving tomato-juice, finger-bowls, and all that went in between. Until ten came, and she was through.

She had just scratched off her last meal-check and was turning to go downstairs and take off her uniform when a new customer pushed through the revolving doors. She groaned inwardly and

Love & Night

waited to see if he would sit at her station. That would mean another half-hour. But he didn't select any table at all. Instead he leaned intimately across the cashier's desk. She glanced over in surprise, thinking he must have a pretty bad cold the way his scarf was thrown up over his chin. Then she saw the cashier raise his hands; his face was white and drawn. He stayed that way without moving, while the customer reached over and did something to the drawer on the inside of the counter where the money was kept.

After that things began to happen too quickly for Ivy to grasp what it was all about. The blast of a whistle sounded faintly outside on the street somewhere. The two or three diners in the place stood up excitedly, craning their necks; a chair fell over backwards. A voice, the voice of that man up front, barked out: "Just stay where you are, all of you!" The revolving door began to spin violently around, and two policemen could be seen flattened against it in a hurry to get in from the outside. On top of all this there was a crashing, shattering noise, as though a giant firecracker had gone off, only much louder than that even, followed by a sound of scampering feet going toward the back, where there was a delivery-exit on the side-street. But by now Ivy was crouching down under a table, her head bunched between her shoulders, as a precaution against whatever might come next.

There were, however, no further explosions like the first one; instead everyone in the place began talking at once, and there was an incessant rushing from front to back and back to front. "He got out the back way!" she heard someone say. She straightened up and ventured out into the open once more. The whole front of the restaurant was boiling with excitement. The night-manager, greatly upset, was conferring with one of the policemen.

"They oughta know better than to build a place with two entrances these days," the policeman was saying disgustedly.

"Mr. Simms," ventured Ivy timidly, "may I go home now?"

"Don't annoy me at a time like this!" Mr. Simms exclaimed abruptly. "Go ahead if your time's up."

She hurried to the back room and down the steps to the locker-room. She quickly opened the locker with her key, took her street-dress off the hook, pulled the Dutch cap from her head, and then sat down momentarily on the long bench to rest her feet and get her breath back. It was then that, glancing into the mirror before her on the wall, she saw his reflection for the first time. He had wedged himself into the corner between the wall and the end locker and couldn't be seen as you opened the door. She froze from head to foot.

"Wait a minute. Keep your head," his voice said. "You know me." And he came out and stood there and, of all things, smiled nonchalantly at her.

"You!" she squeaked. "You—last night!" They stood looking at each other, she up at him and he down at her. It never occurred to her, somehow, to scream for help. After all, when you have danced and eaten a sandwich with a person, you don't usually scream for help the very next time you see him. "I should have known there was a catch in it somewhere," she declared bitterly. "So this is what you are and what you do! And now I suppose you think I'm going to help you get away or something—?"

He kept right on smiling at her; he even seated himself negligently astride the bench, opposite to her. "Go ahead," he invited with a sweep of his arm. "Call them in." He said this with complete indifference. She felt, somehow, that he really meant it; he wasn't just bluffing. "I didn't even know you worked here," he went on. "If you think I'd trade on your liking for me to get myself out of this jam, you're all wrong."

"My liking for you?" she exploded violently. "You'll find out in a minute just how much I like you! You—you criminal!" She leaped up and took a step toward the door, a determined and furious one. Then there was loud knocking and confused voices from outside. "Don't come in. I'm undressed!" she shrieked

Love & Night

wildly, and threw her whole weight against the door to hold it. Over her shoulder she saw that reckless fool still grinning at her, his eyes on the uniform that clothed her from neck to calf. She couldn't help admiring his nerve; maybe that was what made her do what she did.

"There's no one in there but you, is there, Ivy?" the manager's voice called in.

She evaded the question. "How could there be, Mr. Simms?" she shouted back. "I'll be out in five minutes!"

The confusion of voices melted away on the other side of the locked door.

"Such a lot of trouble," he grinned, "to save a criminal!"

"You certainly don't deserve it!" she admitted bitterly. "I don't know what's the matter with me, anyway! Now get out of here before they find you!"

He came up behind her. "All right, let's go," he agreed. "I'll turn my back while you're changing."

"Me, you mean?" she said in a barely audible voice. "Go with you!" And froze in consternation.

"Life is short and sweet; that's the way to live it. Here, slip this on." And that very large diamond ring he had pointed out to her last night behind the glass showcase passed into the palm of her hand. "We'll pick up a car outside, send it back tomorrow C.O.D. We'll make our getaway into Jersey or Connecticut, and what happened upstairs tonight won't happen any more if you don't want it to."

"But it would always be hanging over us. It would only spoil everything," she said. "The only thing I like about you is your suddenness—your courage. Only why couldn't it have been something on the square, like saving a child from fire? Right is right and wrong is wrong." She shook her head. "Hurry up and get away if you can," she pleaded, clenching her hands. "I don't want to have to call them in here!"

He simply saluted her with two fingers at his temple. He opened the door an inch or two with infinite precaution and stood there listening. He crept as far as the stairs to reconnoiter and then looked back at her. He winked. He could think of winking at a time like this!

"They're all up front at the other end of the restaurant," he reported elatedly. "Now's my chance. Watch me go out the back way!" The last thing she heard him say was: "Too bad I have to leave you behind, baby. We were made for each other." Then he slipped from sight and was gone.

She stood there waiting, listening. No disturbing sounds came back to her. He had gotten away. It was over. She gave a peculiar sigh. If only she had had the courage! What was life after all? If you were going to be afraid of it, you were better off dead. Suddenly she found her street-coat wrapped around her uniform, found herself racing up those stairs after him. A skyrocket seemed to have exploded within her, brilliant, flashing; stars were in her eyes.

"Wait!" she gasped. "Wait! Life can't pass me by; it mustn't! Wait, I'm coming!"

Out the back way, from the lighted restaurant into the dark street she sped. Halfway down toward the corner the red tail-light of a car lurched out of a line of parked machines. Instinctively she felt that he was in it, knew he must be. She didn't even know his name, didn't know what to call him. Life has no time in its headlong rush. Her despairing scream rent the quiet night air.

"Wait, wait for me! Take me with you!"

The car didn't stop. He wasn't the kind would stop, ever. Instead it went crashing into reverse and heeled backwards toward her. The door swung open; his arm reached out to take her—to take what he wanted out of life. She found the running-board with one foot and before she could even get in next to him they were careening madly down the street and the city and the world went flashing by, left far behind. Out in the darkness somewhere in back of them came the eerie wail of a police siren. He only laughed, and even in the act of swerving crazily from side to side, so that any minute threatened to be their last, turned to her and their lips met in the bitter sweetness of a kiss stolen on borrowed time.

"Again!" she pleaded. "Again! We may never have time for another—" The windshield cracked and there was a powdered seam in it directly between their two heads—or where their two heads had been only an instant before.

"Crouch down low, darling," he grinned, "and away we go! A miss is as good as a mile!" She slipped down to the floor and rested her head against his knee and never took her eyes from his face after that. From time to time in their long mad flight through darkness he would reach down and stroke her hair with one hand and say: "How does it feel to be alive?" She knew what he meant; he didn't mean because of the bullets—he meant to be alive in this new way, the way she had always longed to live; the way that was to be her way from now on.

• • •

The sleepy-eyed clerk in the little upstate hotel pushed the register toward them at three in the morning, and Eddinger turned to her and kissed her before he signed it. A recklessly happy kiss, an exulting kiss at having outwitted death one more time. The clerk had never seen two people with such shining eyes; he wondered disapprovingly if they'd been drinking. Mr. and Mrs. Smith the book recorded.

"The best you've got," he told the clerk, and carelessly tossed a crumpled bill on the desk.

"You don't have to pay your bill until you leave," said the clerk. Eddinger looked at Ivy and they both laughed, as though they shared some private joke between them.

"You'd better take it now," he said. "There's no telling—"

When the door upstairs had closed upon them and they were

alone, they flew into each other's arms like two wild birds in a storm. Stolen time! Every moment was stolen time. Every minute might be the last. That perhaps saved the situation from cheapness, tawdriness; that made it more than just a one-night stand in a country hotel with Mr. and Mrs. Smith on the register. Though she was inexperienced as far as those things went, Ivy somehow knew the difference just as any woman would have. He wasn't just playing with her; whatever his past had been, he was as sincere tonight as she was. No one could have feigned the real admiration, the basic respect, that showed amidst all the wildness of his kisses. The broken inchoate murmurs he poured into her ears came from the heart; they lacked the smoothness of hypocrisy.

"My kind of a girl, found my kind of a girl at last! You're not afraid of me, are you?"

"No—all my life I've been waiting—you don't know what this means, do you? If you put your head on my shoulder tonight in this room, it means forever, for always. If not, say so now."

"From now on is the word," he said. "It may end in five minutes—it may last for fifty years."

"With this kiss," she breathed, "I thee wed." Darkness suddenly flooded the room. Strangest of wedding-nights, a revolver in a holster slung across the foot of their marriage bed, neither of them daring to undress, every footfall in the corridor past their door a sudden menace.

• • •

When it finally came, just before dawn, there was no warning, not even a stealthy footfall outside. A sudden surging rush of many bodies that buckled their door and almost burst it in. The chest of drawers barricading it alone kept it in place. And then the thundering summons that Ivy heard now for the first time and the last. "Open in the name of the law!" They had leaped

Love & Night

spasmodically apart, torn from each other's arms like a pair of puppets dangling on strings. The gun was already in his hand, aimed at the door, ready, as he swept her toward the wall with one arm.

"Into the closet, sweet, and flat on the floor! Hell's going to break!"

"We know you're in there, Eddinger; open or we'll shoot!"

Vainly she clawed at the knob of the closet-door. "It's locked, Ed. I can't get in!" He took a single step toward it, swerved his gun for a minute toward the keyhole, and fired. It shattered into a dozen metal fragments and the door was open.

"Get in and keep it shut!" Then he dropped flat on his stomach and was smiling as the first thundering volley came crashing through the room door from outside.

That was the last thing she saw—his smile in the face of death. She shrank back into the closet and pulled the door shut after her. Then suddenly she found that there was no wall at her back. It was not a closet at all, it was the next room—that had been the connecting door between that he had blasted open for her. The noise from the room she had just left was deafening for a minute, and then the silence that followed was even more deafening.

"Got him, I guess," said a voice from out in the hall in the midst of the sudden stillness. And a moan escaped from her:

"No—oh, no!"

There was a sudden crash and they had broken in the door. Her heart had stopped beating as she put her ear to the connecting door.

"Got him all right," said the same voice. "Full of holes as a Swiss cheese."

She turned and staggered blindly out into the hall from the room where she had taken refuge and found other guests creeping out of their rooms one by one and no one noticed her in the crowd. As she stumbled downstairs and out into the night, all she could see before her was a smile—his smile in the face of death.

• • •

Half an hour later and a mile away, a big milk truck lumbering toward New York came to a stop beside her.

"Want a lift?" offered the driver. "Something happen to you? Been hurt?"

The girl who had been stumbling along the side of the darkened road took his hand and climbed in next to him.

"Yes, I have," she answered in a quiet voice. "Right here." And she placed her hand over her heart for a moment.

• • •

Her roommate said: "Oh, you had me frightened! I didn't know what had happened to you! You look as though you've been out in a storm. Your hair's all—"

"Yes," said Ivy. "A strong wind caught me up, a wind called life, for just an hour or so. Then it passed on and left a dead calm."

Her roommate wasn't much on riddles; she changed the subject.

"I see they finally killed that awful Eddinger," she said. "It's in all the papers. I'm certainly glad they did, too!"

"Some women," said Ivy with the ghost of a smile, "would stick to a man like that to the bitter end."

"By the way, Walter dropped around to see you last night. He waited hours for you to come home. He left a message for you. He told me to tell you he made the first payment on a ring yesterday. He said you'd know what that meant."

"I do," said Ivy bleakly.

"But," protested her friend, "why are you so downcast about it? You should consider yourself lucky. A steady, reliable fellow who thinks the world of you, wants to settle down. You have no kick coming."

Love & Night

"You're right," agreed Ivy dismally. "I certainly have no kick coming." But she didn't mean it in quite the same way.

[*Breezy Stories*, October 1935]

Distinctive Woolrich elements—insult humor, tinny saxophone music, Thirties song lyrics, even a race against the clock to prevent disaster—overflow in the following tale. The opening scene on the stairs of the dance joint was recycled almost verbatim in Woolrich's classic 1938 suspenser, "Dime a Dance" ("The Dancing Detective").

FLOWER IN HIS BUTTONHOLE

*"Sometimes she thinks she's found her hero,
But it's a queer romance;
All that you need is a ticket—
Come on, big boy, ten cents a dance!"*

Every evening at half-past eight she climbed a long flight of stairs on Broadway. Not on one of the side-streets, but right on Broadway itself. When she got to the top, she always said, "Hello, big boy!" She had learned that expression. "Big boy" was usually leaning an elbow on the shelf of the ticket-seller's window, with one eye on his watch and one on the stairs. He was the manager. As a rule he condescended to nod when she said this. Once or twice he had even gone so far as to grunt in reply.

She had gone in by now, anyway; through a pair of swinging glass doors that flashed closed after her. There was a big empty room before her, with a dark shiny floor and a row of windows curtained in pink and a platform for the musicians. She didn't stop to look at any of this; it was nothing to her. She walked toward a curtained alcove at the back, and as she walked she was already stripping off her hat and coat for action. Sometimes when she felt particularly good and some other girl was there to watch her, and there weren't any men around, she would push her hat far to the back of her head and let her coat slip down her back to her elbows and give a comical shuffle across the floor with her feet spread out. This was supposed to be an imitation of Chaplin. When she hadn't felt so good, she had entered trailing her coat along the floor after her, just like a child with a broken kite.

In the curtained alcove there were a mirror and some chairs ,and there were hooks for coats and hats. No hangers, but just hooks fastened to a board. Hers was the one on the end, and she'd penciled her name under it—Faith. As she was hanging up her things, the brisk tap-tap of high heels sounded across the polished floor outside, punctuated by the swish of the swinging glass doors. She smiled faintly. She knew that walk.

A few moments later the curtain was tossed back and her friend Trixie entered the alcove. With Trixie came a large quantity of red hair, a smaller quantity of Chypre, rebottled at the five-and-ten, a fair share of the town's good looks, and an encouraging feeling that the world wasn't such a bad place to live in, after all.

"Here already?" she remarked. "Not sick or anything, are you?"

"What brings you so early?" Faith asked.

"That's what Simon Legree just asked me at the door. He cracked his whip and handed me this: 'I'm thinking of firing you for being on time.' 'Oh, yeah?' I said."

Faith laughed. "I know; I heard you. So did the traffic cop up at Columbus Circle probably."

Trixie planted her hand dramatically upon her chest.

"Me?" she said in surprise. "I never speak above a whisper!"

Others came in until all of them were there. A preliminary tuning-up sounded outside. It had very little chance of topping the amount of conversation going on in the dressing room, however. They were all talking at once. Half of them were lined up before the mirror powdering their noses, while the rest clustered just in back of them, waiting to get at it. Someone lighted a cigarette and it was promptly snatched away from her and stepped on. "As though it isn't stuffy enough already!"

"Now, now, don't shove! Mamma's nearly through." This from Trixie, who was in the front line and intended staying there until she was satisfied with her appearance, no matter what the cost. Faith insinuated herself at her shoulder and Trixie promptly made room for her at the expense of the girl on the other side. One's friend always came first in a crisis of this sort.

"New?" remarked Faith, looking straight into the glass. She could see it there.

"Yeah, green," replied Trixie. This latter fact was self-evident. Startlingly so, in fact. Beside the gleaming emeraldine hue of Trixie's, the mild green of Faith's own frock paled into nothingness.

At any other time Faith would most likely have retorted: "No kidding? I thought it was red." Tonight, however, she appeared vaguely troubled by the fact that Trixie's dress was the color of her own. "I hope he doesn't get mixed up," she said, as though communing with herself.

"Who?" Trixie asked sharply.

Faith, absorbed in some weighty problem of her own, allowed the question to pass unheeded. "If I had known, I would have picked another color." She tapped her lower lip reflectively. "But I only have green and blue, and Adelaide is always in blue."

Trixie's curiosity, never very weak, had been aroused by this soliloquy. She tapped her friend commandingly on the shoulder.

"Would y' mind telling me what you're talking about? Or is it too sacred for words?"

Faith seemed willing enough to comply. "Come on over in the corner," she said, and added provocatively: "This is just between the two of us. I'm not broadcasting it."

Smoke and flame could not have kept Trixie from following her after hearing that. She extricated herself with some difficulty from

Love & Night

her place before the mirror, not without arousing considerable sarcastic comment.

"Well, well, well! So the Statue of Liberty has moved at last!"

"Are you quitting for good? Or is it just a little vacation you're taking?"

"Look, there's moss growing where she was standing!"

"Ladies, ladies," remonstrated Trixie with an injured air, elbowing her way through them, "you forget who I am." She joined Faith and faced her expectantly.

"Well, you see," Faith explained in a guarded undertone, "I have a date with someone on the floor outside, and I've never seen him before."

"What'd you do, advertise in the papers?"

"Do you remember what I told you one night about someone calling me up by mistake and asking if it was a Chinese hand-laundry?"

"Sure I do!" giggled Trixie delightedly. "And you were feeling clownish that night and said it was, only the management had changed hands and it was now being run by Americans, and begged him to send his wash around and give you a trial!"

"Well, I never told you the rest of it, what happened after that," Faith went on breathlessly. Once started she decided to tell all.

"Oh, was there more to it?" Trixie arched her brows. "I kind of thought so."

"Well, the next day he sent all his wash around, even his socks, and you never saw such holes! The landlady found it in the vestibule and she was going to throw it out, so I told her it was for me and I took it upstairs—"

"Oh, this is swell!" Trixie squealed zestfully.

"Well, when I saw all those shirts with the buttons off, I hated to send the things back to him the way they were, and I thought about it and thought about it until finally—"

"Don't tell me you went ahead and did it yourself!" the horrified Trixie forestalled her, palms lifted. "You did!" she went on, scrutinizing her friend's flushed face more closely. "I can tell by your expression." Then she added dolefully, as one who laments an evil tendency in somebody else, "You always were sort of domestic."

The repentant Faith gazed at the floor in embarrassment, confessing her fault.

"I mended the socks and things in my spare time," she admitted in a small voice. "It was an awful lot of trouble, but it was awfully soothing. I felt just like I was married."

"Only you don't get paid for it then," Trixie reminded her callously.

"Then I pressed the whole batch with a flatiron the lady downstairs lent me."

Trixie covered her eyes in great grief. "Say it isn't true, pal; say it isn't true!"

"But I had an accident. The iron got too hot or something and I smelt smoke and when I looked, his best shirt had a big piece eaten out of it—"

"Served him right, the big chiseler," observed Trixie.

"How was he to know?" protested the victim. "He thought I was really a laundry. He called up and was very angry, of course. I didn't blame him. So I told him I would pay for the shirt, but after a while he said that it didn't matter. He never sent me any more wash, but from then on he used to ring up about once a week and say 'How's the Faith and Charity Hand Laundry getting along?' That was the name I had made up for it in the beginning. He was never fresh or anything over the phone—know what I mean?—and he had such a nice voice that it got so I liked it when he rang up. And tonight he's going to be out there—" she nodded toward the dance floor, already crawling with couples "—wearing a white flower in his coat so that I'll know him when I see him. And I told him I'd have on a green dress." She sighed and clasped her hands.

The white flower had arrested Trixie's attention, it seemed.

Love & Night

"Maybe he's a floorwalker," she remarked apprehensively.

At this juncture a large and none too aromatic cigar thrust its way between the curtains of the alcove and a voice just in back of it inquired truculently:

"What do you two think you're doing in there, holding a wake?"

"We're making mud pies; love to have you join us," Trixie replied instantly, without even turning her head. At this rebuff the cigar was withdrawn. Trixie had a way with her that even kept managers in their place. "Come on, babe," she said, "let's go outside and jump through our paper hoops." Unexpectedly chucking her friend under the chin, she remarked, "I'm wearing a green dress too but don't worry. If he picks me out by mistake, I'll bring him over to you. Lots of luck and bigger and better laundries." Then she sallied forth, shimmying slightly in time to the music.

When Faith came out after her, the glass prisms were spinning around in the ceiling, sending down a shower of sparks, and under them in the dim light couples glided silently over the floor like shadows. She stood still and shut her eyes for a second. She was making a wish, half audibly:

"Make him so that I can like him, will you? Not fresh or wise or anything—"

Her eyes flew open abruptly. Someone had touched her to attract her attention. She gave a single hopeful glance; then her hopes were indefinitely postponed. She reached out mechanically, took the ticket, tore it across, and returned half of it, keeping the rest herself. The dance was on.

• • •

An hour and a half went by. Over each strange shoulder Faith's eyes busily, expectantly roved the room. Looking for a very small thing, looking for a small white flower, as out of place there as a bird or a ray of sunlight. For the fast, "hot" pieces they used magenta lights; for the slow "sweet" ones blue and green lights mixed, causing a sort of dreamy twilight to fill the ballroom as though it were a grotto or undersea cavern. Incidentally, also causing green dresses to appear blue, and vice versa.

She brushed by Trixie, the latter damsel favoring her with grimaces of spiritual anguish to indicate that her partner was a trial to her. Trixie seemed to have a strange attraction for the meek, the halt, and the aged, likewise those who were in need of special instruction, which consisted in leading them to a far corner of the room and endlessly repeating, "One, two, three! Now just watch my feet. One, two, three. That's it!" This was highly lucrative but pretty much of a strain on Trixie. As they swayed close to one another, Faith found time to murmur anxiously:

"See anybody?"

"Not yet," Trixie assured her. "Cheer up, sugar," she added heartenshort. "Not you," she informed her partner coldly. "I was speaking to my friend."

The lights went up, then down again. Half-past eleven and no sign of him. Time seemed to drag so tonight. She had taken these same gliding steps a thousand times before, or maybe a million. Dancing was supposed to be fun. But not when you earn your living at it. Sometimes she wished she would never have to listen to another saxophone again as long as she lived. She also found herself praying that she was invisible, so that no one would come near her for at least half an hour. But someone did almost at once. And stood there grinning foolishly and holding out his ticket.

"What's the joke?" she inquired frostily, as she took it and tore it in two.

"These darned lights," he said. "They blur everything up. What color dress is that you're wearing?" The greenish-blue lights had gone on just before he came over to her, drowning out the shade of her dress.

Her eyes had flown automatically to his lapel but it was barren; there was nothing there. She felt like saying "Oh, go away!" What was he to her, anyway? Still, it was quite a coincidence, his asking her about her dress like that. Maybe he had lost the flower, or forgotten to buy one.

So she decided to play safe and not reveal herself until she had found out a little something about him.

"Blue," she lied. And then, "What made you ask that?"

"Just curiosity," he answered.

"Is there—er—any particular color you were looking for?" she wanted to know.

"Originally, yes," he said smoothly, "but I changed my mind as soon as I saw you." So he was as fickle as all that, was he? Well, she was glad she'd found out in time. He wasn't the type for her, all right. He just didn't click somehow, that was all. But the chief thing was to get away from him before the lights went up again and revealed her in her green dress. Otherwise she was stuck for the night.

Then, at the crucial moment, assistance came to her. She happened to look over his shoulder and catch Trixie's eye and she read unmistakably in it that Trixie had a message for her.

The two couples drew closer, the men still imagining they were leading and not realizing that their footsteps were being guided for them. When they had come up to each other, Trixie nodded vigorously.

"Got him for you," she breathed huskily. "Right here!" All Faith could see was the back of his head and the fairly broad shoulders that cut Trixie off below the chin. She had to take Trixie's word for it about the flower part of it. "Meet me down at the refreshment-stand as soon as this is over," Trixie instructed her in clear ringing tones, and was wafted away. The muscular gentleman stationed in the middle of the floor for the purpose of preserving order and decorum frowned unfavorably upon her as she went by.

"How many more times, Red," he remarked ungrammatically, "have I gotta tell you to quit talkin' on the boss's time?"

"You've got about a dozen to go," Trixie informed him insouciantly. "After that maybe I'll listen to you. And if you don't mind, it's Miss Red to you."

The music stopped at last. Faith had counted each tinny note that came out of the saxophone and thought it would never end, but now the lights went up and she saw Trixie and the man waiting for her down at the end of the room. However, there was an obstacle to be overcome before she could get over to them.

Her present partner stared down at her figure in surprise.

"Why," he stammered, "why, that's a green dress you're wearing! I didn't notice—"

"Yes, it is," Faith interrupted hastily, beginning to back away from him, "but not nearly as green as the one my friend is wearing. See her down there? Much better dancer than I am. Wait, I'll send her over to you." Then she walked away and left him standing there with his mouth open as though he had wanted to say something and hadn't had time.

As she walked toward them, doing her best to be casual about it, all she had eyes for was a little dot of white in the distance; a carnation that had already shed several of its petals, nestling against the coat of the very tall, very likable young man standing beside Trixie. When Faith came up to them Trixie said: "Look what I've got for you," and with a gesture somewhat like that of a referee: "Now remember, Marquis of Queensberry rules and no hitting in the clinches. Anything else I can do for you? Just say the word."

Faith glanced back over her shoulder. "Him," she said unfeelingly. "He's sort of sticky and might come around again."

Trixie appeared to understand perfectly what was expected of her. "A pleasure," she announced, and started over toward

Love & Night

him, a young lady attired so unmistakably in green that even the color-blind would have had to take cognizance of it.

Faith's new-found hero smiled at her, and she smiled back at him, bashfully. "I guess it's you," she breathed almost inaudibly.

"It isn't my brother," he answered. "Well, shall we dance?" he went on.

"Must we?" she smiled.

So they didn't dance. Each time the music sounded, she took another ticket from him and tore it up in full view of the manager. "Anyway, it saves the wax floor," she laughed. They sat together in one of the little stalls provided with tables that overlooked Broadway, a wax-paper cup of untasted orangeade standing in front of each of them.

"I knew you'd be like this," she said softly after a while. "Something told me. You see, I play hunches, and I've never yet been wrong."

He seemed glad to hear her say that and yet at the same time more than a little surprised.

"You mean before you even laid eyes on me you knew what I was going to be like?"

"Why, yes," she said. "I could tell by your voice."

"My voice?" He seemed completely taken back.

"Over the telephone, silly," she explained. "How else?"

He was about to say something to that, but just then the young man with the slide trombone stood up in his seat and emitted noises that drowned out everything else.

Faith was more used to these sudden blasts of melody, if they could be called that, than he was.

"Funny place, isn't it," she laughed, "to sit and try to carry on a conversation with any one?"

"Then let's go to some other place, shall we?" he suggested eagerly. "Someplace where we can be by ourselves and really talk to one another."

This was not the first time anyone had suggested her going out with him. It was the first time, however, that she would go. This was different, this was all right. It had to be, or there wasn't any sun anywhere, there weren't any blue skies, there wasn't any love, there wasn't anything good and decent in the whole wide world. She knew she couldn't be wrong; there was just one man who would and could love her the way she wanted to be loved—and this was the man. She'd waited a long time but he'd come. She was perfectly willing to go with him wherever he suggested.

"You'll have to buy two dollars' worth of tickets if you want to take me out before the session's over," she said. She blushed while she said it. He missed seeing that; he missed seeing a miracle on Broadway—the blush of a taxi-dancer. She blushed because—well, everyone knew what it meant when a customer took one of the hostesses out. Only this time they were wrong; it didn't mean that. Let them think what they wanted to. She knew better.

"I won't be a minute," she said, and went to get her hat and coat. She found Trixie recuperating in the alcove, one leg crossed high above the other, mournfully rubbing her instep.

"Did the stretcher-bearers get here yet?" Trixie wanted to know. "I'm going to try arnica first, and if that doesn't work, Christian Science. Well, how are you two getting along?" was the next thing she asked, getting up and ludicrously pretending to limp toward the mirror.

"I'm going out with him," Faith said, starry-eyed.

Trixie, that peerless judge of the heart's emotion, darted a swift keen glance at her.

"So you've fallen at last!" She acted sort of worried, Faith thought. "Are you sure you know what you're doing?" she went on. "Listen, kid. I'm your friend. I'm the only one here that knows for a fact what the others don't want to believe about you—that you're straight, not like the rest of us. The only reason you've gotten away with it is that it never entered the heads of all the guys that hang around here that there could be such an animal as a virgin dancing in a dime-mill; otherwise you would have

Love & Night

taken the count long ago. Many a time, without you knowing it, I've steered the manager himself away from you by telling him that you were the private property of a guy that went around carrying two guns and wouldn't think anything of turning this place into a shooting-gallery if anyone made a pass at you. Don't ask me why, or what I get out of it. Maybe I'm not so tough underneath. Maybe I keep thinking how I was just like you five or six years ago, and I don't want the same thing to happen to you that did to me." She bent her fingers and looked down at her five bright red nails. When she raised her eyes, they were all wet and shiny.

"Honey," she went on quietly, "there's nothing so lovely in the whole wide world as an on-the-level kid. Stay that way. I don't know why, but just stay that way! Maybe it makes the tough grind a little easier for me to know you're like you are."

"But I am staying that way," protested Faith. "Don't you see? He's not like the others. I know. I know! For months he's been talking to me on the telephone and never said anything he shouldn't, never tried to see me, never tried to suggest anything out of the way. He's the one, the one I've been waiting for, I tell you! I couldn't pass this by. It would never come again." She choked. "I'm sick of dancing night after night, sick of being pawed and kneed, sick of running the gauntlet downstairs at the door to get home alone each night. He's so sweet! Oh, I knew he was waiting for me someplace or other along the way. It all seems too good to be true."

"That's the trouble; it probably is," said Trixie dismally. She laughed but without much enjoyment. Her cynicism, briefly discarded, had returned. "Wet your finger like this and run it down the side of his face; if it's rough and scratchy—and if he talks way down deep in his throat and, and if he's got on a collar and tie and big flat shoes—go home alone. I wouldn't trust anything in pants as far as I could throw that big bass drum out there!"

"They aren't all on the make," protested Faith impatiently. "They aren't all like that—"

"No," agreed Trixie, "but those that aren't haven't been born yet or they're dead already. So you won't listen to me?"

"No, I won't listen, because for once you're wrong."

"Then my advice to you," murmured Trixie, "is to keep your fingers crossed and don't walk under ladders!" And she gripped Faith's arm for a moment, then seeing it was useless, dropped the subject. "Incidentally, who do you think is waiting around outside to take me home? That dark horse you steered me into tonight. Remember him?"

"Is he pretty awful?" Faith asked vaguely. She hardly remembered him any more by now. Just someone who had asked her what color her dress was and hadn't worn a flower in his coat.

"Awful or not," promised Trixie vengefully, "he's going to be taken for a sleigh-ride he'll never forget. I'm going to lead him to that chop suey joint that has a fire-escape right outside the ladies' room—know the one I mean? I'm going to eat my fill of fried noodles, and then when he thinks it's about time to get some return on his investment, I'm going to leave him for a minute and go powder my nose. Long after I'm home asleep in my little beddsie-weddsie, he'll still be sitting there waiting for me to come out."

Faith laughed as she turned to go.

"One of these times one of them is going to come around here the night after and give you a black eye."

"None of 'em has yet," Trixie called after her. "They wouldn't want anyone to know what a fool I made out of them." But as the curtains fell back in place and Faith was gone, her face sobered up again. She stared moodily into the glass. It won't work out, she thought. It never has since Broadway stopped being a cow-path, and it won't tonight. I know what's going to happen just as though I was there in her place. That kid's in for a tough time of it tonight. And tomorrow at this time, just another busted heart— just another little tramp like the rest of us, wiggling at a dime a throw. She shook her fist at the saxophone blaring its summons outside. "Coming, damn you, coming!" she growled.

• • •

Faith went up to where the man stood waiting with that carnation in his lapel and gave him a happy smile and said: "I'm ready." Strangely enough she wasn't tired any more, even though she'd danced miles already tonight. He offered her his arm, the way a sweetheart should, a lover should, and side by side they went down the stairs. He and Faith—Faith of the appropriate name, who had always believed a night like this would come, when there would be someone waiting to take her home, someone special, someone she could look up to and respect, admire and adore. Oh, this was the way to go home all right! The snakes were all coiled up at the door as usual, but tonight she passed through them unscathed, unafraid, head in air. No winks, no leers tonight, no wise remarks, no clutching hands to buck, no one to follow her and try to find out where she lived. She could feel their stares following her as she walked along beside him, could almost but not quite catch what they were saying to one another in whispered undertones. Maybe it would have been better if she had heard, but she didn't know that.

She wouldn't have listened anyway, any more than she had to Trixie.

They walked a block or two along glaring midnight Broadway; it was Broadway's "noon" hour, and instead of one sun there were hundreds to light their way. She gave him another confident smile.

"Everything seems so different tonight. I almost like the lights and crowd—walking through them with you. Do you understand that?"

He didn't seem to. "Shall we hop a taxi?" he said.

"What! And have you throw away your good money? I should say not!" He gave her a peculiar look as though he couldn't believe his ears. "Because I know how it is," she assured him. "I have to work hard enough for my money. Why should we be extravagant? If I like anybody, I like them for themselves and not just for how much they can spend. Chase."

"Chase?" he said blankly.

"Well, that's your name, isn't it? You said it was over the phone. That was the name you gave me when you sent your wash that time."

"Oh—er—yeah," he said lamely. "I forgot for a minute. I wondered how you knew. Yeah, when I sent my wash, that's right." And he eased his neck around inside his collar. They passed one of the glaring all-night Broadway delicatessen-restaurants. It seemed to give him an inspiration. "As long as you want to be economical," he suggested, "suppose I stop in and get some sandwiches and ginger ale and we take 'em around to your room and have a little party by ourselves. We can get better acquainted that way."

She halted momentarily and her eyes sought his. "You're sure you haven't any wrong impression about me?" she asked doubtfully. Trixie's warning returned to her. He was a man after all—and she worked in a dance-hall.

"You trust me, don't you?" was all he said. "You don't think I—" Had Trixie been present she would have sighed impatiently and asked her friend: "What did you expect him to say, you little fool? They all say that. It doesn't cost them anything. You didn't think he'd come out openly and say, sure, I'm on the make, did you?" But Trixie wasn't there; Faith was on her own now.

"You won't let me down," she said. It wasn't a statement; it was a plea. "All right, go ahead; I'll wait here for you. And never mind the ginger ale. I'll make us some coffee to go with the sandwiches. I make very good coffee; wait'll you see!" she said happily. She stood there by the curb while he went in, and she tapped her toe and hummed a little song, she felt so swell. There were a million stars hanging low over Broadway while she waited there for her love. "What did you do, buy out the store?" she laughed when he came back to her burdened with brown-paper parcels, and insisted on sharing them with him.

A brownstone house split up into furnished rooms way over west on one of the Fifties. She struggled with her latch-key and they went in. A flight of stairs painted white, a dim little apricot bulb at each landing, a door on the top floor front.

"Don't mind the way it looks," she said, snapping on the light. "Here, we'll leave the door open like this."

"Nah," he said tersely. "Too much of a draft." And took a step back to close it.

"But that wouldn't look good," she said unsuspectingly. "I don't want to get in any trouble here—"

Almost at once, as though summoned by her remark, a hard-faced, middle-aged woman appeared in the open doorway without any warning sound of footsteps whatever. "Could I see you a minute, Miss Moore?" she remarked, staring vacantly over their heads.

"No, it's me you wanna see," the man said, and he stepped out into the hall and partly closed the door after him. "Here, forget it," he murmured and slipped something into her hand. "You know how it is. The kid works late and don't get much chance to talk to her friends."

"Oh, I know how it is," agreed the landlady with a shrug. "She can talk to her heart's content—only keep the door closed and don't kick up any row. I—er—knew this was coming sooner or later; she's held out longer than I gave her credit for. Matter of fact," she confessed, carefully tucking what he'd given her into the recesses of her wrapper, "I've had a bet on for quite a while with one of the other tenants that she'd give in." She chuckled. "I stand to collect ten dollars on you two tonight."

He nudged her in the ribs with typical Broadway camaraderie.

"It's in the bag," he said behind the back of his hand. Her laughter went trailing down the hallway. He turned and went back into the lighted room. Faith was emptying the contents of the paper bags onto two rather chipped plates.

"Landlady says it's gotta stay closed," he told her, and fitted the door tightly into place behind him. The triangle of yellow light that had splashed out into the hall narrowed, disappeared, leaving only darkness. A key turned slyly in the lock. It couldn't have been heard unless one's ear was up against the keyhole.

• • •

"Only trouble with these little chinkie cups without handles," Trixie was saying, "is you're liable to swallow one whole if you're not careful." She eyed hers comically, then put it down. "Whew! Is there chow mein coming out of my ears? If there isn't, there should be, I'm up to here." He laughed a little. "You're sort of a bashful guy, aren't you?" she went on. "Didn't know they came like that any more."

"Am I?" he said. "I thought you knew that by now." He stared down at the tablecloth. "You know," he said abruptly, "you're not exactly a shrinking violet by any means. I don't mean I expected you to bring along your Bible or anything—"

"Don't have to," she flipped. "I know the whole thing by heart. Read a chapter every night in a different hotel room."

To her surprise he scowled at that. "Quit talking that way," he ordered almost roughly. "Somebody's going to come along some day and take you at your word."

"Am I to infer that you're not going to?" she wanted to know. She loved to bait them even when she knew she was going to give them the slip.

But he didn't seem to have much of a sense of humor.

"What do you think?" he asked her. "Have I been acting phoney with you up to now?"

Love & Night

"No," she admitted, "but you can't always go by that. Still waters run deep, you know."

He flung his napkin down irritably and signaled for the check. Trixie collected her things and prepared to put her disappearing act into execution. "I'll be right with you," she said, "just go back there a minute and powder my nose—"

"Don't bother making yourself beautiful," he said suddenly. "Not for me, anyway. We're not going any place together. I'll just take you downstairs and put you in a taxi at the door—"

"What is this?" she cried in amazement. "Am I getting the bum's rush?"

"That's what I want to know," he told her. "We got our wires crossed, I guess, that's all. No offense, but you're not my type at all. You had me fooled completely until I met you tonight. You weren't this way at all, all these months over the wire. I had you figured entirely different. So suppose we just call all bets off and chalk it up to experience." The waiter brought his change and he pocketed it. "Coming?" he said without even looking at her.

But Trixie had suddenly stopped kidding. She was a little white under her rouge and staring at him with unblinking intensity.

"Let's get this straight," she said in a hoarse voice. "You—you had a blind date on the floor of that shimmy-palace tonight, with—with a girl in a green dress. Am I right?"

"Why the post mortem? You know that as well as I do."

She was almost incapable of speech. She pointed at the lapel of his jacket.

"Flower," she said incoherently. "You were supposed to—"

"I did have one," he said shortly. "Must have dropped it coming up the stairs. I'm not used to wearing them anyway. What's the difference? I ran into you, didn't I—for all the good it did?"

She shaded her eyes with one hand for a minute. Faith flashed through her mind. My God! she thought. My God! That kid went off with the wrong—. She whipped her hand across the table and seized his wrist convulsively.

"Will you do something for me?" she panted.

"I thought so," he said wearily. "It's right in character." And reached for his inside pocket. "How much—Your little brother's sick of course and has to have an operation."

There was no time to explain. She cleared the misunderstanding out of the way by slapping his hand aside impatiently. The gesture would have been funny at any other time but this.

"No; you don't get me! All I'm asking you to do is—sit tight, will you for a minute, until I come back. Please don't leave this table—please!" She jumped up and ran toward the back instead of the main entrance. She knew that if he saw her leave, go out into the street, he'd never stay there and wait; he wasn't interested enough in her for that. He wouldn't believe she was coming back and he'd get up and go—and she'd never be able to find him again. There was no time to tell him where she was going and what she was trying to do—and even if there had been, he wouldn't have believed her, so foul was the impression he had of her by now. She fled toward the dressing-room at the back, wailing over her shoulder: "Wait for me, now! Wait for me!"

If only she could tip off Faith in time, let her know that she was with the wrong man! She remembered him vaguely now; she had danced with him first herself. Too good-looking to be trustworthy, and just the type who would be able to put one over on a kid like that. And no good, he had n.g. written all over him for those who could read. That was why she'd put up such a beef about it in the dressing-room when Faith had told her she was going with him. She'd known instinctively but hadn't known how to get it across to Faith.

The good old fire-escape window was wide open, the way it always was, to give a little circulation of air to the stuffy place. She climbed through it, the way she had so very many times before—but for a different reason this time. The colored woman

Love & Night

in attendance looked up from her newspaper. She knew Trixie by sight and wasn't at all concerned.

"Whut, again?" she drawled. "Thass the third time this week for you, ain't it? Happy landing!" she waved.

"Leave it open. I'm coming back in again in a little while, I hope," Trixie explained. She started down the side of the building, dropped lightly to her feet in a narrow cement alley below, skirted a couple of garbage cans, and came out on Broadway looking fresh as a daisy. "Taxi!" she shouted and dived in head first. "West Fifty-first, hurry up!"

• • •

"What did you close the door for?" Faith rebuked mildly. The man didn't answer but the smile he gave her spoke for itself. Something about that smile chilled her a little; the first premonition of something ominous struck at her, but she wouldn't admit it even to herself. She was just imagining things. She mustn't begin finding fault this early in the game. When they got to know one another better, little things like this wouldn't alarm her; she'd understand him.

She turned to prepare the sandwiches. The two arms that dropped over her shoulders and coiled around her like snakes a moment later were anything but imaginary. Their grip hampered her breath, and sudden stark fright dissipated what was left of it. She tried not to lose her head.

"Don't!" she said, and even tried to force a friendly laugh. "It's late—I want to get going on these sandwiches."

"You and your sandwiches!" he muttered thickly close to her ear. Then in a louder voice, "I ain't in the sandwich mood. Skip it." His lips were like hot pincers on the cool back of her neck, forcing her head down. Kisses that almost bit, they were so fervent. Panic descended like a blinding curtain; she struggled and writhed in such sheer animal terror for a moment that he released her without meaning to. She whirled and faced him, her face gone white. What was he trying to do, make something furtive, shameful, out of this love she had so freely given him? He mustn't; she wouldn't let him; she hadn't given it for that; it wasn't that kind of love! The suddenness of the transformation he had undergone shocked her to the marrow.

She had entered this room a few minutes ago with a sweetheart, a sweetheart whose image she had built up in her heart over a period of months; now she suddenly, hideously, found herself behind a closed door with a gorilla. The image began to rock, to sway. There was still time to save it, the misunderstanding could still be cleared up, but if once it toppled, shattered, then she had nothing left.

She struggled frantically to preserve it, prop it up. She tried to beat the barrier that he was building between them like a brick wall, that rose until it all but hid him from her.

"You don't want me to think you're like all of them, do you? You—you shouldn't act like that," she panted. "I wouldn't have let you come up here with me. Don't you remember, on the street I asked you not to misunder—"

He wouldn't let her finish. "What are you trying to do, hold out? Where are your wings, sister, and where's your halo? Two nickels rents you where you work, and now you're trying to act hard-to-get!" She shrank back; her eyes were so big they suddenly seemed to cover her whole face. He took a step after her, caught her by the wrist. "Who d'ya think you're kidding?" he said brutally. "Come over here!" She saw his other hand go back, groping for the light switch.

"No!" she pleaded agonizedly. "No! Don't let it turn out like this!" But the plea was no longer to him; it was to the vault high above the two of them. "I've waited so long for you; you've been with me night and day—"

"And in the morning you'll wonder who the hell I was and what the hell I looked like!"

Love & Night

He said that!

He didn't hear the crash within her, as the image crumbled to dust and left her—nothing. She was so limp all at once, so like a rag, that his arms dropped as though she had slapped him. His ardor cooled; there was something here he couldn't understand; it chilled him. He reached for his hat, dented it, and slapped it on. He was going. There were too many other fish in the sea. He chucked her briefly under the chin.

"You're a lovely kid and all that—but what a disposition!"

She gave a moan so low it could scarcely be heard. She staggered to retain her balance.

"No high-jinks," he warned her. "I've got the landlady eating out of my hand—" He watched her, waiting for the scream that he felt sure was coming. He was going to clip her one across the mouth and shut her up. It had worked lots of times before. But no scream came. She just stood there shivering.

"All right, all right," he grunted sourly. "If you didn't learn the facts of life at that place where you work, better buy yourself a book and study up on 'em." The real horror of the situation lay in that. She couldn't make him understand what he was doing to her, turning everything sordid, killing everything in her. There was no heart there for her to touch no matter how hard she tried; nothing there for her to appeal to. They didn't speak the same language at all.

"Get out!" she said hoarsely. The shivering had become almost epilepsy. "Get out, I say, get out!"

He saluted her grimly by flicking his index finger at his temple. The door closed after him. A moment later the empty sandwich-plate shattered against it. Then the other one. She was beside herself. She kept saying "Get out!" over and over long after he was gone. Then the sobs came, dry sobs like hiccoughs, like the rustling of dead leaves on a windy day. They brought no relief; they stopped again.

She was still dressed in the tawdry satin thing she wore at work, that she'd come home in tonight. She bent close to the glass, made a horrid scar with lipstick over her mouth as though she was going out again. She was, but not by the door, not to dance any more. She threw up the window as wide as it would go, looked out, looked down on Fifty-first Street four stories below. Everything was dark, the sky was dark, the street was dark, the world was dark, her soul was dark. What was that she had said to herself? No sun anywhere, no blue skies, no love, nothing good and decent anywhere in the world—if this went wrong. Well, it had.

She slipped sidewise across the sill, brought her legs over, took her hand off the window-sash above her head. She felt like a little girl dabbling her feet in cool water on a very hot day. That cool water was eternity; when she slipped into it altogether, it would refresh her, wash her clean.

A piercing scream welled up from the dark street. Someone had seen her, sitting on a fourth-floor window-ledge in a dance frock at four in the morning.

"Faith! Fa-a-aith!" It was like a nail-head scratching glass. She looked down. A cab was parked at the door of the house and Trixie was standing there directly under her. You could hear everything she said—how strange! "No—wait, wait! Don't jump! Just give me a minute; let me tell you some—"

Faith only shook her head and smiled down at her. The light coming from the window behind her showed the smile. She'll go in, try to run up the stairs, thought Faith; then I'll do it before she gets up here.

But Trixie craftily stayed where she was, directly under her, and cleverly changed her plea. "Don't! You'll hit me; you'll kill me! Don't. You'll fall on top of me!"

"Then get out of the way!" warned Faith. Arms suddenly whipped around her from in back, around her slim waist, around her throat, pulled her back into the room. The door stood

Love & Night

open. The landlady and a male tenant held her between them, slamming down the window.

"Now you quit carrying on, young lady, or I'll call the police!" warned the landlady tersely.

"Why couldn't you mind your own business?" Faith sobbed.

Trixie came hurtling in, collapsed into a chair as though it was she who had just been rescued.

"Thank God you two heard me!" she panted. "I was afraid to budge away from there." And then to Faith, ferociously: "What's the idea? You trying to frighten the wits out of everyone?" She thumbed the other two to the door. "She'll be all right. Just let me talk to her. I've come to take her some place." And when they had gone: "Now, honey, listen to me very closely and pay attention to what I say."

It wasn't long after that the two passed the other pair still lingering at the front door to talk over what had happened. The taxi Trixie had come in was still waiting there. Trixie ushered Faith into it; the latter was docile now but still acted as though she were sleep-walking.

"Where you going with her?" whispered the landlady curiously.

"You won't believe me," answered Trixie, "but I'm taking her to a chop-suey joint."

The landlady nearly fell over. "These dance-hall girls!" she bleated. "Well, see that she stays there; she can't stay in my house any more."

"She won't have to!" snapped Trixie, banging the cab door. "She'll probably have a little flat of her own in Flatbush before the week's out and be darning her husband's socks a mile a minute! Let that hold you, poison-face!"

They walked into the Chinese restaurant a few minutes later, a very frightened girl with her arm around a very dazed one. Trixie was the frightened one. Then she saw him still there at the table and she wasn't frightened any more. He was a gentleman to the end; he'd intended ditching as soon as they left, but he'd had the decency not to leave without her, was still waiting there for her. So many things could have gone wrong; one of the waiters could have tipped him off that she, Trixie, always left like that and never came back. But he hadn't asked and he hadn't been told, so he was still there. God had smiled down on a little taxi-dancer tonight.

"Go over there, darling," she urged tenderly. "See him? That's him. Go over there—you've got a little back happiness coming to you; go over there and collect."

"But what'll I say?" whispered Faith.

"You don't have to say anything; just look at him, and he'll look at you—and you'll both know. They tell me," Trixie added wistfully, "that love is like that. They tell me that love is—pretty swell. I wouldn't know personally." She gave Faith a little push forward and then she turned and walked slowly out to Broadway again—alone.

[*Breezy Stories*, November 1935]

Until the mid-1960s the only ground for divorce in New York State was adultery, and the kind of raid on a phony love nest Woolrich depicts here was commonplace. In one of his last stories, "Divorce—New York Style" (1967), written before, but published after the law was changed, he recycled the situation with murder added to the mixture. The earlier crimeless version with its Machiavellian stunt strikes me as much better.

PICK UP THE PIECES

The assistant manager, who had come up in person, opened the door and stood aside to let Mr. Smith see the room he had just bought. "This has two exposures, cross-ventilation, circulating ice-water; you can't hear a pin drop this high up," he babbled. "I think you'll like it. You going to be with us long, Mr. Smith?" He ground his hands together expectantly.

Mr. Smith came in after him carrying a small satchel. He showed no interest whatever in the advantages just pointed out to him, in fact did not even look about him. He put the small satchel down.

"Just for tonight," he said briefly. "It'll do. My wife'll be up in about half an hour."

The assistant manager's face fell a little.

"Oh, just overnight?" he said disappointedly. "In that case I'm afraid the rate will be a little higher—"

"That's immaterial," said Mr. Smith impatiently. "Put me down for whatever you think it's worth." He rested one hand on the door as though waiting for the man to go.

The manager's face had brightened again. "Yes, Mr. Smith. Hope you'll be comfortable, Mr. Smith." He pointed toward an outlet in the wall with a cord dangling from it. "There's a three-station radio there, to help you pass the time."

"I'm not in the mood for music," said Mr. Smith tartly.

The assistant manager left the room backwards and closed the door after him. Mr. Smith promptly went over to his satchel, unlatched it, and took out a pair of pajamas, a bathrobe, bedroom slippers, and a toothbrush in a holder. The satchel, empty, he kicked under the bed. He opened the door, glanced at the number on the outside of it, and closed it again. Then he went over to the phone and put through a call. While he was waiting, he opened a flat hammered-silver case and took out a cigarette. The initial on the case was not S, any more than was the monogram on the pajamas and robe. Mr. Smith evidently spelled his name different from most people.

"Hello, this the agency?" he asked. "This is Walters. You can send the young lady over whenever you're ready. I'm in room fourteen-ten. . . . What?. . . . Oh, Smith, of course. I wasn't in the mood to pick a fancy name." He hung up.

Mr. Smith's statement to the manager about his wife's arrival proved accurate. Mr. Smith evidently had that rarest of all things, a wife who didn't keep him waiting. Her knock sounded on the door half an hour after he had checked in, almost to the very minute. He had meanwhile discarded his coat, vest and necktie, unbuttoned his shirt at the throat, and put on the robe over it. The pajamas he left neatly folded on the bed beside a corner of the turned-down covers. Mr. Smith said "Come in" and the door opened. Mrs. Smith entered the room.

She was blonde, blue-eyed and almost twenty-two—a good five years younger than her husband. Her swagger black-and-white checked coat was tightly belted around the waist, and in one hand she carried the feminine counterpart to his own satchel, a patent-leather overnight-case. The Smiths traveled light, it seemed.

"Good evening," she said formally, and closed the door behind her.

Love & Night

"How do you do?" her husband answered with equal formality. "Make yourself at home."

She had gone ahead, however, without waiting for his permission. She placed the overnight-case on the opposite side of the bed from his pajamas and began to unpack it. From it she took a cobwebby negligee, frilly pajamas, mules with pompons, a nail file, and no less than five magazines of the motion-picture type, plentifully illustrated. She wasn't, evidently, counting on his being very good company while they were in the room together.

"Those your own things?" he asked with a faint flicker of curiosity. "Or do they lend them to you?"

"Oh, we're supposed to supply our own," she answered matter-of-factly, slinging the lingerie over her arm. "But if you take care of them like I do mine, they last a long time. I don't wear them at home; you see, that saves them." She went toward the bathroom. "I'll change in here," she said, and closed the door after her.

When she came out again, she looked attractive enough to wreck anybody's home. The bare room had become suddenly intimate, cozy, with this vision in peach-color chiffon shuffling across it, hanging up her dress and coat in the closet, sinking comfortably into a chair, and fluttering the pages of a magazine, one leg crossed over the other. She reached for a cigarette without taking her eyes off what she was looking at. Mr. Smith extended his case toward her, but she was already lighting one of her own.

"Thanks just the same," she said. "I always bring a pack with me—some of 'em smoke cigars." She looked up. "I would like to use the phone though. Do you mind?"

"Help yourself." Mr. Smith waved his hand generously.

She got up, went over to it, and asked for a number with a Washington Heights exchange. "They sent me out in such a hurry," she apologized. "I didn't have time to make this call before I left. Trouble is they charge ten cents in a place like this—"

"Forget it," Mr. Smith condoned.

Someone got on the line and she called eagerly: "Oh, hello, is that you, Mrs. Conway? Yeah, this is me . . . Listen: I'll be working late again tonight; will you see that Mickey drinks his Ovaltine before he goes to bed? . . . I left it on the stove already mixed. Thanks, will you?" She hung up and found Mr. Smith's eyes fastened upon her curiously. "My little boy," she explained. He sat up a little in his chair. "Sure," she insisted, smiling fondly but not at Mr. Smith. "Don't you believe I have a little boy? Three years old. One of the neighbors looks after him when I'm out on a case."

The bigamous Mr. Smith cleared his throat tactfully. "Your husband—er—living?"

She showed no emotion whatever. "He took a powder," she said flatly. She returned to her chair and they sat facing one another from opposite sides of the room.

"Care for a drink?" he asked.

She shook her head firmly. "I never drink while I'm working." She looked around thoughtfully. "But you ought to have a bottle in the room for atmosphere; most of them do. They might flash pictures or something."

"Oh, Lord no!" he said. "Nothing like that. Everything's under control."

She shrugged. "It wouldn't make any difference to me whether they did or not. They always give me time to cover my face with a handkerchief or something anyway. It wouldn't be fair not to," she explained.

"I'll send down for a quart and two set-ups," he said, getting up. "Have you had any supper? Would you like something to eat?"

"Oh, don't bother," she said politely. "I usually stop in at a cafeteria on my way home and get myself something—"

"May as well have it now while we're waiting," he urged. "There's lots of time."

"Just a ham on rye then," she said, almost bashfully.

Love & Night

When the bellboy had brought the order, he glanced at the distance that separated the two chairs. He didn't venture to grin outright, but it was easy to see there was a grin on his mind. He seemed to be under the mistaken impression that their aloofness had something to do with his presence, would thaw the minute his back was turned.

It didn't. Mrs. Smith sat on the edge of one chair, nibbling her sandwich in a ladylike manner. Mr. Smith leaned back in the other, all the way across the room, slowly sampling a very little rye in a great deal of ginger ale. The desultory remarks they exchanged from time to time were purely of a professional nature, had nothing sentimental about them whatever.

"This Mrs. Conway that takes care of your little boy, does she know what you—uh—work at?"

"Of course!" She gave him a surprised look. "It's an honest living—what's wrong with it? My name's never mentioned. I'm always 'an unknown blonde.' I don't have to put up with half the familiarity a taxi-dancer does, and I don't have to take off as much as I would on a burlesque runway—" He seemed to have hurt her feelings. "It's not my fault if people can't get along with each other. If they'd loosen up the laws of this state a little, there wouldn't have to be any set-ups like this. But as long as there has to be, why should I turn down good money? It's just a form of acting really, anyway, only instead of using a stage it's done in a hotel room with detectives for an audience. I get a commission on each assignment."

His mouth twitched a little at that, but he steadied it with his lower teeth.

"How can you be sure you're not being gypped?" he wanted to know.

"They know better than to hold out on me," she declared. "All I'd have to do would be to step up to the referee, whisper 'collusion,' and the client's case would be thrown out and the lawyer disbarred maybe." She brushed the crumbs of the late sandwich off her fingers. After a while she said: "You're younger than most of the cases I get."

"Yes," he sighed, "I guess I'm not so old." He looked down into his highball. "But young or old, I lost my drag it seems."

She studied him in silence for a while. Finally she asked: "Is she coming herself or just the detectives?"

"She'll be here with them. Take a look at her; let's see what you think of her."

"You used to be awfully proud of her, didn't you?" she said quietly.

"How do you know that?" He laughed wryly.

"I could tell by the way you said that just now. I bet you used to go around when you were first married saying 'Take a look at her. Isn't she swell?' Maybe you didn't say it, but you thought it just the same."

He looked down at his glass again. "Doesn't everybody feel about like that—at first?"

She studied him some more and again they fell silent. Presently she asked: "Is she in on it or will she really think—?"

"It was her own idea," he said, "or at least a friend of hers." He poured a thimbleful more rye into his glass, drowned it with ginger ale, stuck his tongue into it. Then he sat warming it between his two hands.

She narrowed her lids at him shrewdly. "You can shut me up if I'm out of order," she murmured, "but you still love her, don't you?" It was a statement, not a question. His own eyes narrowed back at her.

"Little one," he said abruptly, "mind-reading isn't what you're here for tonight."

"All right, it's your party," she agreed tonelessly, "and none of my business. But you're not fooling me any; it's written all over your face. I've been present at too many post mortems. How do I know? Because you're the first one hasn't tried to pass the buck and tell me how misunderstood you are."

Love & Night

His color mounted a little and he set down his glass with an impact.

"Suppose we go back to talking about you or the weather or the World's Series," he suggested pointedly.

She kept smiling, though. "You're the boss, Sir Walter Raleigh."

"Why do you call me that?" he wanted to know.

"Oh, I don't know, maybe to show you I'm not as dumb as I seem to be." Then she asked innocently: "Wasn't he the one got down in the mud and let some dame walk all over him?"

He was getting more annoyed by the minute. "As far as I'm concerned," he said curtly, "he's just a cigarette!" Then, to get back at her possibly, he snapped: "And who doubled for you, by the way, when your own affair went boom? I forgot to ask you that."

"I never got one for myself," she said quite simply. "Oh, no. I don't believe in divorce. You see, I've seen so much of it."

He was still trying to recover from the shock of that when the long-awaited pounding on the outside of the door came at last. She was sitting there demurely shaping her nails with the file when it sounded; he was sitting in his own chair across the room, staring thoughtfully at her, thinking about what she had just said. He signaled warningly with one finger. "Here they are!" She tossed the file away, dragged the negligee invitingly down off one shoulder. He grabbed his highball-glass, jumped up, and went to perch intimately on the arm of the chair she was in. He bent over her lovingly, slipped his free hand behind her back. "Let's give it some music," she whispered, and plugged in the radio-outlet. Then she let her head fall caressingly against his shirt-front. The whole thing was done in a minute.

The thumping wasn't repeated a second time. A pass-key turned in the lock, the door shot open, and two men and a woman came in. They stopped just over the threshold and stood there looking. The two in the chair didn't stir. "Well?" said Mr. Smith quietly.

One of the men turned up his palm; the middle of it showed silver instead of pink; then he put it back in his pocket again.

"This your husband?" he said to the woman.

The second Mrs. Smith was a little older than the first, a good deal prettier, and unquestionably better dressed. A silver-fox piece was looped dashingly over her shoulder. She was not angry; in fact she even had a whimsical little smile for Mr. Smith, as though there was some understanding they shared between them.

"Unquestionably," she said in a clear, cool voice. "But maybe you'd better ask him yourself, hear what he has to say about it." The detective was too busy poking at the pajamas on the bed and taking in the peach negligee to notice the peculiar smile on her lips. He indicated her with his head.

"This lady your wife?" he asked.

"You heard what she said," admitted Mr. Smith.

At this point his companion in the chair gave a phoney little peep, took her head off his chest, and struggled to her feet. She shrank back against the wall and tried to look guiltily embarrassed without being any too good at it. Even the best of actresses, however, need a minute or two to warm up.

"Well," said the detective, making notes on the back of an envelope, "I guess that about covers everything. Pardon the intrusion. Shall we go now, Mrs. Walters?"

The second Mrs. Smith was still smiling at the corners of her mouth. "You can wait for me down in the lobby," she said. "I'll be right down." The detective went out and closed the door after him. The minute he was gone, her smile broadened. "Let's all have a drink together to show there are no hard feelings. What he doesn't know won't hurt him."

"And here," spoke up the second of the two men who had come in with her, "is the wherewithal." He held up the bottle of rye and sniffed it critically.

The second Mrs. Smith laughed indulgently.

Love & Night

"Just leave it to Fred," she remarked knowingly to her husband, "to find out if there's any liquor in a room."

"You were the one suggested a drink, Peggy," Fred reminded her with a grin.

"You're using Fred for a witness, I suppose?" her husband asked.

"Yes, but he's not writing any of it up in his paper, are you, Fred?"

"Good old Fred!" said the husband sardonically, throwing a cold look at him. The first Mrs. Smith glanced at him searchingly as he said it. Then abruptly she went to the closet, removed her dress and coat, and locked herself into the bathroom. Neither of the three paid any attention to her. When she came out, dressed, they each held a glass in their hands. Mr. Smith offered her one.

"Join us?" he invited. Mrs. Smith the second was smiling fatuously, her arm linked in Fred's. The first Mrs. Smith took the glass that was handed to her and crossed the room toward him.

"Don't say hello or anything to me, Fred," she complained bitterly. "That's right, act like you never saw me before!" He stared at her open-mouthed in surprise. "I didn't mind your not speaking to me while the detective was in the room, but now that he's cleared out, I think the least you might do is say good evening, after what we've been to each other—and for so long!"

The second Mrs. Smith had stopped smiling all at once. "Have you two met before?" she queried with a puzzled look.

"Have we! Have we!" The girl in the plaid coat was getting into her stride now, face flushing with excitement as she turned again to Fred. "What's the matter, don't you want them to know you know me? Ain't I good enough to associate with any more? Maybe you think you're going to get rid of me that easy!"

Fred's face had gone from white to red and back to white again. He finally managed to get his breath back.

"What do you mean?" he shouted angrily. "I never saw you

before in my life! I never set eyes on you at all until I came into this room tonight! Either you're crazy or—or—" He began to shake with excitement. "What's your racket anyway? What is this, a frame-up?"

The second Mrs. Smith had slipped her arm from his, however.

"You should have told me, Fred," she murmured in a low hurt voice.

"I tell you, Peggy, I never saw the girl before; I don't even know her name!"

"Just listen to that! Just listen to that, will you?" cried his accuser shrilly, filling the room with her voice. "I wish I had a penny for every time he'd called me Janey!"

"You're a damn liar!" exploded the man.

Mr. Smith rose from his chair. "Listen, Fred," he said wearily, "would you and your girl-friend mind getting out of my room and doing your fighting someplace else? We've got our own troubles." The second Mrs. Smith had turned her back to them and gone over by the window, holding her gay handkerchief to her chin.

"Yes, I think you'd better go, Fred," she said in a muffled voice. "I certainly don't want to be dragged into that kind of a mess."

The deadly blonde in the checked coat delivered the coup de grace. "But don't think you can come back to me!" she squalled violently. "Little Mickey and I can get along beautifully without you! We don't want any part of you if that's the way you feel about us." She got the door open, slipped out, and raced headlong toward the elevators.

He caught up with her outside on the street, just as she crossed to the other side and looked back to stare up at the hotel windows.

"Hey, wait a minute!" he said wrathfully. "You little four-flushing, double-dyed—!" He knotted his fist and held it under her nose. "If you were a man I'd—!"

"Don't try any rough stuff," she advised coolly. "There's a cop

Love & Night

just down the street; one well-placed scream and he'll be on your neck." She gazed across at the hotel entrance. "There goes your friend the detective," she remarked contentedly, "on his way home alone. She must have phoned down and told him not to wait."

"I want to know what your idea was, doing that!" he bellowed. "You know you never set eyes on me before tonight!"

"I know that and you know it," she admitted calmly, "but you couldn't get her to believe that, not now any more, for love or money."

He took her by the arm and started to shake her back and forth. "You're coming back up there with me and tell her the truth, d'you get me?"

She paid no attention to him; she was judiciously counting the hotel windows from the street up.

"—thirteen, fourteen. Those must be the windows of the room, up there." As she spoke, two of the lighted squares suddenly went black. "Sure, those are them all right." She turned to him then. "I wouldn't disturb them now if I were you. I think they'd rather be alone. No use waiting around either, pal; she won't be down any more tonight."

[*Breezy Stories,* March 1936]

The second Woolrich short-short collected here is one of the finest of his few tales at this length. The opening with dozens of people waiting in the Astor lobby for their dates prefigures the similar scene in Rendezvous in Black *(1948), while the clock motif was recycled earlier in* Deadline at Dawn *(1944). The story's two scenes are mirror images of each other, taking place respectively in 1929 and 1936, but as published in* Breezy Stories, *the lapse of time between them was described as five years. Was Woolrich that bad at simple math? More likely he wrote this tale in 1934, and two years later both he and his editor didn't notice that they needed to change the five years to seven. Neither did I until just before this collection went to press!*

THE CLOCK AT THE ASTOR

It was raining and the lights of Broadway gleamed upside-down from the shiny sidewalk. She came hurrying along from the direction of the Fifties, hanging on to a dog-eared suitcase with one hand. It was fairly large but it must have been fairly empty, for it swung lightly against her thigh with every step she took. She kept her head down to keep the flying drops out of her eyes. There wasn't anything about her to attract attention; she was dressed just like everyone else. Her skirt just missed her kneecaps by about an inch and her hat looked like an inverted bowl jammed down on her head. A flashing sign across the street proclaimed "Garbo talks!" Another one a few blocks down retorted "Barthelmess sings!" There were hardly any silent pictures being shown any more.

The illuminated news-belt around the middle of the *Times* building was laboriously quoting President Hoover. Something about two chickens in every pot. News vendors, hugging doorways to keep out of the rain, were selling papers date-lined 1929.

She didn't pay any attention to any of this as she hurried along, grip in hand, bucking the traffic that cut across her path at each side-street. It was nothing to her. She was leaving it for good. "For better or worse" was the way the words went. She'd hear them said to her, right to her face, by a man holding an open

Love & Night

book in his hand, tomorrow about this time, a thousand miles away from here, where they used lights just to read by and not to turn night into day on the streets. That was what he'd promised, and she believed him; she didn't care what anyone said.

"But if he is the quaint old-fashioned marrying kind," her chum had said, with eyebrows way up to here, "why not do it right here? What's the matter with New York? Why go all the way out to the sticks?"

"Because," the girl had tried to explain, "he's had a job offered to him in his home town and he's taking me back with him; he wants his folks to be there at the ceremony."

Even her landlady, when she had checked out of the rooming-house just now, had warned her: "You better bite that minister and make sure he's not stuffed with straw before you go through with it."

All of which fell on deaf ears as far as she was concerned. She knew what was the matter with them. Broadway had gotten under their skin; they thought there was a catch in everything. That was why she wanted to get away while the getting was good, before she herself got that way.

A taxi-fender just grazed the calf of her leg as she scurried across Forty-fifth Street. Ahead the marquee of the Astor offered shelter, had kept a big patch of sidewalk dry under it. She was going in there anyway; that was where he'd told her to wait for him. He was bringing the tickets with him and had promised to pick her up at eight-twenty at the latest. Their bus pulled out at eight-thirty. Now that this rain had come up, she was glad he'd made it the Astor instead of the bus-terminal itself. It was just an alley between two buildings; bus-lines didn't have much in the way of accommodations yet, and you had to take pot-luck with the weather. As she guided her valise in through the revolving glass door ahead of her, she looked very young and rather inexperienced—at least for Broadway.

She looked around her as she entered the lobby. He wasn't

there. There was the usual crowd, standing, sitting, pacing back and forth, lounging against the columns, everybody waiting for somebody else. The Astor lobby has always been New York's favorite meeting-place and probably always will be until the building comes down around it. Tonight the rain had increased their numbers. She went through to the back as a precaution, first of all, and glanced up and down the transverse alley that runs through Forty-fourth to Fifth. He wasn't there either. He'd said the front anyway. She went back and she was in luck. Somebody's appointee showed up just then and one of the big chairs fell vacant. The girl with the valise sank into it, tucked her grip under her legs, crossed her knees and relaxed with a sigh. Any minute now he'd be here.

But he wasn't. Minute ticked after minute into eternity and the glass door facing her kept turning endlessly, and yet he didn't show. The group about her changed imperceptibly. All the faces that had been there when she arrived had been called for and delivered one by one, and Broadway kept feeding it new ones. She had no wrist-watch to consult like most of the others. Even that dollar-and-a-quarter alarm back in her room had gone out of whack weeks ago. She had to keep turning around and looking over her shoulder at the clock high up on the wall behind her. It was so imposing one didn't dare dispute it. A million pairs of eyes have sought it in their time and tried to read their fate by it: "I haven't been stood up, have I? . . . Is he through? . . . Doesn't she care any more?" And still the hands go slowly round through the years, ticking off New York's evenings. Still the same two gilt cupids hover lovingly above it, one on each side, heartless under their gold-leaf.

More frequently and yet more frequently she began to turn and glance at it, each time with more of a jerk of the head. The five-minute intervals became one-minute intervals; then she was looking every thirty seconds, twisting and untwisting a handkerchief that had come out of her pocketbook. Eight-

Love & Night

twenty-eight . . . eight-twenty-nine. . . . They couldn't make the bus now, not even if they broke their necks hurrying. Eight-thirty—the bus had gone. What was the matter—what had happened to him? If she only knew where to reach him! But he'd checked out of his own room hours ago just as she had hers. Maybe he'd been run over on the wet street—

Panic lapped at her slim ankles but she kicked it back, took a grip on herself. No use losing one's head. Maybe there was a later bus; maybe he hadn't been able to get reservations on the first one. Still, why didn't he come and tell her, why did he let her stew here like this in her own juice? He knew where to reach her; he knew she was waiting here for him. Didn't he want to go through with it? Was he backing out? Needles of ice ran up and down her spine. He wouldn't, he couldn't do a thing like that to her! He knew she'd given up her job last Saturday, let her show start out on the road without her, on his account, and that there was no chance of getting another until the beginning of the new season. He knew she'd given up her room tonight and told everyone the reason why, and that she couldn't go back there and face them, tell them she'd been ditched. The few things she'd bought she'd blown all her savings on. He'd stranded her high and dry, and if he didn't come through, where was she?

Twenty-five to, twenty to, a quarter to. Her small chest was moving up and down like a bellows now, with fright and resentment and scorn all mixed up together. The things they'd said to her, her friends and the landlady and the stage manager, all came back to her now and got in their dirty work at last. Sure, they'd been right, why hadn't she listened, why had she let him make a fool out of her? Broadway mightn't trust its own mother, but at least Broadway knew its human nature.

She'd stopped looking now; there was no use any more, and people had begun watching her curiously, especially that elderly guy over there with the black ribbon holding his glasses and the stock-broker set-up. She was steeped in dismal apathy now, and without knowing it her chin was low, just missed the five-and-ten crystals round her neck. As the hands behind her up on the wall passed the quarter-hour and went into the homestretch toward nine, she clung to one last shred of hope. It wasn't much consolation, but it was all she had now. It was this: he had no reason yet for doing this. If she'd given in to him last night or the night before, or any of the other nights he'd tried so hard to get to first base, the motive would have been clear. But there wasn't any so far. She'd heard of them getting cold feet after they'd got what they wanted, but never, until now, before.

Little by little the fear subsided, left her. This wouldn't kill her, she'd live through it, she'd pull through. Suppose she had no job and suppose she had no room, tomorrow always came. At least he hadn't had the last laugh on her, that last masculine laugh that has gone echoing down Broadway through the years. She could hold her head up! But replacing the first fright that was gone now came a fine walloping anger. A little home of their own with a porch and a front lawn! Yeah! And morning-glories round the door! Yeah! And chickens in the back yard! Yeah! And his mother and sisters would love her, would show her how to bake her own pies; she'd be one of the family! Yeah! God, how she hated him!

"Pardon me, you dropped your handkerchief." The benevolent-looking old gentleman with the glasses had finally worked himself up to the point of tackling her. She didn't blame him at that. Twenty-after. She'd been here a full hour now. People didn't come to an appointment that much ahead of time; he knew the coast was clear.

"Thank you," she said, and took it back. She could hardly see him at all through the waves of heat that were coming out of her smoldering eyes. But visible or not, he didn't go away.

"Would you be insulted if I asked you to join me in a bite?" And then very quickly, before she could show her claws, "I don't mean any harm."

"That's just as well," she said in a flat voice that she'd never heard herself use before, "because it wouldn't do you any good even if you did."

"I can assure you I don't make a habit of this," he faltered, "but there was something about you as you sat here, you seemed so disappointed—shall we say?—that it made me come over and speak to you almost against my will."

"Oh, I don't doubt it," she said stonily. "You fought and you fought until finally you had to give in." She gazed morosely out through the glass door. "It's still raining," she said absently. Her words meant nothing—her thoughts were far away.

"I have a car," he murmured deprecatingly.

Her lips twisted into a peculiar bitter sort of smile. "And don't you want me to look at your etchings? No? Well, you will later." Suddenly she had risen to her feet. She heard herself talking the way she had heard other girls talk in the show she'd worked in. "Save the build-up. I'm ahead of you every step of the way. You have a car. And I haven't had any supper."

"Boy!" he motioned commandingly. "Check this grip for the young lady. It will be called for later."

She preceded him out through the revolving glass door just as the hands of the clock reached nine-twenty.

• • •

The town car drew up in front of the Astor. It was raining, and again the pavements glistened with the reflected lights. News vendors were peddling papers date-lined 1936. She stepped out, dropped a careless word to the chauffeur, and went up the steps into the lobby. Heads turned as she went by. The sleek fur that draped her shoulders was mink; the flower pinned to it was an orchid; the flashing at her wrist was diamonds encircling a watch. She still looked young but not inexperienced.

The usual evening crowd was there and instantly she became

the center of all eyes. She acted used to that. She glanced around her, evidently didn't see whoever it was she had come to meet. A chair was offered her and she sank into it with a nod of thanks as though such attention was hers by right. She frowned slightly as though she were not used to being kept waiting. The spiked heel on one custom-made shoe tapped a little on the marble, the manicured nail of one forefinger drummed on the arm of her chair. That light at her wrist flashed, and she glanced at her watch.

The man who had been watching her more closely than all the rest edged nearer. He seemed to be trying to place her. There was a startled, questioning expression in his eyes. She seemed to become aware all at once that someone was standing directly in front of her. She looked up.

"I—I don't suppose you remember me?" he faltered.

She didn't answer for a long cold minute while her eyes bored into his. Then like the crack of a whip she uttered the single word:

"Perfectly!"

"I—I thought it was you," he said, or something like that.

Again she didn't say anything for a long time, seemed to be about to ignore him altogether. There was a look of cold disdain on her face. Her eyelids drooped with indifference.

"The same place and the same time," she said finally, "but you're just seven years late. What detained you?"

He looked surprised. "Don't you think it's up to me to ask you that? I waited here right on the spot that night until the bus had gone and it was too late. No sign of you."

She sat up a little straighter in the chair. "I had my grip all packed. I waited here a full hour. One of us is lying."

They both forgot themselves a little, were back in the past, intimate again, not just strangers, in the heat of contention.

"Twenty after eight I came—!"

"You couldn't have, I tell you! That's just when I got here. And it was twenty after nine when I walked out of here!"

Love & Night

"Wait a minute!" he said suddenly. He turned and looked up at the two gilt cupids on the wall. "Did you go by that thing?" His hand shot out and touched her.

"Of course! I had no watch of my own."

"It was in April, wasn't it?"

She nodded. "It was in April, but why bring that up now?"

"Because don't you see? I know what happened now! That was the night they changed to daylight-saving time. I remember they warned me when I bought the tickets. And they forgot to adjust the clock here. You came an hour too soon and left just before I got here!"

Her mouth dropped open. She glanced at her wrist, then compared it to the clock on the wall.

"It's an hour slow," she breathed in amazement. "The same thing must have happened tonight again!"

He glared up at it and his face contorted. "Damn the clock at the Astor!" he muttered.

She glanced down at the orchid nestling on her own shoulder, at the diamonds on her wrist; she rubbed her chin lovingly against the soft mink of her collar. She suddenly felt how much life meant to her.

"God bless the clock at the Astor!" she answered thoughtfully. She smiled a little. "Tell the truth," she said. "That was a set-up, wasn't it? You can tell me now; I've been around."

"Yeah," he admitted at last, "it would have been a frame."

She shrugged philosophically. "Well," she said, and got up and moved away as the glass door spun around and the gentleman with the black ribbon on his eye-glasses came in. He looked a good deal older but as prosperous as ever. She was frowning as she went to meet him. "You're a nice one! You can't treat me this way! Remember, I'm your wife, not one of those floozies you used to run around with!"

[*Breezy Stories*, April 1936]

Anyone who experiences a sense of deja vu *on reading this story should know that Woolrich recycled bits and pieces of it in his unfinished novel* Into the Night, *which was completed after his death by Lawrence Block and published in 1987. The Sharlee in this tale has no relation to the Sharlee of "Gay Music" earlier in this collection.*

HIS NAME WAS JACK

The room was adorable, a dainty boudoir all in coral and gray. The girl waiting there in the room was adorable. The tea-rose moon that shone outside the window was adorable. Everything was adorable but one thing—the way those two hands on the clock were pointed, at 3 and at 6. Half-past three in the morning.

Three-thirty isn't necessarily a tragic hour. But when you've been waiting alone since midnight for a husband that doesn't come home, it isn't exactly a consoling hour either. And when the husband's an almost new one, dating only a year or so back, it's more than tragic. It's catastrophic. At any rate you don't feel like laughing about it. Sharlee Milburn wasn't laughing; she was prone across the bed crying her poor little nineteen-year-old heart out. The tangerine satin negligee rippled as her childish shoulders shook under it; one pomponned mule had fallen off, the other clung by just one toe. A Madame Pompadour doll perched at the head of the bed looked commiseratingly down on her as if it too would have liked to cry. This was her fifteenth crying spell since twelve o'clock, and still he didn't come.

The first one had started in almost the minute she closed the door on the last of the gay housewarming guests. A fine housewarming of the new apartment that had been—without a husband! Why, she'd had to smile and lie to them through the

Love & Night

long endless hours, keeping the tears back. "Oh, Craig'll be here any minute now. He—he had to go out on business." Gulp. "At least that's what he said." Which wasn't what he really said at all.

What he said, when she timidly asked him where he was going, was "That's my business!" There is, you will notice, a slight difference between the two statements, but it was the best she could do; she wasn't very good at deceit. And at that it failed to be very convincing. She saw them all look at one another and change the subject. She knew they must think it strange. But she didn't care what they thought if only they'd go. If only they'd go and leave her alone! She couldn't hold out much longer; that glazed smile was cracking her lips and any minute the tears were going to come. Then finally they went, with their banter and their laughter and their good wishes and their noise, and she got the door closed after them. She tore into an adorable but empty boudoir, bounced on the bed, and cried as she'd never cried before.

Then right in the middle of it Stella Hart had to come back for something she'd forgotten and caught her at it. She knew it wasn't Craig; he had his key; he wouldn't have knocked. She just had time to powder her nose and snatch a cigarette for an alibi before she let Stella in. Stella was a funny sort of person, cynical and hard-boiled, wearing her divorces like beads around her neck, a sort of up-to-date rosary which she told off with the least encouragement and absolutely no embarrassment. She'd been watching Sharlee closely all through the evening; maybe that was why she'd purposely left her gloves behind.

"Oh, it's you again, Stella," Sharlee managed in a strangled little voice at the door.

"Forgot my gloves," said Stella. But she didn't seem in any hurry to look for them. Instead she kept scrutinizing Sharlee's tear-bright eyes and nodding to herself as if she'd expected that.

Sharlee tried to bluff it out. "I—I just had a coughing fit on this cigarette," she explained feebly, holding it up to show Stella.

"Peculiar," said Stella, "seeing it isn't lit at all. What do you do, chew them like gum? Who do you think you're fooling?" she said harshly. Harshly but with an undertone of kindness. She didn't wait for Sharlee to answer. "Not me anyway. Now just say the word and I'll butt out again. I know this is none of my business, but I'm ten years older than you, and I hate to see anything as good-looking as you suffer on account of one of those things that wears a necktie and goes around talking way down deep. That's what it is, isn't it? Me, I've made 'em suffer. I've got nothing coming to me. I've collected. But I'd like to help you. I'm great for sex-solidarity. Why don't you tell sister what he's doing to you? Sister'll put a few bees in his bonnet!"

Sharlee tried to be loyal to her year-old husband to the bitter end.

"Help me?" she tried to say coolly. "Why, I don't know what you mean!" Instead all that came was a new gush of tears, and before she knew it, Stella's arm was around her consolingly and she was sobbing out the whole story. "Why does he treat me like this? I don't know what I've done to him! Comes home at all hours, blind drunk! I think he must have married me to spite somebody else, that's what I think!"

"But you've only been married a year!" Stella gasped.

"Every night he leaves me upstairs alone and he's down at the bar until they had to carry him up to our suite. When it began, I used to phone down, but he'd send back word that he'd come when he was good and ready. So I stopped that. Then he got a telegram; I think it was from her, whoever she is! Then we moved to this apartment Daddy and Mom had fixed up for us—"

"Do they know?"

"No, thank heavens, they couldn't come to the housewarming tonight. I wouldn't dare tell them either—Daddy would kill him!"

Love & Night

"Then what are you going to do?" asked Stella. "Are you going to buck this thing alone?"

"It's my marriage so I guess I'll have to." Sharlee sighed. "I've never thought much of girls who ran home to mother the minute anything went wrong. I couldn't face them at home. I want to be so proud of him—and he won't let me!"

"To be proud of him," said Stella acidly, "you'd have to have a helluva good imagination, if you'll pardon my French." She pondered for a while, puffing at a cigarette. "Suppose we try the old jealousy racket," she said finally. "It works wonders, you'd be surprised! You know, what's sauce for the gander is sauce for the goose, that sort of thing."

"What would I have to do?" Sharlee looked sort of doubtful.

"Nothing, I'll do it all for you; just leave it to me. I tried it on my third, no, I guess it was the second, and I had him eating out of my hand in no time! Now let's see, we'll start with—Does he smoke cigars?"

"No, never," Sharlee assured her, mystified.

"Good, then we'll start with that." She went to the house phone and called the doorman. "Run out and get me a good ten-cent cigar," she commanded. "Just one will do—and bring it up here, Mrs. Milburn's apartment." This must have surprised him a good deal, although apartment-house doormen usually expect anything and everything. Next Stella stalked into the dining-nook, studied it gravely, then decided. "This is as good a place as any. We'll set the scene of your misdeeds in here. Got any champagne in the house?"

"No, but somebody brought a bottle of Scotch to the house-warming."

"We'll use that then. Bring two empty glasses in here—and two of everything else, plates, napkins, left-over sandwiches. Now, while I'm fixing the table so it will have that guilty, give-away look, you take a piece of stationery and scribble this on it: 'Jack, darling, come back after the others have left and I'll give you your answer. The door will be on the latch.' Can you remember that?"

"Jack darling, come back after the others have left and I'll give you your answer, door will be on the latch," Sharlee repeated, looking at the ceiling.

"Better sign your name to it too, so there'll be no mistaking who it came from," the satanic Stella added. "Then bring it to me and I'll show you what to do with it."

"But I don't know anyone named Jack!" protested Sharlee.

"Of course you don't! But how does he know that? Go ahead and do what I told you."

Sharlee flitted out and Stella arranged the table. Into one glass she poured a drop or two of Scotch, smearing it around so it would make it sticky and the odor would cling. That was "Jack's." Then into the other she poured a regulation highball and let it stand. That was Sharlee's, who didn't drink much whiskey but had poured herself one just to keep "him" company. She took a bite out of each sandwich, then dropped them on the plates that way, with half-moon dents in them. That meant they'd been too much in love to bother with food.

By the time she was through, the hallman had come to the door with a long black cigar wrapped in cellophane. She tipped him, then ordered crisply:

"Strip it, bite off the end, light it up, and pull on it until you've got it going."

"Chee, thanks, lady," he murmured gratefully.

"Wait a minute," she forestalled, grabbing him by the arm. "Don't go away. I'm not making you a present of it!" She withdrew it from his teeth, closed the door in his face, and carried it in with her to the table. His reactions to this strange behavior must have been highly informative had anyone been out there to listen.

Stella parked the smoking cigar in an ashtray beside "Jack's" glass. It would burn undisturbed for hours, she knew, turning

Love & Night

slowly to ash but not crumbling. Her fourth husband had been a heavy cigar-smoker; that's how she knew.

Sharlee came in with the lover's note and Stella proofread it, then instructed her:

"Now drop it just inside the door, written-side up, where he's bound to see it when he comes in. The idea being that Jack dropped it out of his coat pocket as he was leaving. If it doesn't work that way and he misses it, then here's a surefire way to make it register. You give a little scream, snatch it up and hide it behind you, looking guilty, until he demands to know what it is." Stella evidently knew how it was done.

"You think of everything," Sharlee sighed admiringly.

"Now I'd better get out before he finds me here; he's liable to show up at any minute—" Stella bustled toward the door, Sharlee trailing after her, mewing questions.

"But—but suppose he really believes I've done something wrong behind his back? Should I tell him then that it was all a trick?"

"Under no circumstances!" snapped Stella. "Anyway, not for days or even weeks! Until he's stopped this business of staying out all hours of the night and treating you like a door-mat. Mind you, be careful not to admit there was anyone here, no matter how he storms and raves, but don't deny it either—let him form his own conclusions. That ought to give him something to worry about, make him appreciate you a little more. If he gets too nasty about it, just throw this other woman up to him! That ought to hold him. It's the swellest come-back you could want!"

"And if—if it doesn't work, if he doesn't seem to care?"

Stella threw up her hands. "Then it's hopeless and you may as well give up. You're nineteen and a raving beauty; there are other men in the world, thousands of 'em. I'd just walk out the door in that case and pitch your whole marriage over your shoulder if I were you." She gave her a peck on the cheek. "Well, lots of luck, little Sharlee. Call me up sometime and let me know how it worked out."

It was one by then. Sharlee closed the door on her fellow-conspirator and for a while felt considerably braced up. She went in, put on a dab of lipstick, touched a drop of Chypre to each ear, changed to one of her trousseau negligees, daringly pulled it down off one shoulder so she'd look flustered when he showed up. Then she just sat back and waited nervously while the note lay face-up just inside the door and the cigar filled the dining-nook with acrid fumes and the clock ticked on and on.

By two she was beginning to wilt again a little, now that Stella's moral support was lacking. Not that little Sharlee Milburn was any dope or slouch herself under ordinary circumstances, but anyone very much in love is working under a terrific handicap. By quarter after two the tears were already playing a return engagement, and from then on they took nothing but curtain-calls until the clock reached three-thirty.

There was a lurch against the outside door; it banged open and there he was—the object of all the plotting. His hat was shoved to the back of his head, and he was in one of those "cold" drunks, that is, knew everything he was doing and saying and was ready to show his true colors. He wasn't lovely to look at, but then he wasn't handsome even when he was sober. His mouth had a sullen, cynical twist to it, and only the slight stagger with which he moved betrayed his condition.

Sharlee had gotten off the bed but had no time to dry her eyes before he was standing there looking in at her. He saw that she'd been crying—tactical error number one.

"Oh," he said resentfully, "the water-works again, eh? I can see what kind you're going to turn into in a couple years' time, one of these cry-baby wives!"

He spotted the note when he turned back to close the door which he'd left open. She saw him pick it up and squint at it. She

Love & Night

remembered Stella's instructions; she squealed, ran out, jerked it away from him, tried to look properly guilty.

"Who the blazes is Jack?" he asked indifferently.

"Jack is—is Jack!" she stammered, looking at him with big round eyes. It didn't seem to be going over any too well so far.

He sniffed the air, traced the odor to the dining-nook, went in. The cigar was mostly ashes. "Whew!" he said disgustedly. "Tell him I'll treat him to a good cigar next time he comes around. This one smells like fried fish." He dumped it out, noted the careful stage-effect on the table. "Little party, eh?" he commented. "Good for you! That's the spirit!"

She nearly sank through the floor. Oh, something was wrong; didn't he care at all? Wasn't there even a spark of jealousy somewhere in his make-up for her? She averted her head, more bitterly humiliated than he could have guessed.

"It doesn't seem to matter to you—what I do," she said in a low voice.

"It's all to the good," he told her. "You have your little parties and I'll have mine, and heigh-ho the merrio! But yours didn't seem to turn out much of a success judging by the way you were bawling just now when I came in. Or is that the reaction you always get, moral indigestion after you've eaten your cake?"

"I'm not sorry for—for whatever I may have done tonight," she flung at him defiantly. She would have died now rather than have him find out the whole thing was a frame-up. "Can you look me in the face and say the same, with somebody's face-powder all over your shoulders and a lipstick-smear at the corner of your mouth and one of your garters trailing down over your shoe top?"

"Yes, I can say the same!" he bellowed angrily. "I can go even further than that! I was not only with someone just now, but I'm going to be tomorrow night and the night after and every night! How do you like that?"

"What did you marry me for?" she fairly screamed.

"On the rebound!" he said callously. He picked up "Jack's" highball-glass and took a gulp from it. He sneered at her over the rim. "Who do you think you're fooling anyway? I wasn't born yesterday! I've had this tried on me before—it's a racket with your sex! You should have a lover—you, married a year and crying every time I step out the door! There isn't any Jack and you know it! You cooked up the whole thing yourself to try and get under my skin. Tell you how I know—if you'd really been guilty, you wouldn't have been so damn careless, leaving things around wholesale like this! That cigar alone, you can smell it all the way down in the vestibule. The first thing you would have done would be to air the place if there'd really been a man here. Your technique," he said scornfully, "is lousy."

But she wasn't in the room any more with him; her face was white now, and she didn't look nineteen any more, and she was in the boudoir, getting dressed at a mile a minute.

"I'll show him!" she panted. "I'll show him whether there was someone or not! I'll throw myself at the first man I meet outside that door tonight! Heigh-ho the merrio is right!"

Off came the tangerine satin negligee, splitting down its seam in her hurry; off came the pomponned mules with a vicious kick. There remained practically nothing to speak of for a moment, but friend husband wouldn't have been interested even if he had been in the room at the time; he liked them thirty, experienced, and well-rounded—as he might have put it himself. Not nineteen and straight up-and-down like willows. On went what she considered the suitable costume for a young wife leaving her home in the small hours to throw herself away on the "first man she met": a little blue tailored suit, pumps, a jabot, a funny little hat with a feather, and a purse with thirty-five cents in it.

He had finished "Jack's" highball by the time she got the front door open but was still in the same derisive mood.

"Going home to mother, eh?" he called out to her. "Give her my regards."

Love & Night

"I am not!" she wailed. "I'm—I'm going to him! And you've driven me to it! You've made your own wife into a—a two-timer!"

"Hah!" he laughed insultingly. Below them somebody began rapping on the steam-pipe. "You'll probably wind up at the nearest Y.W.C.A. Be sure to look under the bed before you turn the light out; that's your speed! Well, come back when you're tired of play-acting, you little lame-brain! I'm going to bed, and I'm not getting up to answer any doorbells either so you better take your key with you!"

She closed the door with a shattering boom and stood there with her finger on the elevator push-button, heaving with anger. "The first man I meet!" she kept hissing. "The first man I meet!" A moment later, as the car came up for her, she realized there would have to be amendments. For instance, people like this hallboy—who was cross-eyed and had pimples—didn't count; she'd better rule out all—er—employees and people like that, such as taxi-drivers, news-vendors and milkmen, or there was liable to be some kind of a catastrophe in no time at all. So the lift-man was eliminated, and she marched out into the before-dawn street head up and with a determined look in her eyes. She'd show him; she'd get even! Lame-brain, was she?

But the streets were not only deserted, they were chilly and misty and depressing as well. Still, she couldn't show up at her parents' at this hour, and she wasn't going back so he could have the laugh at her. She could have gone to Stella's, she supposed, but Stella was probably asleep hours ago, and she had a husband, and it seemed like an imposition. I suppose, she thought, the best place to—to throw myself at someone would be a night-club. But that was out too, for several very good reasons, the chief one of which was she only had thirty-five cents with her. And then she couldn't think of any night-club offhand, and even they were probably closing down by now too.

She began to wonder as she walked briskly along, getting

further and further away from the apartment-house, what they meant by always saying it was so easy for women and young girls to go wrong, go to the dogs, become a prey to temptation. Here she was out looking for it, and it seemed to be avoiding her.

A policeman strolled past just then, and she could feel him turning around to stare after her as she went by. But she quickly ruled him out, he was a sort of city employee, wasn't he, and he hadn't looked like a very flirty sort either, in fact rather suspicious and hard-hearted if anything. After that she didn't meet anyone for several blocks until suddenly, of all things, she came upon a woman walking alone just as she was. They were coming toward one another, and as they drew abreast the other party addressed her.

"Pardon me, dearie," she said, "could I touch you for a cigarette?"

Sharlee stopped and murmured politely, "Oh, I'm so sorry. I don't think I have any with me."

"Skip it," said the other girl philosophically. Then she surveyed Sharlee from head to foot. "How are tricks?" she demanded, not unkindly.

"Terrible!" Sharlee blurted out without stopping to think twice. "I'm so sore and disgusted—I've just about got things up to my neck!"

"Tell me what your trouble is," the other commented critically. "You're going around looking like somebody's pet corn. Y'wanna flash a big smile, see—like this, give 'em the bridgework. And what's the matter with your war-paint, did you run out of it? No wonder you're not getting any breaks! Here, come on over by this street-light; I'll lend you some of mine and fix you up. Now stand still—" She proceeded to take out a well-worn lipstick and an eyebrow pencil and began grinding them in on Sharlee's delicate features. What emerged was a terrifying mask of red, white and black that could be seen a mile off.

"And there's no flash to your clothes at all," she went on. "You look like you're going to a wake. Where'd you ever get that rig from? Tell you what I'll do. I'll trade this garden-hat for yours and that pocketbook, whaddye say?"

"All right," said Sharlee, "if you think they'd be more attractive on me."

"Think? I know what I'm talking about. Empty your purse and here goes!" She saw the thirty-five cents, shook her head, offered with sudden sympathy: "Want a loan of fifty cents? I'll never miss it."

"Thanks," said Sharlee, "but I don't think I'll need it." But she was grateful.

"Yeah, you'll be in the money in no time now," the other agreed. "I've improved you a million per cent." They parted and the girl went her way with the noble feeling of someone who has just performed a good deed.

Sharlee tipped the gigantic threadbare black velvet cartwheel over one eye and proceeded in the opposite direction. Wasn't she nice, she thought gratefully. I wonder what she was doing out so late?

For about five minutes more nothing happened, and then things began to happen with great rapidity. She was practicing the "bridgework flash" the other had suggested and not thinking much about her surroundings at all when suddenly a loud jovial voice assailed her:

"Well, look who's here! Come to poppa!" and a sailor was lurching toward her with both arms extended in an intended bear-hug. Where he came from she never afterwards found out; he seemed to have sprung from the ground at her feet. Instantly he was ruled out. She seemed to be doing nothing but ruling people out, but he was an employee, an employee of the government or something like that, and he'd been drinking too much beer, and—she turned with a squeak and tried to flee but the bear-hug closed around her and he deposited a loud loving "smack" squarely between her eyes. The squeak turned to a loud screech and she squirmed and tried to kick at him. He seemed hurt by her lack of cordiality.

"Don't you 'member me?" he said thickly. "Don't you 'member your old flame Bilge Braddock? And after I had your name tattooed on me all the way from here to here! That's a woman for you!"

"I never saw you before!" she wailed. "I'm not your old flame!"

"I'd know your face anywhere! What're you trying to do, throw me down?" Hurt turned to indignation. "Deny that you're Lily from Honolulu! Stand up there and deny it to my face!"

"I do!" she howled, struggling to get away from him at a forty-five-degree angle. "I'm Sharlee from New York and I was never in Honolulu in my life!"

"So I ain't good enough for you any more!" he shouted wrathfully. "So you ain't been true to me, after I bought you them earrings with real imitation poils and brought you back a live humming-bird from Bonus Airs! Well, this is what I do to broads who try to ritz me—"

He swung one powerful arm back over his shoulder and got ready to pound some affection into her.

"Here, you!" a voice said sharply. They both looked around. A taxicab had halted nearby and a young man in evening clothes was leaning out of the open door, eyes fixed threateningly on the nautical Romeo. "Don't you let me catch you hitting her while I'm around," he added.

"She's Lily from Honolulu and she's my woman, at least she's my favorite one, and I can do what I want with her," the sailor growled truculently. He let go of her, however, and turned to face the intruder.

"She may be all of that, and she certainly looks it," commented the young man not very flatteringly, "but if you were any kind of a man at all—"

But Sharlee put in her two-cents-worth at this point. "I'm not

Love & Night

Lily from Honolulu and I'm not his woman and I never want to see him again!" And she punctuated it by taking a vicious dig at his instep with her sharp-pointed slipper.

"O-woo!" he bayed, and began to hop around on one foot, holding the other up with both hands.

Sharlee fled toward the cab for sanctuary. "Let me ride with you," she pleaded urgently. "Just a block or two, so I can get away from him."

He helped her in, slammed the door and said: "Go ahead, driver." They left Bilge Braddock staring mournfully after them and shaking his fist.

"Well," smiled Sharlee's rescuer, "you seem to have a taste for cave-men."

"Why, I never saw him before in my life!" she said indignantly.

"I know, I know, you're just misunderstood," he purred. And he dug the point of his elbow jocularly into her ribs. "You're really just a lady-picket or something, aren't you, but you forgot your sign, and after he saw you walk back and forth in front of him about twenty times, he got the wrong impresh—"

She stared at him curiously from under the brim of the big floppy hat. What was he driving at anyway? He sounded vaguely disrespectful; in fact, plain disrespectful without any vaguely about it.

"I think this is far enough," she said suddenly. "We're a mile away from him by now." And she reached toward the latch on the door.

His hand suddenly covered hers. "What's your hurry?" he grinned. "Why not drop in for a while? I'm a bach, perfectly all right!" And he added: "I like you. I really mean it, something a little different about you, don't know just what it is."

The funny part of it was she liked him a little too. He was a gentleman, and although he was being altogether too familiar on short acquaintance, somehow she wasn't afraid of him. Not like with that menace a few minutes ago, for instance. And anyway, wasn't this what she'd threatened to do? He wasn't an employee; there really didn't seem to be any excuse for ruling him out this time.

"It's awful late," she condescended formally, "but I'll drop in for a little while if you insist."

A minute later she wondered why he slapped his knee that way and bent over double, roaring with laughter as though she'd just said something very funny.

"You're cute!" he gasped. "No matter what you are, you've got personality—that's what counts with me."

Which didn't make very much sense, but she let it go. They got out in front of a rather swank apartment building, and she saw him exchange a wink with the doorman as he ushered her in. The doorman just said "Good night, Mr. Herndon" very respectfully, and that told her his name.

He had really a very tasteful apartment, more expensive than hers and Craig's in some ways, but more subdued of course on account of being a bachelor's.

"Like it?" he grinned disarmingly.

"Do you live here all by yourself?" she wanted to know incredulously.

"The building furnishes maid-service," he explained. "Take off your hat. What can I get you?" He opened one of those portable bars, and she'd never seen so many different decanters and flagons in her life.

"What's that—that red one on the end?" She pointed blindly.

"Port," he said, and she heard him comment to himself: "True to type all right." He brought her a glassful and then perched on the arm of the big chair she was nestled in with a very weak and short Scotch in his own hand. He looked down at her and she looked up at him. "Poor kid," he said suddenly, and rumpled her hair with his free hand. "You know, you're much younger than I took you for at first." He sighed and turned his head away.

Love & Night

"I'll be preaching at you in a minute if I'm not careful. Well, it's your life, I suppose—" He got up and refilled his glass, brought her back another port. "You'd better drink this and go," he said curtly. "I don't feel right about the whole thing. Frankly, this isn't my sort of stunt at all. I don't go in for it, don't know what got into me tonight, impulse I suppose." Then he picked up her hand and folded something into it. When she tried to see what it was, he wouldn't let her. "Skip it," he said. "There's something too damned innocent about your eyes."

The port was making her sleepy. "First you ask me to drop in; then you ask me to drop out. You're awfully funny, Herndon! I never had anyone treat me that way before."

He pitched his glass over his shoulder and it smashed somewhere in back of him. Suddenly both his arms had folded around her.

"Hell," he growled close to her face, "I was only trying to be noble, not to take advantage of you—or something. Don't forget I'm only human too." But she didn't hear the rest of it; her head tilted against his starched shirt-front and a minute later she was soundly, childishly asleep.

He stared at her in amazement. "Well, I'll be—" he ejaculated. Then he picked her up in both arms and carried her inside to the next room. "Maybe some guys would wake you up and throw you out," he said softly, "and maybe some would wake you up and not throw you out, but I haven't the heart either way." And when he came out again, closing the bedroom door on her, he added: "I could like that little tramp an awful lot—worse luck!"

• • •

Sharlee opened her eyes in a strange room, in a strange bed—and with her clothes on under the covers. A clock staring her in the face said it was after eleven. She remembered Craig first of all. Then she remembered Stella. Then a very pleasant dream she'd had came back to her, about someone who'd put both arms around her.

She got up and looked at herself in the mirror and all but screamed. She looked a fright, her face was all cheap red and white. She bolted into the bathroom and there was a great sound of splashing and scrubbing. When she came out again, she was herself once more. She ran a comb through her hair a couple of times and then she opened the door and looked out into the other room. There was a form huddled on the sofa under a topcoat, dead to the world. She tiptoed over and looked closer. It hadn't been a dream after all. But she was smiling as she straightened up again. The name came back to her suddenly, Herndon. So I did it after all, she thought elatedly. Even if nothing happened, I kept my word. And he was nice, from what I remember; I couldn't have picked anyone nicer if I'd tried.

The usual thing to do in a situation of this kind, she recalled from somewhere or other, was to make breakfast for him and have everything all ready when he opened his eyes. But when she looked around, there wasn't even a kitchenette in the place, or a crumb of bread. That, however, wasn't going to keep her from showing the right spirit. She phoned down in an undertone and had breakfast for two sent up from the drugstore below. Then she shook him gently by the shoulder.

"Herndon, wake up!"

He took lots of shaking but finally he grunted, rolled over and sat up. When he looked at her, his eyes popped.

"Who—who are you?" Then: "My gosh, you can't be! Not that little hustler I brought in here last night!"

She gave him a mildly rebuking look. "One lump or two?" she asked.

He waved the coffee-cup aside and caught her by the wrist. "I've got to talk to you. What is all this? What's it all about?" Suddenly his face was flaming red. "I ought to have my face slapped! The things I've been saying! But why the masquerade, why the get-up? But why did you let me go ahead thinking what I did? Any fool can see you're not!" And then, almost savagely, "D'you know what could very well have happened to you here last night? Haven't you any brains at all?"

"If you'll let me get a word in," she protested, "and a mouthful of coffee, I'll explain." And she did.

"He oughta be shot!" he scowled when she was through. "And that woman-friend of yours oughta be horsewhipped. And you yourself—oughta be spanked!"

She went ahead spreading marmalade. "But if it hadn't been for them, I—we wouldn't have met each other. I'm not sorry I met you. Are you sorry you met me?"

He didn't answer, he couldn't, straining her to him the way he was. After a long time he said: "At midnight I didn't even know you, and at noon I—don't laugh at me—I very much think I love you." He gulped. "Damned if I don't!"

"I like you more than I ever liked anyone before," she breathed. "And I guess they call that love—the beginnings of it anyway."

Nestled there in his arms, somehow she knew what the ending of this was going to be. Oh, not today and not tomorrow but soon, someday very soon now. Craig and her marriage would be a thing of the past. An annulment or arrangement of some kind would take care of it. And then there'd just be herself and Hern.

"What's your given name?" she murmured. "Here I am in your arms—and you haven't even told me yet! Don't you think I'd better begin practicing up on—"

"Jack," he said. And then he looked at her in astonishment, the way she had thrown her head back against his shoulder and was laughing, laughing until the tears came. "What's so funny?" he grinned. "You little feather-brain."

But all he could get her to say was: "Doesn't life play the craziest tricks on us sometimes?"

[*Breezy Stories*, July 1936]

This is the earliest of three Woolrich evocations of a pulp mystery writer alone in a furnished room, working feverishly on a story. In "Murder Story" (1937) we get to read the complete tale the protagonist is writing, but here and in "The Penny-a-Worder" (1958) Woolrich gives us only fragments, which aren't at all like the pulp fiction he actually wrote. Anyone who wonders what Woolrich was like when pounding the keyboard will find a vivid answer here.

THE GIRL NEXT DOOR

It was like rain on the roof at first, licketty-split, licketty-split, licketty-split. Mr. Theodore Cobb came back from another world to his present surroundings with a wrench. The other world, of swift sudden homicides, of many many homicides per typed page, faded away beyond hope of immediate recapture.

Cigarette in the far southeast corner of his mouth hanging by a thread, hair a bird's nest, collar open, shoes unlaced, fingers poised predatorily above the keys, he blinked and looked about him dazedly. It wasn't coming from above. This was the top floor of the Plantagenet-Turret Furnished Apartments, Mrs. Olivia Everard, manageress, so it couldn't have been coming from above. Now it was going licketty-split, licketty-split, licketty-split, getting faster and more furious all the time. There was an undercurrent of music in it somewhere.

Mr. Theodore Cobb got up and went to the window to see if it was hailing out or something. He had to; the room was too thick with smoke to be able to tell from where he had been sitting. It definitely wasn't; the sun was going down in perfect propriety. He opened the window and let a little of the fog out. Instantly, page 23 left its mates and went volplaning flatly across the room. Pages 22, 21, 20 and 19 in that order went migrating after it. He

Love & Night

closed the window again hurriedly, just in time to keep the rest of "Murder on a Dark Night" from following suit. All this was very bad for an artist's nerves.

He picked them up, frowning, patted them together again, got down to the business of blood-letting once more. At a cent-and-a-half a word, "keep it fast, keep it clean, keep it unexpected." But his gory muse seemed to have deserted him. He had cooled off just as he was getting nicely steamed up. He couldn't remember for a moment who had killed whom, nor why. He couldn't even remember who was next on the list.

The cause of this professional catastrophe, the licketty-splitting, was working itself up into a fine frenzy. It was like a roomful of crickets, all mixed up with woodpeckers, and all being very busy at one time. He ran a hand through his Fiji-Islander coiffure, peered at what there was of page 25. Right at the climax, that had had to come along—whatever it was. His fingers plunged; the roller shot over to the left; a tiny bell rang warningly. Then he stopped, aghast. He had killed the wrong party. Someone who wasn't in the story at all. Someone who had been killed last month, in last month's story.

Out came page 25 with a rip, in long tatters. The cigarette left his lips for the first time since it had been lighted, hit Mrs. Everard's floor with a bounce and a shower of sparks. He ground it out on his way to the door and the hallway outside. Anyone not knowing him and seeing the look on his face at the moment might have taken him for a character from one of his own stories. As a matter of fact he fed horses sugar on the street, but he wasn't in a sugar-feeding mood just now.

It was louder out there in the hall. Like a train going over split-rails. Clicketty-clack, clicketty-clack! Sure, it was coming from right next door, on his left. What the hell were they doing in there anyway—roller-skating across the bare floor boards? He scowled darkly at the oblivious door. He controlled the urge to go down the hall and give it a good, swift kick. He'd follow the proper procedure about this, relay the grievance, although he longed for personal contact, devastating contact at the end of a fist.

He gave his own door a bang, picked up the house-phone, asked for Mrs. Everard.

"Look," he said, "I've got a deadline. What's going on next to me in 6-C, riveting? I can't hear myself think!"

Mrs. Everard clucked soothingly. "Oh, I guess that's your new neighbor," she said. "I guess maybe she's practicing. I told her she could—"

Visions of personal contact at the end of a fist faded reluctantly from Mr. Cobb's inflamed mind.

"She? I might have known it," he echoed cynically.

"She's a lovely little dancer," placated Mrs. Everard, who had strong pacifist tendencies as long as you paid your rent.

He was already, even this early in the game, strongly disinclined to agree with this opinion.

"What does she practice with, ball-bearings?" he wanted to know.

"I put her in there because, well, there's no one under her, you know, and I didn't think you'd mind, well, on account of your typewriter, you know—" said Mrs. Everard, by way of a gentle hint.

"I do mind," he said severely. "If you'd come up and listen to it—"

"It's only six in the evening," she said distressedly. "I don't like to inter—I tell you what," she said hurriedly, as a way out of the dilemma offered itself. "If it keeps you up, you call me back and I'll let her know. I'm sure she wouldn't want to—"

She hung up before she had finished, before he could protest. "Yeah, but if I put a burn in one of your rugs, I never hear the end of it!" He glowered at the disconnected phone.

He went back to his death-dealing machine, opened the flat tin of cigarettes, stuck one into his gums, put a new, bloodless page 25 into the roller.

Click-click-clop, click-click-clop, it was going now. He gave the wall a lethal look over one shoulder, hitched up his trousers, began whacking at the keys.

Duke squeezed the trigger and lead whistled at the dick. His own gun talked back in the same bullet-language. Suddenly Dolores was standing there in the same beautiful evening-gown as when she'd killed Mickey. She had a gun in her hand too. Click-click-clop, click-click-clop—

He'd put in a whole line of the things before he caught himself. He said bad language, very bad. Language worth a dime a word, not just a cent-and-a-half. He hit out a concealing row of X's, shrouding the mishap.

Rat-tat-tat, rattety-tat-tat came blithely through the wall. "Call me back and I'll let her know!" he mimicked Mrs. Everard savagely. "I'll let her know myself!"

There was quite a heavy glass ash-tray at his elbow. Cheap but substantial. Mrs. Everard got them wholesale. It was the nearest thing at hand, and it was just about ideal for the purpose anyway.

Sock! it went, like a cannon-ball, and dropped to the floor in two neatly-split halves. There was a sudden stunned silence. Muted music continued for a bar or two; then that stopped too.

"That did it!" said Cobb with grim satisfaction.

He tore out the second page 25 and put in a third. He washed his hands without soap and water. He pressed his nails back and blew on them vigorously like a pianist. He poised them clawlike over the well-worn keys that had slaughtered their thousands—

Wham! It sounded as if a battering-ram had struck the other side of the wall behind him. He jumped a full two inches above his chair, came down again limp. He was a very high-strung young man. Most crime-story writers are. Then, twice as loudly as before, in defiance, in despite, in open animosity, it resumed where it had broken off. Clackety-bang! Clackety-bang! Clackety-bang!

It was the beginning of a beautiful feud.

• • •

He saw her for the first time two days later. They hadn't placed each other yet, coming up together in the automatic elevator, so there was no hostility displayed. He sized her up with an open mind, unprejudiced as it were. Not a bad-looking girl, not a bad-looking girl at all. In fact sort of swell-looking. Lithe and lissome. Copper-colored hair in the three-quarters length he liked best. Nice hazel eyes. He was even wondering whether he should risk some remark about the weather to this prepossessing fellow-tenant when the car stopped and they both got off at the same floor.

He put his key in the lock, then turned his head to look after her. The corridor was empty. He looked up the other way and there she was, right in front of that hostile door to the left. Identification was mutual and instantaneous. A mutual glare followed. A sizzling glare that should have set the hallway afire in spontaneous combustion. Two doors slammed as one like a double-barreled sunset gun.

He got to the typewriter first. Maybe she had to change to practice clothes or something. The head start was only a matter of seconds. There was a warning blast of music and then sounds suggesting a Spaniard with St. Vitus dance playing the castanets.

There was temporarily a dearth of ash-trays. He'd broken two in two days. "Miz Everard ain't gonna give you no mo'," the dusky chambermaid had announced that morning. "She say you run through 'em too quick." He picked up one of his unlaced shoes instead and flung that. One thing about a shoe, you can

Love & Night

use it over and over again. This time there wasn't even a pause in the complicated routine.

He flung the door open and stood there peering out aggressively. "Am I a man or a mouse?" occurred to him. He stepped quickly down to the offending door, bopped it commandingly with his knuckles. Then, taking most of the courage out of the act, he retreated halfway to his own. To neutral ground, so to speak. But the Rubicon had been crossed. The feud was out in the open now.

She was flushed and panting when she stuck her head out to see who it was. She had on shorts and a blouse. The copper-colored hair was delectably awry. To an unjaundiced eye she might have seemed quite lovely. Both of Cobb's were a vivid orange as far as she was concerned, though.

"Say, d'you have to practice all the time? I'm trying to get some work done in here!"

She regarded him balefully. Up and down and back up again. "Work!" she scoffed.

That hit home. "It takes brains!" was all he could think of. Which was not only beside the point at the moment but gave her a swell opening. Too late he saw his mistake.

"Exactly," she said icily. "When are you going to get wise to yourself?"

• • •

For the next hour he thought up beautiful come-backs, one after the other, but since she'd closed her door again immediately afterwards and he'd closed his, he didn't derive much satisfaction from it. "Murder by the Yard," the masterpiece in progress at the moment, suffered considerably as a result. He put her into it and cut her throat on page 3, then brought her back to life and had her thrown off a ship at sea on page 10. Which made him feel a whole lot better, vicariously if not otherwise. But no matter how often he slew her on paper, the tap routines went on unimpeded on the other side of the wall. He had never known anyone could practice that much—and live through it.

"It couldn't," he cried aloud more than once, running both hands through his brambled hair, "be a soft-shoe dancer. It couldn't be an adagio-dancer, or even a fan-dancer. No-o! It hadda be a tap-dancer!"

He could have moved out and found other quarters. But almost at once it became a point of honor not to. He'd been here first. He liked it here. It was reasonable and comfortable and Mrs. Everard was easy-going. No leggy hoof-swinging stage-struck chit of a girl was going to drive him out like a whipped cur!

Their hours unfortunately seemed to chime almost to a T. They were never in at different times; they both always seemed to be at home simultaneously and busy at their respective arts. If not, then they were both out at once, and the lesser mortals around them got a much-needed reprieve. On the rare occasions when Cobb was home and the menace wasn't, unkind nature arranged it so that he wasn't in the mood for writing, couldn't take advantage of the lull. Her tapping seemed to act as a sort of spur on him, driving him to a point where he had to type or bust. And the same was true of her. She could be in there without a sound, reading a book or washing hankies maybe, but he no sooner got the lid off his machine, batted out the first couple of words, than bingo! She had dropped everything and was practicing again a mile a minute. As much as to say, "You're not gonna get ahead of me, Smarty! I've got a career too."

Cobb was not a particularly vindictive young man. If she had only gone one day, one whole day, without practicing, his feelings might have had a chance to cool off. Maybe that was the exact way she felt about his typing, herself. One sure thing, if she had come to him and proposed that he knock off for a day, he would have resented it to the point of apoplexy. The way it was, they each took turns adding fuel to the fire, so it really had no chance

Love & Night

to die down. The wear and tear on ash-trays, coat-hangers, shoe-trees and all other easily movable objects within reach was something terrific.

But when she held up his work to ridicule, aloud and publicly, that was more than adding fuel: it was pouring gasoline. He certainly didn't intend eavesdropping. You didn't need to where she was concerned; you usually needed cotton stuffed in your ears. But there was something vaguely familiar about those cadenced phrases coming through her transom one night as he stepped out of the elevator. Pressed, he might have admitted people didn't actually talk that way in real life.

She had a couple of girl-friends in there for her end-men. Mrs. Everard had evidently passed on one of the pulps with his stuff in it. Perhaps she had been asked to, out of malign curiosity. The menace was doing the reading aloud—she would!—and her voice sounded strangely thick, almost strangled.

"Lead spat over his shoulder. He swerved in the nick of time, fired behind him under one arm. There was a clump as a body hit the floor. Mercedes' screams were coming down from the roof where the Chinamen had dragged her—"

Gales of laughter drowned out the rest of it. They were laughing at something that was meant to frighten you! At something that thousands—well, all right, hundreds—of people sat up in bed shivering over at night, with their hair standing up!

"Can you stand any more? Or have you had enough?"

A choked voice begged, "Don't—please! My ribs hurt as it is!"

"And can you imagine? He gets boiling mad every time I—I thought I must be living next door to Shakespeare, or at least Anatole France. When I asked Mrs. Everard, she passed me this!"

Righteous indignation, and maybe just a touch of something else besides, sent the color flaming to his neck and ears. He funneled his hands, megaphoned: "Not a brain in a roomful!" and banged the door shut after him.

If she was only a man! Oh, if she was only a man! Or if he only had a good husky sister, or even a female cousin, to take up the cudgels for him! He visualized a scene in which the latter planted a punishing foot where it would do the most good, but swiftly, against the offender's person. And then stood threateningly over her. "You gonna tap-dance any more? You gonna so much as put a cleated shoe to the floor? Just you lemme catch you!"

He sighed. Most of the girls he knew were fragile little things, totally unfit to be proxies in any physical combat. Especially with someone who had the endurance she had. Anyway, you couldn't very well go to a girl and ask her to—

In the end he took it out on her in the same old way as before, the only way he really had. He thought up such horrible predicaments for her that night, never at his own hands, of course, that was beneath his masculine dignity, but at the hands of malign Orientals and such, that it really made a story. He jotted it all down from force of habit.

His phone rang the next day and it was Elkins, his editor. Privately known to him as Simon Legree, the Man with the Whip. A rejection of course. Well, no wonder, trying to work next to a female Fred Astaire!

"Say, you're going good. What's come over you lately?" Elkins' voice boomed out jovially. "Just thought I'd let you know. Boy, are you getting bloodthirsty! That last one nearly scared me myself when I read it! Wow, what you didn't do to that poor girl!"

"So then how about a boost in rate?" Cobb managed to get off instinctively, while the rest of his mind was trying to adjust itself.

Elkins' voice instantly lost lots of its ill-advised enthusiasm. "What? Oh, sure," he said glumly. "Er—I'll jack you up to a cent and five-eighths; how'll that be? Now don't let it go to your head. G'bye."

Love & Night

Cobb hung up, turned and glared at the blank wall. A glare that was meant to go through it to the other side. "See? Laugh at me, will ya?" he said pugnaciously.

Almost as though by mental telepathy, Blah! went the introductory music, and then tappity-tap, tappity-tap—far into the afternoon.

He had one of those allegorical struggles with himself, like in "Pilgrim's Progress," that night. It was participated in by his Better Self, his Worse Self, a pair of pliers, and a radio-antenna outside the open window that led diagonally downward and over toward hers.

She can have it repaired inside a half-hour, said his Better Self; but it's sort of a dirty trick any way you look at it.

Afraid, huh? sneered his Worse Self. Are you a man or a worm?

He reached out, caught the wire, and snipped it neatly in half. "And now," he gloated, reverently closing the window again, "for a little peace and quiet around here!"

If he was a trifle ashamed of what he'd just done, he refused to admit it even to himself, kept it severely soft-pedaled. That's the trouble with allegorical struggles.

She came back inside of half-an-hour; he could tell by the challenging bang she gave her door. Came the usual change-of-clothes pause. He forgot to type for a minute, waiting for the pay-off. Bla-ah! blared out familiarly. And then, allegro fortissimo or something, clacketty-clack, clacketty-clack!

He just sat there with a very funny look on his face.

"No, there's no radio in 6-C," explained Mrs. Everard the next morning, collecting the two dollars the people on the third floor insisted he owed them for the repair of their aerial. "She uses a portable phonograph and records. You really shouldn't be so impulsive, Mr. Cobb," she rebuked mildly. "It's not a nice trait." At the door she turned and added: "You should try to meet her halfway. She's really got a heart of gold."

"Silence," he seethed, "is golden too. Doesn't she ever," he wanted to know hopelessly, "work at it—I mean somewhere else except where she lives?"

Mrs. Everard promptly came to her defense. He was not in particularly high regard just then, after the discovery of the incriminating pliers on his desk. "She has lots of offers—lots!" she championed stoutly. "She's waiting for the right thing to come along. She doesn't want to do night-club work. She's a refined girl, here on her own, and so many of these fly-by-night offers have strings attached. I think she deserves a lot of credit."

"A lot," he agreed sombrely, "but just a little soundproofing too."

Mrs. Everard coughed apologetically. "I have a nice little one-room available in the rear. You wouldn't, er, consider—"

He rose to his full if somewhat lean six feet, behind the portable. His fist came down soggily on a bunch of carbon paper.

"Never!" he stormed. "A man's home is his castle! I wanna be where I can see the sun go down!"

Mrs. Everard coughed again through the layers of fossilized cigarette-smoke that all but veiled the window-frame itself, let alone what lay beyond. She didn't press the suggestion.

However, every dog has his day. Opportunity with a capital O arrived only two nights later. The barrier to physical onslaught was suddenly removed. The outlet he craved was given him. His heart's desire was granted. Although he had been unable to conjure up a sister or female cousin to manhandle her, she suddenly supplied herself with a male retainer or familiar of some kind whom he could deal with personally. Which was a whole lot better. Not too old or decrepit, either, to make it worthwhile.

The tap-dancing had been unusually unbearable the night this male first appeared on the scene. She seemed to run through the whole gamut of her routines, from clicketty-click to biff-bing-bang! Almost as though she were giving a private audition there in her room.

He had learned by now that throwing things at the wall was no deterrent; she took it for applause, gave encores. Besides, there wasn't much that was throwable left around unbroken any more. Half-insane, he jammed the lid on his machine, went out to get a glass of beer, or three, or even six, as a surcease for his suffering ear-drums. The monthly deadline was due tomorrow, and he wasn't half-way through "Murder in a Dreadful Way." He was grinding his teeth like the leading character in it.

It was while he was waiting for the car to come up that he discovered she had finally gotten herself an audience. A male voice came through the transom above the din of hoof-beats.

"Tricky, that," it said judiciously. "Very good, sweetheart, very good!"

Cobb clenched his fists. "I'll very-good-sweetheart you if I get my hands on you, whoever you are!" he smoldered. "Coming around encouraging her! I only hope I run into you some-time—"

Coming back an hour later, he did. Mars must have been in the ascendant that night. He went into his room quietly and heard something. Something very different from the tap dancing and the sweetheart stuff. It was a muffled scream from his next-door neighbor. He stopped and listened. Beauty in distress, he thought, rather sneeringly, and then he wondered, what was the matter with the girl? He couldn't help listening.

"Oh, oh!" she was saying. "You leave me alone!" Then came mutterings from the man of which Cobb couldn't make sense, and the girl's frantic, "I'm not that kind! No! No!" There came a sound of scuffling and the girl's voice full of terror: "Get out! Oh, get out!"

Then Cobb, who was listening breathless, heard a foul word and a door opened. That nasty word did things to him. Calling a girl that—any girl! And that kid was a nice girl! Yes, he really thought that, much as it amazed him. He pulled open his door and stepped out into the hall. A man stood there, a very Broadway-looking man, trying to adjust his collar and tie. There was a long red scratch across his face and Cobb was pleased. Serves him right, he thought.

Cobb had six beers in him but he didn't need them in a good cause like this. He moved to the man. "Who ya crowding?" he demanded pugnaciously.

The man looked surprised, fell back another step, didn't answer. "Oh, yeah? Izzat so!" said Cobb. Her door had opened again and she was looking out. That was about all he needed if incentive had been lacking until now. He gave her a belligerent stare over the shock absorber's shoulder, he wasn't doing this for her, and then gave the man a punch in the jaw. A beauty.

The man went down flat. He didn't know it but he hadn't been hit by a fist; he had been hit by thirty days of accumulated tap-dancing as well as that nasty word.

"Dance-hound!" hissed Cobb, shooting daggers over at her. Then: "Calling a girl such a name!"

The only reason he didn't give the man a second biff was because he had never seen anyone get up and scramble into an elevator so quickly in his life before. Whisht! and he was gone. He left a shattered gardenia behind him on the floor.

She came out into the hall step by step as though drawn against her will. He could tell at a glance, right through the beer and all, that this had had a salutary effect on her. Gone was all her arrogance, her cocksureness. She acted sort of droopy, as if she wanted to cry and was looking around for a nice comfortable shoulder to do it on. There was a rip in the shoulder of the beach-robe she wore over her practice clothes; her hair was tousled, her face streaked with tears.

Cobb felt a lot better, a whole lot better than he had for weeks. He felt like a new man. He felt swell. He stared at her unrelentingly so she wouldn't get the idea he was weakening or anything.

"Thanks," she conceded grudgingly, twisting an edge of the robe around in her hands and looking down at it. "I don't know how you knew but thanks anyway. He was horrid. I was afraid of him."

Cobb wasn't interested. It wasn't her—it was that name—a man pulling a girl about!

"Ah, shut up!" he growled half audibly.

Her morale instantly improved. Her dispirited eyes blazed up anew. "Shut up yourself!" she snapped back. Again as so many many times before, two doors banged as one.

It was a sort of farewell salute, although he didn't realize that at the time. He was at his old machine-gun next day ready to go, tin of cigarettes at his elbow, stack of blank pages beside him, shoes unlaced, when he first noticed that something seemed amiss. He couldn't place it for a moment, looked around, even looked under the desk. Slowly it dawned on him what was holding him up. Silence. He was waiting for the counter-blast from next door ,and there wasn't any.

"Sure put her in her place," he murmured approvingly. But his typing sounded hollow in the strange stillness. He kept waiting for that racket to chime in and it didn't, and after a while he lost interest, quit trying. He blamed it on last night's beers.

There wasn't a peep, or rather a tap, all the next day either. Mrs. Everard was formal to the point of stiffness when he encountered her.

"She moved out the first thing yesterday morning," she told him cuttingly. "I pleaded with her not to but I can't say that I blame her, you know. She told me what happened. She said she was too grateful to you for putting that low-down night-club man in his place, after the way he came here and insulted her, to wish to annoy you with her practicing any longer. And of course she isn't ready to give that up for anyone. She was a sweet child. You might have," she added, fixing him sternly with her eye, "been just a little more tolerant."

"She didn't have to move out on my account," he growled shamefacedly.

Victory, now that it was his, didn't have as much savor to it as he'd expected. That was just like a woman, always going to extremes when there was no need to, and always managing to put you in the wrong too.

"I hope you'll find conditions more suitable for your work now," Mrs. Everard said with a distinctly unfriendly toss of her head.

But that was just it; he didn't. They should have been but they weren't. The strange oppressive stillness weighed him down. He couldn't seem to get warmed up any more. One thing about that erstwhile din, it had managed to heat him to boiling-point almost instantaneously each time it occurred. Trying to work without it now was like an actor walking on "cold," without a cue. He got stage-fright every other paragraph, went ahead by fits and starts. It was like pulling teeth to drag the stuff out of himself. Doors didn't bang around him any more; things didn't hit the wall. All was silence. It—it didn't seem like home any more.

On the way back from mailing his latest bunch of junk to Elkins, he paused in front of his door, looking down at that other one. After a while he went over, stood there by it with his hands in his pockets. "I'll be damned," he said softly. "You'd think I actually missed her or—or something." He leaned the side of his head and one shoulder up against the door disconsolately. He hadn't suspected there was this streak of sentimentality in him. He who slaughtered his characters so ruthlessly right and left. A variation of a poem passed through his mind.

> *"Noisy feet I loved*
> *Beside the Shalimar,*
> *Where are you now—?"*

Love & Night

It didn't scan very well but it fitted his mood. Not that he really loved her of course, or anything like that, he hastened to explain to himself; but anyone who penetrated one's consciousness as loudly as she had, you sort of felt lost without. Like a sudden shut-down in a boiler factory. He sighed gustily.

Just as he was about to straighten up, he was saved the trouble. The door fell in unexpectedly and he all but did too with it. A stoutish, severe-looking person wearing rimless glasses stood holding the knob.

"My goodness!" she stated. "What next? Sniffling through people's keyholes!"

"'Scuse me," he said hastily, and slunk back where he belonged. No other word would describe it, the way his knees were bent under him.

Elkins rang up next day, within twenty-four hours of submission.

"I might have known it!" he boomed. "Raise you an eighth of a cent and you go soft on me right away! There wasn't a single violent death for ten whole pages! Whaddye think I'm running, Godey's Lady's Book? Of all the wishy-washy stuff! Matter, you in love or something?"

Cobb scorned to answer this rude editorial thrust. "So it's coming back," he said indifferently.

"It oughtta be there already, the speed I kicked it outa my office! Now for Pete's sake, stick a pin in yourself and get good and sore, if that's what makes you turn 'em out the way I like 'em!"

Cobb went from the phone straight downstairs.

"Where'd she go?" he demanded without preliminaries.

"Where'd who go?" asked Mrs. Everard.

"That girl. Where'd she move to?"

"Now, young man," she began sternly. "Hasn't there been enough trouble between you two already? I call such a thing willful persecution! It so happens that she left no forwarding address, but even if she had, I'm not sure that I'd care to—"

"She take lessons?" he snapped. He seemed to be in a great hurry.

"Lessons? Oh, you mean dancing-lessons. No, she didn't need them any more; she'd learned everything they—"

"Well, did she have a trunk then?" he interrupted.

"She had two trunks," Mrs. Everard said boastfully as though he were trying to disparage one of her favorite ex-tenants. "A little one and a big one."

He grabbed a classified directory from her desk, began calling express companies one by one.

They met again in the hall that night. Blocks away from where they'd last met. All the way across town as a matter of fact. Hers, naturally, was the greater surprise of the two. She stood stock-still and surveyed him darkly.

"It's me," he admitted so she wouldn't take him for an apparition and faint or something. She dropped her purse to the floor, poised both hands at her hips.

"Well, of all the nerve! And right next door to me again! I'm going to see the management about this right now!" She took an infuriated step toward the elevator. "Deliberately hounding me! There ought to be some way of stop—"

"You—you can practice all you want," he said hastily. "Tell you the truth, that's why I did it," he blurted out. "I got so used to it I found I can't work without it now. I even paid 'em a premium to get in next to—where I could hear it good and clear."

She deferred her intention of going downstairs. "Mm," she said undecidedly. She went back and picked up her purse. Hostility gave place to pensive abstraction as though she were mulling something over in her own mind. "I noticed something like that myself," she admitted guardedly. "I haven't been practicing nearly as conscientiously since I came here where no one objects."

Love & Night

"Maybe we need each other for inspirations," he said hopefully.

"Maybe," she said noncommittally. "But mind you, the first ash-tray you slam against the wall—the very first!"

Two doors closed as one, tactfully, restrainedly, yet with a jaunty fillip to them.

It occurred to him that it was really very uneconomical for two young people like themselves, trying to get somewhere in the world, to keep two separate apartments going side-by-side when for a mere two dollars, the price of a license, they could cut their rent in half. He must mention that to her, see whether she agreed with him. Not right away of course, but some day real soon.

[*Breezy Stories*, July 1937]

The first scene of this strangely moving tale comes straight out of the opening of Woolrich's 1936 pulp classic "You Pays Your Nickel," better known as "Subway," only in this rough sketch there's no mad gunman or runaway train. Delaney's love for the woman he meets on the job and does a good turn for is no less intense for being, like the love of so many Woolrich men, nonsexual.

I KNEW HER WHEN—

At six-fifteen an alarm clock sounded vigorously in Mrs. Delaney's dark silent bedroom. Mrs. Delaney's own voice answered it. "All right, creature, I heard ye the first time." The alarm clock nevertheless continued to signal raucously. "Shh, that's enough now!" Mrs. Delaney commanded it. It was several moments, however, before the light flashed on and revealed Mrs. Delaney in person. She had miraculously attired herself in the dark, for the light like the clock was at quite some distance from the bed, and every minute counted. The alarm by now was running down anyway. It had sunk to a metallic growling. Mrs. Delaney interrupted the tying of an apron about her slim figure to reach out and silence it with a click of her thumb. "Y'd go on all day if I didn't stop ye," she commented. With this remark all conversation between herself and the clock was over until the following day.

She now passed into the adjoining room and proceeded to do a number of things at once yet far from noiselessly. A coffee-pot that had evidently been filled the night before began to simmer over a blue gas-flame, two eggs started to hiss in the preliminary stages of frying, and a knife, fork, spoon, cup and saucer, one of each, appeared in tinkling, crashing succession on the white enameled table-top. When this much had been accomplished, Mrs. Delaney paused her first pause of the day to brush the back of her hand before her forehead and remove the slight moisture that her efforts had accumulated thereon.

She next returned to the threshold of her own room and called sonorously through it:

"Jerry! Be getting a move on." A door opened and her young and good-looking husband appeared, attired in trousers and shirt and blinking his eyes. "That's the bye," Mrs. Delaney remarked encouragingly, and returned to her duties.

When he joined her presently, he was buttoning a dark blue coat over the trousers. A coat with brass buttons in two rows down the front. A coat that was more than a coat. A coat that was a badge of distinction, a symbol of authority and competency that set him apart from the common herd, that empowered him to tell people that South Ferry trains did not go to Brooklyn and to stand aside please, don't shove, and watch your step. The coat that proclaimed this, and the visored cap he had brought in with him and thrown on the seat of a chair, the cap that bore on a metal disc the numerals 01629, were to Mrs. Delaney objects of justifiable pride.

She loved them. They were to her what a silver tea-service would have been to other women, or an invitation to a ball, or the mention of one's name in the society column. With the thought of them in mind she could tilt her chin in air and say to Mrs. Ross across the fire-escape, "Oh, haven't you heard? My husband works for the Interborough," and say to Marco, the greengrocer on the next corner, with an air of conscious superiority and patronage, "Twenty cents for a pound of string-beans? The life of me! What'll you be asking next?"

She flounced around her husband, giving the sacrosanct coat a tug of the hem in back to straighten it, smoothing down each shoulder with a little sliding caress.

"It needs pressing," she said sadly. "I'll have the iron out when ye come back tonight."

"Inspection don't come again until March," he reminded her,

miraculously speaking through his coffee-cup. Jerry Delaney's ideas on the subject may have erred on the side of indifference; he had been lukewarm as regarded his occupation and the prestige attendant on it for many months now, even going so far as to remark upon his return in the evening: "Whew! I'm glad that's over for today." A point of view which Mrs. Delaney failed utterly to share. It wasn't much, no; but just think if he had been on the night-shift, or on one of those surface cars that stopped at every other corner. "Then ye'd have something to kick about."

Young Mr. Delaney groped for a metaphor with which to answer this. A come-back was the designation he applied mentally. "All I do is get a look at the sun at New Lots Avenue; then I gotta go all the way back to Van Cortlandt before I see it again." Which was geographically inaccurate; the sun was visible from Dyckman Street on. When there was a sun.

"Sure!" countered Mrs. Delaney with affectionate raillery. "And if ye were on the night-shift, it would be the moon you were missing."

He was whistling as he left her and went down the long dim stairs, the visor of his cap jauntily over his eyes. He had stopped being Jerry Delaney now and was simply 01629. It was only beginning to grow light when he emerged onto the street, but it was doing it slowly and beautifully, as though it had purposely waited until he appeared to show him what he was missing every day of his life. But he gave no heed to the pink that had started to creep down the upper stories of the tenements nor the attenuated white of his breath as it escaped in little steam-drifts with every step he took. At 125th and Broadway he climbed the subway stairs, climbed not descended, for it bridged the street at this point above the level of the rooftops. One of the incalculable advantages of his occupation as Mrs. Delaney saw it at once became evident, for scorning the turnstiles, he simply loosed a chain that barred his way and passed through unhampered.

At the end of the line, more prosaically known as 242nd Street,

Love & Night

he got up, stretched himself, thrust the delightful tabloid into his pocket, and stepped off the train. He removed a small pass-book from his rear pocket, made his presence known to the gentleman who made up and detailed off, out of his own unaided creative ability and good judgment, mind you, the personnel of the various southbound trains, and this rite—"shenanigans" Jerry termed it—attended to, joined a group of his mates sprawled about on benches until the necessary ten minutes preceding his assumption of duty had elapsed. At precisely seven-twenty he stepped into the waiting line of cars that would soon be a vehicle and placed himself exactly over the coupling-irons of the second and third cars from the end, one foot on either platform like an Atlas astride his own little world. A small group of passengers entered and dispersed themselves over the seats, seats made doubly welcome by the knowledge that after the first station or two they would be unobtainable. The signal was given and Jerry bore manfully down on the pneumatic lever. Six doors in all, three to the left of him and three to the right, slid sibilantly closed. He plucked at a cord overhead to relay the knowledge to the next guard in line, two cars away. When it had reached the motorman, the train began to move. The day had begun.

The last seat in any of the cars went immediately after the third station had been reached. That was simply a preliminary to what was to follow. Long before the train sought subterranean darkness at Dyckman Street, the aisles were crowded with rhythmically swaying bodies. At Ninety-sixth Street the overflow from the locals—Jerry's train now took on the dignity and questionable alacrity of an express—was waiting to get on. Most of them did, too. No individual passenger on the train was now free from contact at some point with the body of another. Which is putting it mild. Jerry himself, wedged solidly on the brink of the two cars between a prickly pony-coat and a caracul one that smelt of recent mothballs, received the benefit of their shouted remarks with great, not to say painful, distinctness. His eyes took on a fixed blank stare as he learned all the details of "What sort of a time ja have with Al las' night?"

At Seventy-second Street it had become a sheer physical impossibility for any additional people to enter the train at any point. But there was nothing to prevent them from trying. The few unfortunates obliged to get off here had to bore their way writhingly toward the direction in which they last remembered having seen the doors, with agonized supplications of "Getting off! Getting off!"

Forty-second Street brought a measure of relief. They streamed out through the doors. The pony-skin coat had gone with cyclonic adieux. The caracul one was powdering its nose and getting Jerry's coat-sleeve all white. At Pennsylvania the great garment industry called to its devotees. Fourteenth Street helped too. But the real improvement came with the last Manhattan stations, Fulton and Wall. The aisles were cleared, seats shyly appeared here and there. It was over until tomorrow.

His ears hummed a little as the train plunged him below the waters of the East River for the first time that day. Beyond there it was all velvet; the tide was going the other way. Once more he sprawled comfortably on the seat nearest the door, lost to the world. The amount of reading he accomplished in the course of the day's routine would have provided a liberal education in itself. Especially topics that had not the slightest bearing upon himself and his surroundings, such as storms at sea, airplane mishaps, and the birth of three-legged roosters at Wichita, Kansas. Mechanically, he rose at last and reversed the stenciled slats in the end-windows of the car announcing its destination, stepped out as it reached there with a sigh, and went upstairs for a breath of air and a look around.

Returning Manhattanward, the cars filled slowly. There were matrons bent on shopping (and the Roxy), and those whose occupations called for no such stated regularity of hours, such as radio repairmen, piano tuners, picture-house ushers, employees

Love & Night

of the Consolidated Gas Company starting out to read meters, a Western Union messenger, and a prosperous professional beggar or two on their way to their morning beats. They chose the midtown street-corners, being wise, where the dimes were thickest and where they would practice standing on one foot and then the other for the balance of the day. The majority of these vanished at Times Square. Into Jerry's car in their stead came a gentleman with a beard, two chattering Puerto Rican damsels, a somnolent Negro bellboy in a dark green uniform, a rounded gentleman in plus fours with a bag of golf-sticks bound for the public links at Van Cortlandt, a fatigued youth who had ladled orangeade all night, and a very pretty girl carrying a suitcase.

She selected the seat next to the door as though her stay was to be a short one. Several times she made a false move to get up. Jerry sensed an impending inquiry and sighed resignedly. At length, as the train proceeded uninterruptedly on its way, she made up her mind, did get up, and presented herself before him, suitcase still in hand.

"When do we get to Forty-second Street?" she said. She had to shout to make herself heard.

He had expected something not particularly brilliant, none of these requests for information were, but this was the worst he had heard in months.

"What's the matter, you asleep?" he said gruffly. "We just passed it."

"But that was Times Square," she said innocently. "I got on there."

His sense of the fitness of things rose in rebellion at this. "Are you trying to kid me?" he demanded pugnaciously. Was nothing sacred in the eyes of these people, not even the uniform of a guard? But her eyes were so startled at the tone he had used, and at the same time so limpidly ingenuous, that he decided after a moment that she was more to be pitied than censured. She was a greenhorn; and not just a pale green one, but one of the deepest dye. "Where d'ye want to go?" he said with impersonal brusqueness.

"Here," she said. "I have it right here." She extracted an envelope from her handbag and held it before him. On the back of it was penciled a name. Also an address. A Forty-second Street address. "This gentleman's going to put me in a show," she explained happily. Jerry studied her gravely, without comment. Just where, he was wondering, had he heard this story before? "When he was staying at my Uncle Ed's hotel up at Patchouli last summer," she informed him, "he told me any time I was in New York to look him up and he'd put me in a show. So here I am!" This last with a triumphant toss of the head.

"Well," said Jerry, who found boredom had strangely departed from him during the last few minutes, "as long as you're going into a show, you'd better change at Seventy-second for a downtown train." He said it almost regretfully.

She thanked him and took back the envelope. They arrived. The doors slid open and she turned to go. Then catastrophe! A lady who would have been the pride and joy of any side-show was waiting to get on. She did, too, sweeping everything before her. She was rotund, monumental; when she died, she would have to be lowered out of the window like a piano. She filled the doorway from side to side; not a crevice remained. Not even a moth could have made its way out. The future stage performer was obliterated, satchel and all. When the living mountain had gone by, she reappeared in its wake, gasping for breath. She had been turned completely around, so that she faced the other way, away from the door. Meanwhile the door had closed upon her once more, doubly imprisoning her. Had she stood still and simply let him reopen it for her once more, all would have been well. But involuntarily, she took a step toward him, to call his attention to the fact that she was still on the train (he was leaning far out in the space between the two cars, craning his neck and wondering where she had gone to so quickly), and as she did so, the sound of rending silk came to all ears. She paused horror-stricken, with dreadful surmise written on her face. Surmise turned to certainty as she turned to look. The rear end of her dress had been guillotined by the door. What was left now resembled an apron in reverse, revealing the seams of two silk stockings up to where the stockings ended, and after that an inch or two of unblemished skin, quickly followed, in the nick of time, by some intimate apparel trimmed with lace. She gave a bleat of inexpressible woe and shrank back, with her back to the wall of the vestibule.

The train meanwhile was under way again, and Jerry descended from his perch and stepped back inside the car. His eyes opened in astonishment as he saw her still there. Pleasant, gratified astonishment. He even went so far as to beam at her, probably the first guard to beam at a passenger in the twenty-five-odd years the line had been in operation.

"Oh, you changed your mind, did you?" he said.

She pointed despairingly to the detached fragment of dress-goods that had remained caught in the door.

Jerry whistled. "Well, you can't go to the show that way," he said.

"I can't even get off the train now," she wailed, and her eyes shone wetly under the electric lights.

His official manner had become a thing of the past. He indicated the grip.

"Haven't you got anything in there you could put around you?"

"Only some pictures of me when I was in the school show up home. I—I came away in a hurry."

"Can't you even pin it until you get home?" he queried commiseratingly.

"But my home's upstate in Patchouli," she explained wanly. "I just got off the train a little while ago and started straight for the show."

"Oh, devil take the show!" he exclaimed with strange irritability. "You should never have left Pa—what is it, now?"

"Patchouli," she said helpfully, with a little sob.

"Now, don't be crying," he commanded, and lifted his cap to facilitate the scratching of the back of his head. At length a gem of thought seemed to result from this friction. "You could go around to the little lady," he remarked, "and see what she can do for you. She's a great one with the needle," he added proudly.

"What little lady?"

"My little lady, who did you think?" He leaned toward her confidentially. "Tell her Jerry sent you and show her what's happened to you and tell her he says will she please baste it up for you so they won't be arresting you walking on the streets." Then, reluctantly, he began unbuttoning the brass buttons of his jacket. "You get out at 125th," he said. "Delaney is the name; it's four flights up in the rear—you can't miss it." The coat was off now, and but for the visored cap he would have been no better than any mere passenger on the train. The heart of "the little lady" would have been wrung at the sight of him stripped of his glory and insignia. "Put this over you till you get there," he said, and passed it to her. "And be sure you leave it behind you at the flat or I'll be out of a job in the morning."

She hurriedly thrust an arm into each of the ample armholes and buttoned it around her. "Oh, thanks again and again," she said gratefully. "I don't know what I would've done if it hadn't been for you, Mr.—Mr. Delaney." The result was somewhat as though a blue-serge tent had suddenly deepened and enveloped her. The bottom of the coat came below her knees, hiding all traces of her own mutilated costume, and her hands were lost somewhere above the cuffs, not a fingertip visible.

Jerry himself had not been appreciably improved by the exchange either. He now consisted largely of dangling arms in shirtsleeves, girdled with crocheted blue garters. He scowled defiantly at the curious stare a newsboy passing from car to car flashed him. 125th Street bore down upon them. He turned to the muffled figure beside him.

"This is yours," he said, and carefully gave her the house-number, then with most un-Walter-Raleigh-like pessimism added: "I'm taking a chance on you. But I guess the coat's safe enough with anyone who would believe the first traveling salesman who told her he could get her in a show."

"I'll take good care of the coat, Mr. Delaney," she promised. She thrust forth one enveloping cuff and pumped his hand grotesquely. "I—I'll see you later," she said, picked up her grip, and scurried off the train. At the turnstile, oblivious of the attention her outfit was attracting, she turned and waved her appreciation to him.

"Don't forget the number, four flights up. Go straight there!" he bawled after her as he manipulated the doors shut. The rest of his ride was spent in a rosy haze. Little unseen cupids rode with him perched on the roofs of the subway cars.

It was not without misgivings that, several round-trips later, he presented himself before the agent at 242nd Street, passbook in hand. That individual, fortunately a personal acquaintance of his and one who had more than once in the past partaken of Mrs. Delaney's corned beef and cabbage, took in the shirtsleeves and crocheted armbands with wholehearted and not unfriendly curiosity.

"Warm, Delaney?" he was moved to ask. "Where's your coat?"

Jerry smiled inscrutably. "I've hung it up on the top of the car to dry."

His overlord nudged him in the ribs. "So at last ye'll own up to being all wet, will ye?"

Young Lochinvar returning home from the wars, or wherever it was he returned from, had nothing on the youthful Mr. Delaney as he stalked up 125th Street a short while later, whistling ebulliently. If it occurred to people that it was still rather early in the year to be without a coat, they wisely kept their thoughts to themselves. "He's lost his job," commented a lady on a fire-escape to a lady shelling peas at the window below. "It don't seem to bother him none," replied the latter.

His ascent of the four murky flights of stairs completed, he stopped abruptly at the rather intimate sight that presented itself when he had flung open the door unannounced. Mrs. Delaney, ensconced in her favorite rocker, was busily rocking and stitching at a garment lying across her lap. Opposite, legs tucked up under her, sat the late wearer of his uniform jacket, wearing it no longer. She now boasted his Rosemary's bathrobe instead, which fitted her rather better.

"Go in and watch the sausages, Jerry," Rosemary commanded, "until I get through with Peggy's dress. Peggy's staying to supper."

He whistled with the ardor of a whole cageful of birds as he turned the sausages over and over with a fork—So her name was Peggy and she was staying to supper, was she?

She helped Rosemary with the dishes afterward, as any well-bred guest should, and then the three of them sat talking in the homey little living-room. Or rather she did most of the talking; Jerry and Rosemary just sat and listened. All her dreams, all her plans.

"I want to get somewhere, be somebody. I want to be a big star and have my name up in lights. Peggy Parker, for all the world to see. Oh, I know it won't be easy. I know there are disappointments and heartaches ahead, but I'll buck them all and I'll get there, you'll see. I was born unknown but I'm not going to die that way, and that's about all anyone can do for themselves in this life."

It was like a breath from another world; what did they know about those things, the two of them? The little blue-eyed, red-haired Irish housewife whose interests were the price of string beans and the blue uniform jacket; the handsome dark-haired boy she'd married, whose half-articulate grumblings at his lot

Love & Night

would soon be beaten down by habit? Yet it was thrilling to listen to, like something said on a movie-screen. Although the words might be strange, the language of youth needed no translation. The animation, the gestures, the bright determination in her eyes, the confidence that had not yet met its first setback.

Then finally she said, "My goodness! It's after ten already, and I'm sitting here jabbering away. I'll have to get out and find myself a room—"

Rosemary said quite firmly: "See if ye can rig up that old cot in here, Jerry, so it won't fold up under her. I'm keeping her here this night. 'Tis no town for a girl to be walking around looking for lodgings by herself."

While she was inside hunting up sheets and a pillowcase, Peggy confided above the noise of the hammer-blows with which he was whacking the cot into shape: "I think your wife's the sweetest thing I ever knew. And up home they always said New Yorkers were inhospitable!"

"And is she the only one in the family you've a word of thanks for?" he probed, with typical Celtic humor.

She smiled shyly without answering, but an unseen warning spark seemed to crackle in the air between them.

The last thing Rosemary did, after she and Jerry had gone to their room, was tiptoe out again with one of her own nightdresses folded over her arm for the use of her guest. The poor always make the most generous hosts.

In the morning, before he left for work, Jerry drew Rosemary out of earshot into the hall. "She's going to come back here this afternoon and cry her eyes out when she goes down to that place and finds it was all a lot of blarney. Do what ye can for her. Tell her—tell her it don't amount to so much; she can be happy without being in a show."

Rosemary Delaney gave a keen searching look at the wall before her as though she had just seen something there. As a matter of fact, it was perfectly blank. But maybe she had seen handwriting on it. She didn't answer him.

Peggy wasn't there when he got back that evening.

"Maybe she isn't coming," said the preoccupied Rosemary presently. "Should we go ahead and eat?"

"She left her bag," he pointed out. "Maybe she's ashamed to come and tell us. Maybe she's walking the streets this very minute, not knowing which way to turn. It hits them hard when they've got the acting-bug that bad."

"Acting—or love—they do hit hard, now," said Rosemary, addressing the platter of steaming cabbage she was carrying in.

A rattle of light, hurried footsteps echoed on the stairs outside. There was the briefest tap on the door, then it pushed inward. Jerry stood up hastily. Rosemary braced one slim shoulder for possible weeping upon. In came Peggy. She was breathless with something she had to tell and had been saving all the way uptown with no one to tell it to.

"I went there—" she gasped, and could go no further. She opened her small mouth to inhale all the air possible, seated herself on the edge of a chair and leaned magnetically toward them. "I went there where the envelope said and—oh, Mrs. Delaney, how could he lie to me like that?—it was nothing but an old park in back of the library." Young Delaney's demeanor had become noticeably commiserating; willingness to console shone in his eyes. "So then," the object of his sympathy went on, "I asked a policeman where the show was rehearsing, and he was very nice and considerate to me. He told me that the only reason they don't have them out in Bryant Park is because traffic would probably be all tied up and a lot of people trampled to death. And he told me that nowadays they were having them in a theater further up, on Forty-fifth Street, so that the lives and limbs of passersby wouldn't be in any danger, and so that the old ladies that sell tangerines wouldn't have to go out of business. Then I threw away the envelope that man had given me and

Love & Night

I went to the place where it really was," she concluded simply. She stood up and removed her hat as though there were nothing further to talk about. "I'll help you set the table, Mrs. Delaney," she said. "I'm sorry I was so late."

The look on Jerry's face was now a definitely grim one. And how bravely, he marveled to himself, she was taking the disappointment. Not a tear, not a whimper. She certainly had—er—stamina.

"But why don't ye go on?" persisted Rosemary, dealing out plates with mathematical precision. "What happened after that?"

Peggy opened her eyes as though surprised at such a question. What else was there to tell, her attitude seemed to imply. "Nothing," she said. "They told me to come tomorrow for rehearsal and then I came straight up here."

There was a squeak from Jerry's chair as though he had risen above it involuntarily and then come down again.

"Oh, they took you, did they?" Rosemary said.

Peggy looked slightly amazed, as though it had never entered her mind that anyone could doubt this for a moment.

"But I told you they would," she remonstrated. "He fooled me; I had the wrong address at first, that was all. I'm only in the chorus but by next season maybe—That corned beef smells good," she added wistfully.

Midway through the meal there was a stentorian bellow from somewhere below-stairs that easily penetrated the thin flat-door.

"Mrs. De-laay-ney! Oh, Mrs. De-laaay-ney! Sure your sister from Flatbush is on the phaon!"

"Janitor's wife," explained Rosemary, jumping up hastily. "I'll have to run down a minute." Her hurried tread descended the four flights to where the only phone in the house was located, the janitor's apartment, over which all the tenants in the building received their calls. The janitor and his wife didn't resent this;

they even encouraged it; it gave them a very swell opportunity to know everyone else's business—and then some.

They went ahead eating. "Fifty a week," she said. "Of course we don't get paid till after we've been rehearsing three weeks, but I'd go into it for nothing if they only knew. It's the beginning, the start, the springboard." Her eyes were shining at him like two stars across that tenement meal-table. "Oh, and I looked at all the others; I've got something that none of them have! I can't miss, can't go wrong! I knew it, felt it in my bones, as I stood there on that stage-apron, holding my skirts up over my knees for the stage-manager to see how I'd look in costume. He was going to turn me down, I could tell that; I'm so green yet, it's written all over me, I guess. And I'd admitted I had no previous experience of course. He was already starting to motion me over to the left where the unacceptables were grouped and then he looked into my eyes. He seemed to see something there. He just kept looking into my eyes. Then he motioned me over to the right instead, and before I left he came up to me and said such a funny thing. He said: 'I have a hunch this show we're doing will be only remembered for one thing, some day. Because a kid like you, half-hidden in the back row of the chorus, was in it, got her professional start in it.' Wasn't that a strange thing to say?"

Rosemary came back, breathing from the climb. "It's Tom again. Oh, the good-for-nothing that he is! Sure he got drunk again, she says, and fell in the gutter! Oh, the shame of it! That me sister should be married to anything like that!"

Jerry didn't look unduly alarmed. Tom was an old story in the Delaney family circle.

"So he's in jail again?"

"No, this time he's in the hospital. A milk-wagon went over him lying there and it's a broken arm he's got." She was putting on her hat. "I've got to go over there and be with her a while; she's taking on that bad!"

"We'll do the dishes for you," Peggy offered.

Love & Night

Then later on, passing them to him, one by one, to be wiped, in the stuffy little cupboard of a kitchenette, she said: "You know, Jerry, I think you brought me luck. I'm superstitious that way. Ever since I tore my dress yesterday afternoon in your car, everything's gone right for me. Whatever happens, whatever comes later, I'll never forget you. After all, you were the first person I met when I got to New York. I may forget your name and I may even forget your face—but I'll never forget you."

The dish he was holding shattered on the floor like a firecracker.

"You've got that devilish way about you; you'll go far," he said huskily. "But oh, before you go too far, out of my reach, here are my arms around you now!"

It happened as suddenly as that. Without either of them meaning, intending it to happen. One minute he was holding the dishcloth, standing beside her, the next they were locked in one another's arms. For that moment they forgot everything except the amazing fact that they were in love and that love was sweet. There was no Rosemary, no time, no honor, only young love and passion. It passed like a breath.

Then they separated again. She didn't thrust him from her; they released one another automatically. They weren't confused, embarrassed. They both seemed to realize it was an impossibility. Two paths had crossed for a moment, the paths of two who could have loved one another, not for long maybe but for a while. But they were two divergent paths, two utterly divergent paths, on different planes, pointing straight away from one another. Polar antitheses.

Somehow, to him, this didn't seem to have anything to do with Rosemary. Neither sneakiness nor treachery nor disloyalty. It was such a different thing. If it had been some girl of their own kind, living their kind of life, some girl who lived above them or below them or next door—but this was like a man falling in love with a star over his head in the night sky.

"I'm sorry," he mumbled, but without really meaning it.

She put it into words for him. "No, don't say that! Don't spoil it. I'm glad you did it. It's like a seal upon the whole thing." She touched him friendlily on the arm as she went by. She said: "I'm going now—out to my future. One of the girls in the line-up offered to let me share her room with her until I start getting paid."

"I've driven you out," he said remorsefully.

"Driven?" she contradicted gently. "Why, what's pulling me is a magnet stronger than any love that ever flamed!" She picked up the little bag she'd been carrying in the subway when he first saw her. "Thank Rosemary for me," she said. He went out to the landing after her and saw her start down those grimy stairs. A golden glow, a radiance, almost seemed to come from her, lighting her way. As she turned the corner of the staircase, their eyes met for the last time. But she didn't see him any longer; the dazzle of what lay ahead was too bright.

He was sitting there alone by the window when Rosemary came in. She looked and saw the broken dish lying on the floor where it had fallen. She seemed to understand. They said the little things that they would say all their lives. After a while she came over and stood behind his chair and her hand strayed fondly in his hair. He reached up and pressed his own upon it with clumsy fondness. They both stared down into the street.

Someone has to buy the string beans. Someone has to open the doors of subway-cars.

• • •

That was all long years ago. There's a theater marquee on Forty-eighth Street now that has in big bright lights PEGGY PARKER, and underneath in smaller letters the name of some play. The play doesn't matter; the PEGGY PARKER does. It does!

Love & Night

Each season it gets bigger, brighter. Underground the trains still run. And all those funny little hats the wedged-in figures wear are copied from the one Peggy Parker wears.

"What kinnova time d'ja have last night with Eddie?"

"Swell time. He took me to see Peggy Parker, second row inna balcony."

"Gee, I'm crazy about her, aren't you?"

And 01629, squeezed between them, just smiles a little and seems to hear a voice in his ear again: "I may forget your name and I may even forget your face, but I'll never forget you."

He says to himself: "They can't take that away from me. Who else in all these seven millions can say as much?"

[*Breezy Stories,* October 1937]

This last of Woolrich's pulp romances might easily have become a bitter tale of economic and sexual exploitation, but—well, I'd better not give anything away. The octagonal mirrored room in which the Broadway star first meets the girl from the dresssmaker's shop would be moved a few years later to the isolated house where, in Woolrich's 1941 noir classic "And So to Death," also known as "Nightmare," the doom-haunted protagonist comes close to death twice.

THE INVINCIBLE

She lived on the roof, Vivian Lane did. Her friends called it a penthouse but she herself, whenever she spoke of it, called it simply the roof. When she was through at the theater each night, the theater that had her name up in electric lights on the outside, she used to say, "I'm going home to my roof now." She always said it with a sigh of relief, as though she was glad she was through for that night, glad to be alone.

To reach this rooftop home of hers, you had to go up twenty stories or more in an elevator, her own private elevator, inside a tall sleek white apartment building. That was what Sybil Jenkins was doing, and doing it very much against her will too. In fact her unwillingness to make this call on Vivian Lane had nearly cost her her job. The call was not by invitation—for Vivian and Sybil did not know each other—it was not even by request. It was by command. And Sybil had brought the reason for her call with her; it was a flat oblong cardboard box with *Chez Lorraine* marked on the cover in small neat letters. Within, Sybil knew, for she saw it being done up, were endless layers of dainty, faintly scented crepe paper, and within those in turn nestled the pride of the firm of Chez Lorraine, the apple of its proprietress' eye—a gown designed specially for Vivian Lane.

Love & Night

Two weeks before, out of a clear blue sky, she had telephoned the shop and said, "This is Vivian Lane. I want a dress; something different; something that no one else in town has." Mrs. Lorenz, the proprietress, had nearly strangled on the spot in an attempt to get all the honeyed words she had to say out of her windpipe at one time. Then later she had clasped her hands together repeatedly in an attitude of prayer and jubilation while she marched back and forth from reception room to fitting room and from fitting room back to reception room again. "Think what this means to us! Think of the prestige this will give us! Oh, that dear sweet darling young woman! She's going to have the most stunning dress New York ever saw!" Later she had called on Miss Lane herself with pencil, ink, and water-color sketches which three of the firm's crack designers had toiled over day and night and submitted them in trembling and trepidation. The whole staff had been kept in after hours that night to learn the fateful decision. "I'll need everyone, everyone!" Mrs. Lorenz had said. "If this goes over, you get a bonus, every one of you!"

It was almost seven before she returned, tottered out of the taxi, and collapsed weakly in the first chair at hand. Her assistants gathered anxiously about her, picking up the assorted sketches which she had dropped all over the floor. "A glass of water!" she gasped, and then, somewhat restored, went on: "I've lost five or ten pounds, my hair has turned gray, but—we're going to make a dress for Vivian Lane!" A polite murmur of rejoicing and congratulation filled the shop.

Two more visits followed on Mrs. Lorenz' part after that first fateful interview, both conducted in person, one to obtain Miss Lane's measurements and the other for the only fitting that the busy star could find time to concede to her, and then the fateful day of delivery arrived. "Have it here at seven," Vivian Lane commanded briefly and imperiously when informed by telephone that her gown was ready and waiting her approval.

"Not a minute sooner and not a minute later. Your check will be in the mail Monday morning," and hung up.

It was at this point that everything had started to go wrong. First the gown was done up and carefully put, box and all, into the safe in Mrs. Lorenz' private office. "If anything should happen to it at the last minute," she explained, "I think it would kill me!"

Next the delivery-man was called in and told to report to Mrs. Lorenz in person at six-thirty for a special assignment. "On a Saturday night?" he gasped. "Not much. I'm through at five."

"I'll pay you for the overtime," Mrs. Lorenz promised seductively.

"I can't," he protested. "It's my wife's birthday."

Mrs. Lorenz had been under a nervous strain all week. She lost her temper. "Very well," she snapped, "you're through here. I'll deliver it myself."

Six o'clock arrived and everyone had gone home except Mrs. Lorenz and Sybil Jenkins. The porter had even appeared with his pail and mop and had begun to slosh water about on the marble foyer to have it clean for Monday morning. The priceless dress was extracted from the safe and Mrs. Lorenz, hugging it jealously under one arm, began drawing on her gloves preparatory to leaving. "Don't forget to turn off the lights in the showcases before you go," she called in to Sybil Jenkins. A moment later there was a scream of horror from the direction of the door, a crash of tin, and a heavy thud.

Now what? thought Sybil in fright, and she came running out and across the long carpeted reception room. In the foyer, beside the overturned bucket of water, Mrs. Lorenz was seated firmly and catastrophically in the exact center of the floor, surrounded by what appeared to have been a young cloudburst and holding the package containing the dress desperately above her head with both hands.

"Here, take this, quick," she cried to Sybil, "before it gets wet."

Love & Night

But when Sybil, assisted by the penitent porter, tried to help her to her feet, she moaned. "I can't stand up! He left that pail right in my way. I've turned my foot or something!" Anxiously they both led her to a chair near the door and seated her in it. "Don't stand watching me!" she shouted irritably. "That dress has to be delivered! Get a taxi, you fool!" This last to the dumbfounded porter, who promptly turned and darted through the door.

"Oh, but Mrs. Lorenz," protested Sybil, "you can't think of going up there now!"

"I'm not," agreed Mrs. Lorenz bitterly. "You're the one who's going to deliver it instead. Hurry up! There's no time to lose—it's got to be there at seven sharp!"

A look of panic appeared on poor Sybil's face, and she drew back momentarily as though she had been bitten. "Oh, but Mrs. Lorenz," she wailed, "I can't! Any other night but tonight! I have a date with the boy I'm going with. I should have been home half an hour ago!"

A taxi meanwhile had drawn up in front of the shop and stood waiting dramatically.

"Miss Jenkins," announced her employer majestically, "there are a million boys you can have dates with, but there is only one Vivian Lane and she has got to have her dress tonight. Now your work here has been highly satisfactory up to now, but unless you are in that taxi on your way to Park Avenue in five minutes, you needn't come back here Monday morning. Take your choice!"

Sybil had a brief struggle with herself. The job won.

Half an hour later she was standing dejectedly in Vivian Lane's private elevator, slowly going up twenty stories to the roof.

The elevator stopped at last and Sybil stepped out. She found herself on a roof under the open sky. But what a roof; Vivian Lane's roof! Above her all the stars of the night gleamed like jewels. Sybil had always thought a roof meant tar and chimney-pots and perhaps clothes hanging on a line to dry. This roof meant plants and flowers, a little fountain of tinkling water in a pebbled basin, and a white-sanded path, soft as silk, leading toward an arched doorway beyond which inviting gold and orange lights gleamed. She went in there, past a long fringed Spanish shawl hanging diagonally from the doorway in place of a door, and looked about her uncertainly. Almost at once Vivian Lane's maid appeared from somewhere or other and beckoned to her.

"Right this way, please." Each room they passed through seemed more attractive to Sybil than the one before until at last they stopped in the loveliest room of all and there was Vivian Lane herself. "Your new gown, Miss Lane," said the maid and disappeared once more, leaving Sybil standing nervously alone in there.

Vivian at first sight was just a very beautiful but partially unclothed back, from where Sybil was standing. Beyond her the reflection of her face was repeated eight times, from left to right, by eight lighted mirrors ranged about her in fan-shaped formation. All eight of them spoke at the same time, saying politely but indifferently, "Oh yes, my dress. I'd forgotten about it. Be right with you." Poor Sybil was quite startled by the effect these multiple mirrors managed to convey; the whole room seemed crowded with Vivian Lanes.

"Sit down," Vivian added after a moment or two. "No use tiring yourself."

But just as Sybil was about to carry this suggestion into effect, a new one was forthcoming. "Suppose you try it on for me; we seem to be about the same size. That'll save time. You can step behind that screen there." And Vivian Lane pointed with an eiderdown powder-puff set on the end of a long ivory stick.

Sybil, too taken aback to protest at this rather unusual idea, found herself behind the screen a moment later, obediently slipping off her own garments and then untying the package containing the dress. Oh, my! she thought frantically, if anything happens to it while it's on me, what will Mrs. Lorenz say? She got the dress out and put it on with as much care as though it was made of spun glass and might fall apart at the slightest touch. Then, trying to control her trembling, she stepped out from behind the screen. Vivian Lane was preoccupied at the moment doing something to one eyebrow. Sybil cleared her throat timidly.

Vivian wheeled around on the low bench she occupied, opened her eyes and mouth at the same time in astonishment, and finally dropped the crayon she had been using to the floor. At last her breath returned to her.

"A natural!" she exclaimed. She stood up slowly, her eyes still as wide as they could be stretched. "I never—!" she started to say, then changed this to: "My hat's off to your firm, young lady."

Sybil stood there, never so embarrassed in her life, not knowing what to do or say.

"Walk back and forth," ordered Vivian. "Turn around." Sybil turned. "Pretend you're dancing."

Sybil stood stock-still. "I can't," she faltered miserably. "I haven't any partner."

Vivian laughed friendlily. "I'm sorry," she said. "I forgot you're not on the stage. We're so used to doing anything we're told at a moment's notice," she explained.

"Then you like the dress, Miss Lane?" Sybil murmured anxiously.

Vivian laughed again. "My dear child!" she said gayly. "I've been trying to tell you that in every possible way for the last five minutes." She was about to say more when the maid suddenly reappeared and murmured something apologetically that Sybil couldn't quite catch. At once all Vivian Lane's good humor seemed to desert her. "How dare he show up here!" she exploded angrily. "He's never even been introduced to me! I won't see him! I know what's up his sleeve! You go back and tell him I've gone away for a week—or a month—or a year! Get rid of him!"

The maid vanished with bent, repentant head. A moment

later the telephone rang. Vivian went over and answered while Sybil stood uncertainly in the middle of the room, radiant in the borrowed gown. She tried not to listen to what Vivian was saying into the telephone, but she couldn't help hearing most of it.

"George, your brother's here, and I don't know how to get out of the place without running into him. He's camped outside. No, please don't come up and give him a piece of your mind; the two of you will only end up by having a row—and that will set him more against me than ever. Don't let on I told you. Wait for me where you are, I'll find a way of giving him the slip . . . The Carillon bar? Good, don't forget." She hung up just as the maid returned a second time.

"Oh, Miss Lane, what am I going to do now?" the latter quavered almost tearfully. "He knows you're in; he heard your voice in here and told me so. He says he won't budge."

Vivian clapped a distracted hand to her head. "He's driving me crazy! He's pestered me for weeks now to go out with him!"

Sybil, thinking she had overheard just about enough of what was none of her business, made a move toward the screen to change her clothes. It was getting late, and she remembered she had had no dinner herself.

"Wait a minute," Vivian said to her suddenly. "Don't take that off yet. Will you do something for me?"

Sybil stopped and looked at her in surprise. "What?" she asked.

Vivian opened a drawer of the vanity table, rummaged in it, came back with a handful of crisp green bills.

"Could you use a hundred dollars?" she blurted out.

"Nicely," Sybil had to admit.

"First let me ask you something. Something terrifically personal, and please don't take offense. Are you—er—this sounds so silly—but are you a good girl? You know what I mean?"

"I should hope to tell you," bridled Sybil, blushing.

"How good?"

Love & Night

"I haven't had a strike called against me yet."

"Well, here's the point," Vivian said. "Are you good enough to hold out against—well, against the handsomest man you probably ever laid eyes on? Not only that, he's got money to burn. You'll not only have to buck him, you'll have to buck a walloping big fat check, diamonds, furs, a big car, a penthouse, the promises of all those things anyway, and he can make 'em sound awfully real."

"Sure I can hold out," said Sybil sullenly. "I'm no one night stand. I want to get married myself someday."

"Then you're what I'm looking for."

"What do I have to do?"

"Just go in there dressed like that and pretend you're me for one evening until he gets it out of his system."

"But how can I?" Sybil gasped in astonishment.

"He's never seen me except on the stage," Vivian explained rapidly. "In a white wig, with a lot of thick make-up all over my face. He'll never know the difference. What do you say? Is it a go?"

Sybil pondered the matter a moment or two, then suddenly raised her head in quick decision. "A hundred dollars is a lot of money," she said. "But it's a crazy thing to do. I never heard of anything like it before in my life, but I'll do it if you want me to that badly."

Vivian nearly threw her arms around her in delight. Then turning quickly to the maid, she said:

"Tell Mr. Worthington I'll be out in a few minutes. Just as soon as the dressmaker leaves."

As soon as the two of them were alone once more, she confided jubilantly to Sybil: "Now that you've decided to help me in this, I'm going to give you the absolute facts of the case. I couldn't talk openly in front of Yvette." Sybil listened wide-eyed, wondering what was coming next. "The boy that called me just now," Vivian went on breathlessly, wriggling into a trim tailored suit while she spoke, "is this man's younger brother. He's dead stuck on me, and his intentions are as honest as the day is long; wants to marry me and all that. He worships the very ground I walk on, and I think he's aces. So far so good. Now here's where the complications come in. The family has a lot of money, but the older brother controls all of it, at least until George—that's my boy—is thirty. He's threatened to cut him off if he marries an actress. There are a lot of stuffed shirts in the family with these peculiar old-fashioned notions about stage people; another objection would be that I might just be marrying him to divorce him later and milk him for a heavy settlement. Which has been known to happen, I'll admit, but I happen to love the kid. Try to tell them that, though!

"Well, withholding his inheritance wouldn't be enough to stop us in itself, and the older one knows it, so he's decided to make a play for me himself, to prove his point that stage women are all alike, they can all be had if you ring up the right price. In other words, he's out to cure his brother by making me himself and then presenting poor George with a nice little fait accompli. 'You still want her? There she is, old top!' I know just what his little game is, don't worry! And the worst part of it is," she went on, running a tortoise-shell comb sketchily through her gleaming hair once or twice and then crushing a diminutive hat down on top of it, "he's as dangerous as dynamite; he's got this damnable magnetism and charm, what they used to call sex appeal in the old days. He has a reputation for always having been able to get any woman he wanted. That's why the family are using him for their stooge. He's really the wilder and more experienced of the two, but the family doesn't object to that because he never marries any of them, whereas George, who's really an innocent boy alongside of him, respects me and wants to bring me into the family. So what do all the old fogies of the clan do but deliberately set this Jimmy—the black sheep—on to me, to turn me into what they say I am if I'm not already."

"But," objected Sybil astonishedly, "what I can't see is—isn't forewarned forearmed? If you know what his object is, why do I have to take your place? Why can't you go out with him yourself and beat him at his own game, show him he's wrong?"

"Because," admitted Vivian in a throaty confidential voice, "as woman to woman I'm not so sure he would be before the night's over. I've heard too much about him. Two of the girls in my last show went out with him; they had a reputation for being hard-to-get until they put on the gloves with him. They didn't last one round, either of them! And I really love George and I'm afraid to take any chances. I never was told by any doctor yet that I'm suffering from low blood-pressure exactly. I'm playing safe and staying away from him; what you don't go near won't hurt you. When you're out with him, the odds are two-to-one against you; him and you both against your conscience and the way your mother brought you up."

"But you're trusting me to hold out?"

"I'm paying you a hundred dollars to. And of course it always leaves an out for me in the end. Even if you drop a stitch. I can always come back to him: 'That wasn't me, sweetheart; try again!' Now I hope I haven't frightened you too much. How about it? Is it still a go or are you afraid you're not allergic enough?"

Sybil's self-confidence was equal to the ordeal, like that of a raw recruit who hasn't yet been under fire and therefore doesn't share a veteran's instinct for self-preservation. At least not very well-aimed fire; just slingshots, you might say, as opposed to machine-guns and heavy artillery.

"He's met his Waterloo," she announced firmly. "He's going to find out by the time tonight's over there's one girl in this town he can't have. You can look but you mustn't touch or you're gonna get all the enamel scratched offa you!"

"Onward Christian Soldiers!" encouraged Vivian. "Kid, you do the trick and you get another five hundred tomorrow morning, in whichever hospital ward you may be at the time!"

Sybil tapped her lower teeth thoughtfully. "And just to load the dice in my own favor and make doubly sure," she said, "could I have a—let's see—a pair of embroidery scissors? Or anything with a sharp point will do."

"You're not going to stab him, are you?" cried Vivian alarmedly.

"Oh no, I'm not taking them out with me. I just want to use them here in the room for a minute before I go."

Vivian located a pair, handed them to her with her shapely mouth slightly ajar.

"Not my new dress?" she asked apprehensively.

"No, not the dress either," Sybil reassured her. She stepped behind the screen she had used the first time, remained hidden with them a short while. A faint sound of snipping was discernible in the bated stillness of the room. Then she came out again and handed them back with a complacent expression. "There. Now I'm a cinch to outsmart him."

"What on earth did you want them for?" asked Vivian, mystified. She looked her over from head to foot but couldn't see any signs of their having been used on her.

"That's a professional secret," said Sybil airily. "I'll tell you tomorrow—if it works."

Vivian transposed her shapely middle-finger across her equally shapely index-finger, held them up to show her. "These are staying this way—all through the witching hours of the night," she intoned melodramatically. "You go out there now and keep him busy. You can say I'm the dressmaker as I slip by on my way out."

Sybil took a last look at herself in the eight mirrors and was eight knockouts. She drew a deep breath, like a person who is about to dive into a pool of ice-cold water without testing it first, and sauntered regally in the direction of the penthouse living-room where the adversary was waiting. Enemy territory and no quarter given.

Love & Night

Vivian was egging her on in a stage-whisper like a fight-manager's parting advice to his bantam before he climbs through the ropes. "Remember, my whole future is in your hands. Don't give up the ship! Think of your mother. Think of your future husband. Think of your grandchildren. Think of the multiplication table if you have to, or the price of eggs wholesale. Stay away from sofas with too many pillows on them. Make sure there're always at least two lamps on at any given time. Be careful of soft music. Keep your eyes off the moon if there is one, or the stars if there isn't one."

"When better resistance is made than he's going to get tonight," was Sybil's parting assurance, "I'll make it!"

Into the living-room she swept, with that gliding walk she had seen the models use at Mrs. Lorenz' establishment. The long dress was clinging to her body like wet elastic, so perfectly did it fit, and then at the bottom around her insteps it flared out all around her like pale green sea-foam. She was something to see.

There was a startled gasp of admiration from one corner, like this—Uff!—and then the menace rose slowly to his full height of six-feet-one. Sybil knew just how St. George must have felt facing that dragon. Only this dragon was darned easy to take; you wanted to get up close and cuddle and croon, "Go on, blow a little smoke and flame my way." She thought: No wonder Lane sent me in here to take the risks for her. Smart girl! She wouldn't have a chance against this with her artistic temperament. Even I with my Washington Heights morality can feel a peculiar what-do-I-careishness coming on! Turn those eyes off, mister; I don't carry fire-insurance.

"Mr. Worthington?" she said sweetly, making a U-turn in front of him and then braking on the red-light look in his face.

His mouth was open, as though he found the sight of her incredible.

"George didn't exaggerate when he said you were the loveliest thing ever," he began rather insidiously. "Why, you're even more of a treat to the eye than you were the night I saw you on the stage!"

"It is a little hard to make passes with a ten-piece orchestra in between," she purred felinely. "How did you like my singing?"

"Were you singing?" he exclaimed with what seemed like genuine surprise.

"How did you like my dancing?"

"Were you dancing?"

"Well then, how did you like the show?"

"Were there other people on the stage with you? I thought I noticed a kind of blur, a haze around you, but all I could see was your face."

"Damned liar," she said agreeably. "Tell me more. You'll run out of tackle after a while and I'll still be swimming fancy-free."

"The footlights," he went on, "made your eyes seem gray that night, but now I know they're really blue. And your voice is really much softer than it sounded in the theater."

"Why don't you go home with a good book, honey?" she coaxed. "You're wasting a perfectly good evening for yourself this way and getting absolutely nowhere."

"I'd rather read you."

"Sure, I know. The Braille system."

At this point a demure little figure in tailor-made suit, with a hat pulled down close over her eyes, glided unobtrusively through the room toward the outside door. "Good night, Miss Lane," she breathed respectfully in a barely audible voice.

"Oh, good night," Sybil replied carelessly. "Just my dressmaker," she explained indifferently for Worthington's benefit. He glanced around, turned away again. You don't waste time on a sparrow when there's a peacock in front of you.

Behind his back the departing "dressmaker," as she slipped out through the door, held up one hand ostentatiously. The middle-finger was still crossed inflexibly over the index-finger.

Love & Night

Sybil glanced over, imperceptibly drooped one eyelid in a ghost of a wink. The door closed and she was on her own.

"Let's see, where were we, Mr. Worthington?"

"Just call me Jimmy, won't you?"

"What held that up until now?" she asked mockingly. "You're nearly a minute-and-a-half late with it. I'm afraid you need oiling. Very well then, just call me Brrh!"

"What does that mean?" he asked, puzzled.

"I don't know," she shrugged engagingly. "But that's what all the boys say when they kiss me. They get chapped lips."

He shook his head with mock ruefulness. "Gee, you're case-hardened."

"Case-hardened? I'm an armadillo. Even diamonds won't cut my shell."

"I noticed that," he admitted, "the way I got that bracelet back."

"Tired yet? Want to give up? Or would you like to try a little longer?"

His face colored and his eyes glittered dangerously. "You've made the fatal mistake," he told her grimly, "of offering opposition, putting me on my mettle. Now you're in for it; now you're sunk! How about coming out and dining with me while I map out a campaign of action?"

"I've got to eat anyway," she said with devastating aloofness, "so somebody may as well pay for it. One wing tie is pretty much like another, sitting across the table from me. Just let me get my brass-knuckles, be right with you."

She came out again in a borrowed velvet wrap of Vivian's, insolently flicked a speck of imaginary dust from his sleeve with the tips of two fingers as he held the door open for her. "Come, beloved," she said scathingly, "and be sure not to forget the sleeping-powders for my wine."

In the upholstered car he tried to hold her hand. "Never before dinner," she let him know, and took it away. "It's as light as a feather; I can hold it myself."

The restaurant where his driver stopped didn't mean a thing to her. She'd heard of it but that was about all.

"You see, I know all your habits," he said as they got out. She didn't understand in time, and the car had already driven on by the time he added: "I know this is your favorite rendezvous after the theater."

"Oh, couldn't we go somewhere else?" she exclaimed with a clutching gesture after the car as if to pull it back again by main force. "I'm so tired of it here."

"Sorry," he said. "I should have consulted you first. It'll be impossible to get him back now in all this traffic. Surely once more won't hurt," and he looked at her curiously.

She gathered the wrap and her courage more closely about her. Heaven help a little dress-shop employee on a night like this! she thought as she tilted her chin and advanced with grim determination into the brightly lighted vestibule.

A tall distinguished-looking young man was standing in the exact middle of it, evidently waiting for some girl to come out of the powder-room. Sybil passed so close to him their elbows brushed but with chin still in air.

"Aren't you two on speaking terms?" Worthington murmured with a glance over his shoulder.

"How's that?" was the best she could manage, with a feeling of thin ice cracking underfoot.

"Why, he's been carrying you in his arms up a flight of stairs, while he smothers your face with kisses, six nights a week and two matinees for the past eight months—at the end of the second act."

"Yes, but he's very mean; he keeps bumping my—er—the bottom of my spine into the scenery every time he does it. Purposely."

"Oh!" he said. But again he gave her a curious sidelong look, this time with a trace of a grin on his face.

She had an uneasy feeling, as she sat down at the table with him and pretended to scan a menu, that she had bitten off a good deal more than she could chew. She stole a look at him over the top of the folder. Not for nothing had the Worthington clan selected him to do tonight's dirty work. Vivian had known what she was doing in steering clear of temptation. She caught herself wondering: Does he sort of swoop when he kisses, or stand perfectly still and haul you in at him?

He caught her eyeing him. "Yes, I'm still here," he grinned impudently.

...

The following Monday morning the former Vivian Lane, now Mrs. George Worthington, was sitting breakfasting on the terrace with her brand-new husband when Yvette, the maid, appeared and told her someone wished to see her.

"I'm not at home to anyone," said Vivian firmly, "from now on."

"It's that young lady who brought your dress the other night," explained the maid.

Vivian jumped up. "Oh, that's different. I must see her! She's a dear! Come along, George, and meet her. She's the one I told you about, that I used to turn the tables on Mr. Smart-Aleck Jimmy Saturday night."

"Gee, the poor little kid," said George penitently. "We'll have to do what we can for her. It's a foregone conclusion what happened to her if she went out with Indian!"

Instead of just Sybil, however, the terrible Jimmy Worthington had come along with her. Vivian and George took a deep breath when they saw him and edged closer to one another as if for mutual protection against the tirade that was to come.

He looked, however, slightly sheepish and not at all tiradeish.

Sybil was the only one of the four who seemed to have her wits about her.

"I brought your dress back," she told Vivian.

George stepped manfully into the breach. "Now, Jim," he began earnestly, "you and the family can do what you like about it, but I married Vivian Saturday night up at Greenwich, Connecticut, and—"

"Congratulations, old man," said Jimmy meekly.

George and Vivian just stared, mouths open, at this unexpected submission.

"Yes, and now you two can congratulate us," remarked Sybil matter-of-factly. "We got married ourselves at Greenwich Saturday night. Isn't that a coincidence? We must have passed each other on the way, you coming back and we going up."

"You what?" Vivian gasped. When she had recovered somewhat, she put an arm about her new sister-in-law and murmured:

"Could I talk to you alone, dear, for a minute?" As soon as they were out of earshot, she burst out: "How did you ever land him? Him of all people! Why, he was known to be absolutely allergic to marriage."

"Virtue is its own reward," explained Sybil complacently. "When he got tired wrestling with me and not getting anywhere, he suddenly discovered he couldn't live without me even if it meant marrying me, so he whisked me away to a justice of the peace up at Greenwich."

"But how did you manage to hold out against him? He's deadly to women, you know. What will-power!"

"Will-power nothing!" snapped Sybil. "I've got my own little private system. You remember when I borrowed those scissors before I left here that night? Well, they did it. I'll show you what I used them for." She stepped behind the screen for a moment or two, came out again holding what had once been a dainty pair of pantalettes. You couldn't tell what they were any more,

Love & Night

they were as full of holes as if an army of angry moths had been busy at them for months. They were tattered, threadbare, disreputable.

"You did that yourself?" gasped Vivian.

"Certainly! It's sure-fire! You're a woman yourself; you know how we'd rather die than be found out with a hole in our stockings or underthings. All I had to do was think of what my lingerie looked like under that beautiful gown and I was perfectly safe."

[*Breezy Stories,* January 1939]

C.W.